I0609403

Cover design by M.D. Mare
Logo © M.D. Mare

First Edition – 2025
Published by M.D. Mare
Printed in the United States of America
ISBN 978-1-970588-00-2

Connect with the author

madmansays.substack.com

What are you going to witness

This rain soaks my feet, my ankles, my legs. It rises through my veins and floods my belly. I float in this sea.

Beyond a hand's breadth from my eyes, all I see are gray, blurred shadows. The umbrella snatches from my hand, like a bird trapped, desperately trying to fly away, stuck between chin and shoulder. I could let it go, I could let it take my soul with it, beyond the low clouds crushing me in this solitude.

The stream of water running along the sidewalk deepens now, high heels or flats, it doesn't matter anymore, this is a flood, and I'm in it, up to my nose. This apnea that chains me to the ground, pounding from inside my chest with fists of desperation, free me. Breathe me.

It could scream.

A nuclear bomb could explode.

The tall concrete buildings could collapse. And I would still be here, waiting in this liquid prison. Where my boundaries are, I no longer know, and I don't care. Whether this water fills me or empties me. Whether it exists or not.

Whether I am going mad or already insane.

The car stops. There is no procession behind it. Dissolved in the rain. The coffin inside is white. It is simple, without frills or decorations. A man in a dark suit passes in front of me. He runs. He doesn't want to get wet.

With a rapid movement he opens the trunk, three more men appear from the storm stretching their arms into the car. The coffin slides out.

I watch a silent film while the downpour fills my ears. It almost feels like being outside of it all, as if it was a distant representation. The hands, the wet clothes, the dark glasses, the countdown.

It's only the sound of the lifeless body knocking against the wood as it is lifted too hastily onto their shoulders that brings me back here.

Heavy again on my bones.

And as that reckless motion propagates through all dimensions of space, spinning awkwardly in the air while these strangers take charge of the final journey, that's when a wave of nausea grips me at the end of the sternum, and I bend over.

It is colorless, it almost chokes me. There's nothing left inside me to throw out. The spasms seize me violently, shaking me like a dry branch, and I can only watch their black–shoed feet pass by me. They climb the marble steps. And then, out of my sight.

When it all seems to have passed, I stand up, exhausted. The church door has a purple drape hanging on the right side. Inside, only the distant lights of the altar are visible. They place the coffin on the pedestal with more care now.

Only now do I realize it is over. Truly over.
I will not enter this church today.
This is not a church today.

HE LIES ON THE JESTER'S CART

1.

"Good evening, Chief."

The neon light casts a cold glow on the white walls. Bare, except for the photo of the President of the Republic staring serenely into space, a crooked police banner hanging beside it. On the other side of the room the commissioner sits behind a desk piled with papers. He is bent over a newspaper, indifferent.

The uniformed man removes his hat as soon as he enters the room and quickly approaches the edge of the desk occupied by the commissioner. The papers rustle and flutter from the cold draft blowing through the room. The balcony door is open, and the city lights spill in, reflecting yellowish and warm in the glass.

"Chief, you need to stop smoking in here. And it's freezing when you keep the windows open. On top of that, there's a mad draft all through the station. That De Michele is just waiting to cause a ruckus, and you know it. Why do you always provoke reactions?"

The commissioner slowly turns the page of the newspaper. The cigarette butt rests on the edge of the ashtray, extinguished as it reached the filter.

"Can I close it?"

The commissioner dismissively waves his hand.

"God, it's freezing. You want us in pain."

"Listen, Cesarano, are you here just to piss me off? Because I'm really not in the mood to have you buzzing in my ears. So if that's the case, you can go to hell."

"Chief, for God's sake, what are you talking about? You know I'm saying this because I care. You're a good person, but if you're not careful, these guys will screw you over for the smallest things."

The commissioner has a dark overcoat draped over his shoulders, his black hair tousled, long enough to curl at his neck and temples. Arms crossed, resting on the desk, he hunches over the newspaper. The crime section page.

Cesarano struggles a bit with the window latch before managing to close it and walks back. He stops near the desk leaning in slightly to read the large headline in the middle of the page.

"Terrible story, huh?"

The commissioner grunts in agreement.

"What could have been going through his head?"

"I don't know."

"Some people have everything, and it's still not enough."

The commissioner grunts again in agreement.

"Chief, aren't you going home?"

The man lifts his head from the newspaper and stares intently at Cesarano.

"What have you got going on?"

"Chief, there's the game on tonight. Let me be."

"Cesarano, you're the backbone of this precinct. If it weren't for you, this whole building would collapse, and criminals would roam free and unchecked on the streets."

"Chief, they're already roaming free and unchecked. For now, I'm going to watch the football match, and tomorrow we'll see."

"You're wise, Cesarano."

The man stands up. The chair's wheels creak as they roll backward. He reaches for his car keys and walks away quickly.

Cesarano watches him go.

"Did they assign you the case?" He shouts as he sees him crossing the doorway.

In the distance, he hears the commissioner's voice echoing down the hallway.

"Just what the chief needed…"

The sound of footsteps on the wet asphalt is strange, like walking on insect carcasses. He hates it. He tries to glide over it as lightly as possible until he finally reaches the handle and opens the car door. He slips into the car; the seats are worn and the windows should be rolled down to air out the heavy smell of smoke. The only solution is to light another cigarette while the old Twin Spark coughs to life again.

Let's go. Where are we going?

There's little traffic tonight; everyone's home, pounding fists on tablecloths, armchair and beer in hand, distracting themselves from the horror of this night. The road to the highway ramp is clear, and he shifts into third gear, presses the pedal, then shifts into fourth. The fuel gauge needle is dangerously low, dipping toward the left. The ramp is steep and curves, the iodine lights disappearing quickly, leaving only the low beams to light the way. They are low and uneven, bent from too many collisions or rough parking jobs. It's pitch black, a new moon, but the road is familiar, almost like driving on autopilot.

He turns on the service radio, just for company. He hates music, he hates silence. The crackling of service communications flows by like the dashed lines of the lanes, just some public order updates near the stadium, but otherwise, everything is calm. Even the clouds seem to have gone, or at least it seems so, but it's so dark that anything and its opposite could be true.

The industrial area is getting closer, brightly lit like an oasis in this black hole. Large signs with foreign names rise high above the prefab warehouses. Sleek logos and, behind them, chimneys point toward the sky. There's only one gap in this mosaic of light. He stops in front of it.

He gets out of the car and looks at the sign fixed to the green gate.

Prosud S.p.A.

Yellow tape marks the area. From the gate, the fire—ravaged remains of the building rise up, a three—story structure of glass and concrete, blackened and twisted by the fury of the flames. There's a sweet smell in the air, and the wet ash seems to have soaked into everything around it.

Further on, the employee entrance is visible. There's a funeral notice posted nearby. He turns on the high beams and steps out of the car, walking toward it with short strides, hands in his pockets.

It reads:

Marzio Solimena has passed away. His passing is mourned by his mother, his brother, and the entire management of Prosud. The funeral will be held on September 11th at the Church of S. Maria delle Grazie.

September 11th.
Today's date.

2.

Peace I seek within.

The stormy sea crashing against my chest shakes me while I stand still. The damp cotton of the pillow. My body seems to have lost its substance. My limbs have disappeared, I no longer have them. A trunk, then just my neck, and finally, all that remains are my eyes, staring at a gray, indistinct, opaque surface.

I am only myself as long as I can still think my name. I am air. A single breath. I could disappear, but I am still here. I wish I didn't exist, but I can't annihilate myself enough to fulfill this sweet desire. I could be with you now. Beneath the earth, in the dark. In the warmth of your arms and crying in the silence of you who are me, with me. And who left me here alone, believing I couldn't make it. To go mad, drop by drop.

What's normal is turned upside down, what's familiar no longer exists. Life, plans, thoughts of the future. Me, smiling, waiting for you to come toward me, the summer sunset blowing through our hair, the sweetness of knowing we would share the beauty of things together, the simplicity of each morning, that constancy slowly becoming the foundation of my happiness. From here, I would build my future, my serenity. From here, the joys would bloom, adorning my neck like pearls on the most beautiful evening.

It's true, and it was here, in these rooms. I still feel your scent, your clothes folded in the wardrobe, the change of clothes you'd need the next morning when you stayed the night, they're there for you and for me. I dig my nails into my palms. Bit by bit, everything falls apart. It's a world collapsing, silently, without raising dust, and the bricks sink into a white sea. I remain alone in the void. I have nothing to cling to, and even if I did, I wouldn't have the strength to grasp it. An infinite room, the void surrounding me, and this quicksand pulling me down to my waist and leaving me there. To watch what happens without being able to move.

The silence is pure. Crystal–clear. The morning in the suburbs is an untouched gem. I open my eyes. The hours are still young. The light is blue, filtering through the blinds carelessly closed the night before. I laid here and here I remained. A worthless accessory, a new trinket in this concrete hole. I will come to hate everything that exists, even you, even you, if I don't already hate you. If I don't already scythe through the souls of everyone in front of me just to scream at you that I hate you, that if I'm here, it's your fault. That I deserve to be happy with you, and I don't deserve this punishment. I would tear your hair out, your skin, bite into your flesh, and tear you into a thousand tiny pieces, and each one would smile at me, love me, and I would cry, just as I am crying now.

It would be easier. Simple.

It would all be easier if you weren't here with me now.

If you weren't looking at me with those eyes as you lean against the doorframe of my room.

You appeared a few hours ago. As beautiful as I remember you.

You stand still and look at me. Your eyes are cold, you don't smile at me like you always did, but you look at me.

You don't speak.

I got up last night. To believe it was a dream, I reached out my hand, and you stepped back. Then, kneeling on the bed, closer still, and you stepped back again.

Can't I touch you, Marzio?

Standing, facing each other like any ordinary day.

I step forward, and you step back.

This dream of flesh, slipping along my skin like a cold vibration, the numbness of sleep drifting away. I wait, I wait for the eternal seconds for your figure to blur, to disappear, to return where it belongs, in my mind, in the dream, in sleep.

I remain still in bed. Waiting. In vain.

It doesn't happen. You stay there, still, motionless. As my limbs grow stiffer with each passing second. Compressed under the weight of fear. My mind coils around my spine, forcing it to arch. Resist, resist. And finally, admit it. You're going mad. There's no other explanation. You are here, inside me, so strong and vast that I cannot contain you. I project you outward to breathe, to leave an inch of space in my soul. Just enough to find a moment of peace.

And yet, you are so real. You are so close. You are so true.

What do those eyes mean, what are they hiding, what do you want to tell me with your presence?

I dive into them and sink until I surface on a placid lake whose waves are still in the storm, eternal and plastic. What dark secret are you hiding, you cannot scream to me.

What further pain are you asking of me, my love?

Leaving me alone wasn't enough; you're here for something more, to collect your dues. I remain fixed on the bed, without strength. And yet this makes me feel pleasure. Everything is over, but you are still here. Your eyes are cold, it's true, but that's your skin, your face, your white shirt. And I could stay here long enough to forget myself. It's enough for me to know you're watching me, and everything else can be forgotten, food, water, and, eventually, breathing. You will take me with you, we will leave through the door together, and go far away, wherever you want.

"Oh, the world is made of many things that we want, but you can't have them all!"
The voice is shrill, unpleasant. A surge of electricity courses through me, and my lifeless body trembles with fear in every fiber. The hairs on my arms and legs stand on end as if they want to escape.

I shift my eyes, then my head toward the window, arching in tension. Against the light, there is a small figure sitting on the desk, legs crossed, body leaning back, arms stretched out, resting on the surface. The hands are old, wrinkled, the long, bony fingers tapping the wood in jerky movements. Bells dangle from the tips of the hat, glimmering and reflecting the droplets of light seeping through the window. The costume is white, seemingly made of silk, and on the short torso, it splits into two symmetrical parts, one white and the other black.

I don't see the face, and I'm not sure if I can't, or if I don't want to.

My Marzio is still there, I can feel him. He's watching me.

"He's not going to leave."

That raspy, sarcastic voice again, barely holding back from bursting into an evil laugh.

"He asked so insistently to return. And for the devil's sake, he insisted, insisted, annoying! Annoying!" He slams his fists on the desk "He's just a spoiled child. I told him he's a spoiled child, but he kept insisting, insisting, crying, crying." He says, mimicking wiping his eyes with his fists. "And I asked, 'What is it that you need to do? What is it you want to say?' He told me." There's a long pause. "And I replied, 'Alright, alright. Let's go back.' But there are rules to the game, otherwise there's no fun!" He raises his finger and waves it in front of him.

I still can't see his face, but I don't move; I'm frozen, still, paralyzed.

"You understand I don't have all this time to spare, I have many things to do. But you can't refuse something like this. You can't, because you have to know how to have fun while time passes. We're not angels, we're not perfect, we can't always be strict and say no. Every now and then, you need a pastime. Every now and then, you need to find a distraction. Every now and then, you need to play."

He stands up on the desk. He's barely over a meter tall, and now I can see his profile in the light.

He's old, his face full of wrinkles. His nose is long, the tip droops down like a crow's beak, and his ears are elongated, with long golden earrings hanging from the lobes.

"The first rule is that he can't speak" He says, pointing at Marzio, grinning crookedly.

13

"The second rule is that time is short."

"The third rule is" he stops. He gazes into the void, swaying forward on his ankles. He's on the edge of the desk, arms outstretched, raising one foot behind him, teetering in precarious balance. "I have to go now." He says, but I don't see his mouth move. His arms rotate slowly. "But I'll be back to talk to you again. After all, we haven't even begun. But we'll have fun, we'll have fun together!"

He laughs. A shiver runs through me, piercing my spine. I haven't moved, yet it feels like I've been thrown into a centrifuge. The room sways before my eyes, and I have to grip the bedsheets to make sure I don't fly away. I breathe. I'm still alive. I'm here. I breathe.

I turn.

Marzio is still there, standing motionless by the doorframe. He's cold. It's clear that he's dead.

His eyes are ice cold. They hide something.

3.

The music is one of those overused jingles for phone hold lines, identical to that of twelve hundred other switchboards, which irritates him even more.

"Prosud S.p.A., good morning, how may I assist you?"

"Good evening, this is Cardona. May I speak with Mr. Solimena?"

"Which company?"

"It's the Italian government."

"What?"

"Police, Commissioner of Police."

"Who do you wish to speak with?"

"Solimena, Mr. Solimena. The boss."

There's a brief silence.

"One moment, I'll connect you to the office."

The music starts again. The same music. The commissioner starts humming it in his head out of frustration. Then he curses. These three notes will stay with him all day. No matter how much service radio he listens to, they'll follow him into bed.

"Dr. Solimena's office, good evening."

"Good evening, this is Cardona. May I speak with Mr. Solimena?"

"Mr. Solimena is busy at the moment."

"Can I speak with him now?"

"He's busy."

"Will it be long?"

"I don't believe he'll be free soon. But if you'd like, we can schedule…"

"Very well. Goodbye."

The commissioner hangs up the phone and springs to his feet. His coat is already draped over his shoulders.

"Cesarano!" He yells. "Cesarà!"

He walks out of the office, and to his left, Cesarano comes running, out of breath.

"Chief, you called?"

"Cesarà, I'm heading to Prosud."

The officer hurries alongside the commissioner but falls behind, craning his neck to look him in the face.

"Chief, do you want me to come with you?"

"No, Cesarà, you're in uniform. Don't bother."

"And if De Michele comes by, what should I tell him?"

"Tell him I stepped out."

"Alright, Chief. Good luck."

"Take care."

Cesarano stops and sighs.

The road to the industrial area in the morning feels longer, eternally longer. The traffic of trucks blocking his view. That fine mist rising from their wheels, settling like grime on the windshield. Too slowly even for the wiper's lowest speed. So dense it leaves thick streaks with each pass of the wiper. And every time he sighs, every time he adjusts the control behind the wheel.

The sight of that blackened, twisted building should bring relief, it does. His chest swells, a deep breath. And then a sense of conviction immediately buried under the skin out of modesty. Work, the pleasure of work.

The green gate is now open, and the black Alfa 155 slips inside and stops before a barrier. To the right, there is a truck parking area and more green fences still restricting access. On the left, a guard in a blue uniform approaches the car and gestures for the window to be rolled down.

"Yes?"

"Good morning."

"Good morning." The accent is strong, from the northern province of Naples.

"My name is Cardona, Police. I need to have a word with Dr. Solimena."

"Well, please park over there for a moment, see?" He points to the parking area on the right. "Then come into the guardhouse to get your entrance permit."

The commissioner parks quickly and exits the car.

The guardhouse has dark glass walls, and the nearby buildings reflect towards the commissioner as he approaches. He pulls his collar tighter around his neck; the wind is cold today. Humid and cold. His joints shrink with each step.

The door opens automatically, sliding to the right. Inside is a high counter, and behind it, two distracted guards' heads barely poke above.

"Good morning. I need to get in."

"Do you have an appointment?" Asks the guard on his right without even looking up from the monitor.

"Not exactly."

"Who do you need to see?"

"Solimena."

The guard looks up.

"You can't just go and talk to the boss without an appointment!"

"Call and tell them Commissioner Cardona is at the gate."

They exchange a silent glance.

"Can I see your ID?"

The commissioner pulls out his badge from his coat and holds it out in his hand.

"Can I?" Says the guard, reaching for it.

"No." The commissioner holds it up where the other can't reach, the guard keeping his hand outstretched for a moment before giving up and squinting to read it. The commissioner brings the badge closer. The guard exhales deeply, then picks up the phone and dials.

"Francesca? Hi, it's the front gate. Commissioner Cardona from the police is here. He wants to speak with the doctor." He nods once, then again, and once more. "I see, I see, okay, okay. Bye."

He lifts his head above the counter.

"Commissioner, Miss Schiavone is on her way. She'll escort you to the boss. While you wait, I'll just register you. Can I see your ID?"

The commissioner nods, puts his badge back in his pocket, takes out his wallet, and places his driver's license on the counter. He moves towards the row of windows overlooking the site. From there, all that's visible is the burnt—out building. Scattered around the wreckage are chunks of plaster, glass, and charred debris. Yellow caution tape marks the area, fluttering in the wind. He can almost imagine the sound. No shadows are cast on the ground today, nothing has a shadow. A row of red fabric chairs, slightly worn, lines the window. The commissioner approaches and rests a knee on one. He feels the fluid shifting as he puts his weight on it, and a sharp, sweet pain starts spreading through the area. He considers calling the orthopedist.

"Commissioner, here's your badge. You must wear it while inside the facility." The uniformed young man stands up and places a badge inside a plastic holder on the counter."

"You need to sign here."

He points to a piece of paper he's holding down with his fingers and hands the pen to the commissioner.

"What is this?"

"It's a document informing you of the facility's rules, which areas are open to the public, and what to do in case of an emergency."

"Where do I sign?"

"Here."

The commissioner scribbles an illegible signature, picks up the badge, and slips it into his pocket.

"Commissioner Cardona?"

The officer turns around. A woman in a gray suit has just entered through the door. Her brown hair is tied back at the nape of her neck, she wears thin glasses. A black folder under her arm with a few papers inside.

"Yes, that's me."

"Very pleased to meet you. I'm Francesca Schiavone, Dr. Solimena's assistant."

"Pleasure is mine."

They remain silent, looking into each other's eyes.

"How can we assist you, Commissioner?" She smiles.

"I'd like to speak with Dr. Solimena."

"The doctor is very busy today. I'm not sure he'll be able to see you."

"Well then, while I wait for him to be free, I could take a look around the facility."

"This is an industrial site, Commissioner." She says with a sarcastic smile. "It's neither prudent nor allowed under our safety protocols to let someone wander around the premises."

"You could assign someone to accompany me."

"We could schedule an appointment later this week, or maybe at the beginning of next." She opens the folder "The doctor is free on Wednes..."

"No, I'm happy to wait for the doctor. This place is quite interesting." The commissioner interrupts "I can wait patiently. After all, I have the right to access the area under investigation as I'm part of the inquiry, so in the end..."

"I understand. I'll show you to the waiting room then." She closes the folder with a snap "However, I can't promise anything. The doctor may still not be able to see you."

"I'll wait hopefully." The commissioner forces a smile, but it doesn't quite work.

"Perfect, follow me then."

She turns and heads out of the guardhouse.

The commissioner follows her, steps through the door, and walks alongside her.

The facility is vast, with green and gray being the dominant colors. There's a large open area through which Schiavone leads him, heading toward a small two–story building accented with aluminum, giving it a modern look. On the main facade above the entrance, the company logo stands out, made of stainless steel: two intertwining flames.

In the background, tall metal structures loom, filled with tanks and other equipment whose tangled tubes weave together like a poorly wound ball of yarn. Though distant, a low, deep hum can be heard in the air.

"What's that building over there?"

"The management offices. Behind them are the production plants."

"There's a lot of noise back there."

"Not only that, the plants are places only experienced and trained personnel can access.

"They're fascinating places."

"Yes, they are."

"Tell me, what was in that building that burned down?"

"Offices."

"What kind of offices?"

"There was the engineering technical office on the ground floor and administrative offices upstairs."

The commissioner nods and turns to look at it.

"And what do you do here?"

"What do you mean?"

"I mean, what do you make here, what do you produce?"

"Prosud produces polymers and base components for cement additives. We supply them to the major cement companies in Italy and Europe. We like to say that in Italy, there's a part of Prosud in every construction from the 1970s to today."

"The 1970s?"

"The company was founded in 1972, right here in this area. The skeleton of the first production plant is still standing, kept as a memory. It's in the western area."

They approach the building, climb the marble—covered stairs, and stop at the sliding glass door. The woman pulls out a magnetic badge and places it on the reader mounted on a steel column to the left of the door.

"Well, this is a company rich in history, then. You could say that."

"It is." The reader emits a monotone beep, and the door opens. "It really is."

"Certainly, this whole mess wasn't needed."

The woman walks into the hall, at the far end, there is a reception desk. Two women look up at her and give her a slight nod, which she returns, then heads down a long corridor lined with red carpet. The walls are adorned with photos of construction sites and industrial plants, majestic and vividly colorful.

"No?" prompts the commissioner.

The woman seems to tense up, then tilts her head slightly toward the commissioner, who is following half a step behind.

"The event affected everyone. We're all shaken by what happened. But life is like this, and we move forward."

"Exactly. Life always moves forward. You have to keep looking ahead."

They continue walking in silence, their footsteps muffled by the carpet.

"Certainly, I have an odd job." The commissioner resumes "Instead of looking ahead, I'm always looking back, trying to figure out what others did, thought, or said."

"And does that frustrate you, Commissioner?"

"Not too much, actually. I like it. Some others don't though, they feel threatened or powerless" He points to one of the many photos on the walls "Are these your construction sites?"

"Yes and no, most of them belong to our clients."

They stop in front of a glass door with a wide frosted band in the middle. The woman turns to the commissioner and clutches the folder closer to her.

"Commissioner, beyond this door are Dr. Solimena's offices. Please wait in this room." She gestures to a wooden door on her left. "There's a coffee machine and some snacks if you'd like while you wait. I'll come get you as soon as the doctor is available."

The commissioner opens the door. The room is large, with an oval table seating twelve, and chairs along the long sides. At the far end, a giant plasma television occupies most of the wall.

"The coffee machine is on the right as soon as you enter."

The commissioner puts his hands in his pockets and takes a step toward the door, then turns back and leans on the doorframe.

"Alright, I'll wait here."

The woman looks at him, then smiles. She pulls out her badge and places it against the reader on the wall. The glass door opens with a metallic sound, and she steps inside.

The commissioner watches as she walks away on the red carpet, and the door closes behind her. Then he looks down and scrapes his shoe against the soft floor. When he raises his head again, the woman has disappeared into one of the rooms.

"Very well."

He turns and retraces his steps back to the hall at a brisk pace. When he arrives, the two receptionists are behind the desk, one of them on the phone, speaking loudly and annoyingly. The commissioner walks confidently toward the door, which only opens when he is very close. He walks through, descends the stairs, and walks about ten meters to the right, stopping on the sidewalk after passing the building. There are well–maintained flowerbeds around him. He lifts his head and looks around. Three buildings face the west side, opposite where he now stands, on the main road of the facility heading north. He pulls the map the guard gave him at the entrance from his pocket. There's a map on the back, marking the emergency assembly points. It confirms that the facility runs along the main road from the south, where the guardhouse is, to the north, where the plants are. The west side contains the three buildings he now sees in front of him, and behind them is a large open space. In one corner is the structure that is supposed to be the first plant the secretary mentioned. The main production plants are in the north and east. He turns and confirms this. A tall, long building can be seen in the distance to the northwest. Trucks are parked around it, waiting.

Someone passes behind him, and he extends an arm, brushing the person's shoulder.

"Excuse me!"

The man turns. He's in his fifties, with graying hair.

"Yes?"

"Do you know where I can find a coffee machine? I didn't have breakfast this morning."

"The nearest one is in that direction. Otherwise, you'll have to go across, under R&D."

"Where?"

The man walks beside him and points to the first of the three buildings across the street.

"Thank you very much."

"Isn't there anyone accompanying you around the facility?"

"He went to the bathroom!" Says the commissioner as he walks away, raising his hand in farewell.

The road is busy with many trucks and tankers alternating in both directions. Every now and then, a few green and gray cars appear between them. The commissioner crosses, careful not to disrupt the traffic or get honked at. He approaches the door. It's gray aluminum, with the Prosud logo and 'R&D Department' written below. The door is closed and won't open. There's a badge reader on the right side. The commissioner rubs his temples and peers inside through the glass to spot anyone.

There are two women standing in the hallway, talking just in front of the door. The policeman knocks on the glass with his knuckles and catches their attention, miming drinking from a coffee cup. One of the women moves toward the door while the other says something before leaving. The woman reaches out and opens the door, and the commissioner nods in thanks as he enters the building.

"Are you looking for something?"

"Excuse me, I left my glasses by the coffee machine. I'll go grab them quickly."

"Alright, go ahead." She says, leaving the door as it closes and walks away.

The commissioner heads down the hall in the opposite direction from the woman.

"The coffee machines are this way!"

He turns, and the woman is standing there, watching him.

"Sorry! My sense of direction is terrible."

He returns and catches up with the woman.

"You forgot your glasses?"

"They're reading glasses."

"Do you or you don't know where the coffee machines are?"

"If you show me quickly, it'll be faster."

The woman narrows her eyes at him. She's young, with an intelligent gaze.

"At the end, then right."

"Thanks! I won't bother you anymore!"

The commissioner walks quickly toward the end of the hall. A window lets in blue light that tinges the walls with sadness. He turns right and finds the coffee machines. There's one for coffee, one for drinks and water, and a third for snacks. On one side, there are some chairs.

The commissioner realizes a coffee would be nice. He reaches into his pocket and pulls out a coin. Fifty cents. Perfect. He inserts it into the machine and presses the espresso button.

"Did you find your glasses?"

The girl from earlier is leaning against the wall, looking at him challengingly.

"No."

There's a pause. The coffee machine activates the pump and emits a metallic hum.

"You've never been here before."

The commissioner waits for the coffee to be ready. The machine signals the end of the process with a long beep. He reaches inside the compartment, takes out the beige–colored cup, and walks toward the row of chairs along the wall, sitting down.

"I think you're underpaid for what you're worth."

"Who are you?"

The commissioner sips his coffee and watches her as he does.

"My name is Cardona. I'm a police commissioner."

"Oh." The girl hesitates. She stiffens for a moment, then recomposes herself. "For a moment, I thought..." She stops.

"A corporate spy?"

"A journalist."

"A sensible guess." He tosses the cup toward the trash can and lands it perfectly. But no, I'm a cop.

"Are you here investigating Marzio?"

"You knew him?"

"Yes, I knew him. Everyone here knew him."

"What did you think of him?"

"I think he was a good guy. I always saw him working hard, and whenever we did something together, he was always very kind, very smart too."

"The girl has her arms crossed, hugging the papers she's carrying."

"You worked together? On what?"

"He worked here, in Research and Development. I've been here for two years, and he was already here when I arrived. He was Dr. Cardia's assistant, and they always worked closely together."

"Who is Cardia?"

"Cardia was the dean. The head of R&D. He's the one who made Prosud the technological leader in plasticizers, release agents, and waterproofing for concrete. He's the one who built this company alongside Solimena. The mind behind Prosud."

"Ah, I see." The commissioner pulls out his black notebook from his coat. "Can I talk to this Dr. Cardia?"

"No, you can't. He died four months ago."

The commissioner grunts in disappointment and jots down the name in his notebook.

"And Marzio was his assistant?"

"Yes."

"Tell me more about him?" He asks politely.

The girl walks over to the coffee machine.

"I arrived here two years ago. He had been here for a year already, since he finished university. At that time, we were working on UF–10, a new superplasticizer. It seemed promising, and I remember everyone being excited about it. Marzio was part of the development team and worked closely with Cardia. They often stayed late into the night in the labs. It was a great time, coming to work in the morning energized you, filled you with hope and vision for the future." The coffee is ready. She picks it up and holds it in her hands. "Then UF–10 was released, and R&D went back to normal, but I still have fond memories of those days."

"What kind of person was Marzio?"

"He was cordial, always smiling. He didn't talk much, but when we were by the coffee machines and exchanged a few words, he always made you feel comfortable. He was pleasant."

She pauses and sips her coffee, gazing down the hallway, lost in thought.

"Did you like him?"

She hesitates, then lowers the cup from her lips.

"He was a good–looking guy." Another sip. "But he was a good person in general. Honestly, it felt like everyone was a bit drawn to him. It seemed so easy to love him."

"Those are beautiful words."

"Yes, they are. It might seem easy to speak well of someone who's passed. But" She sighs "I don't know, maybe it's true. But these are the memories I have."

She's hunched over as she says these words, then straightens up, her gaze focusing on something. She smiles.

"Hi Agnese."

A blond man enters the room. He's in his late forties, tall and thin, wearing thick black celluloid glasses. He has a prepaid coffee card in hand, which he inserts into the coffee machine and orders one.

"Good morning." He says after noticing the commissioner seated to his left.

"Good morning" Replies the commissioner.

"Agnese, you seem a bit down. What's with that look?" He says, addressing her.

"Nothing, we were talking about Marzio.

The man looks back at the machine.

"I see."

"Gianni, this is Commissioner Cardona. He's here to investigate what happened last week."

Gianni extends his right hand toward the officer.

"Very pleased to meet you, Giovanni Ventriglia."

"Pleased to meet you, Cardona. Have you been working here long?"

"Twenty–one years now, almost twenty–two."

"What's your role?"

"Senior Project Manager."

"You knew Marzio?"

"Yes, we all did. We worked together."

"You mentioned that Cardia passed away, right? What kind of person was he?

"Ah, Cardia. He was certainly... unique." Exclaims Giovanni. "He was tough, demanding, and precise in theory but very practical. You'd often see him on the plants, pushing aside department heads to operate the control panels himself. The entire facility hung on his every word, and he knew it well. He had complete authority. No one could object; every word was law."

"He was tough, but he knew how to give credit where it was due." Says Agnese, throwing her empty cup into the trash.

"Yes, that's true. But it was hard to be around him."

"But Marzio handled it well, didn't he?" Asks the commissioner.

"Yes, he did." Agnese replies.

"I don't recall him ever reprimanding Marzio in public, to be honest." says Ventriglia.

"Maybe he never needed to, but after all, Marzio wasn't given special treatment. At least, I don't think so." She responds.

"Well, they had a special relationship anyway. Especially after Mr. Solimena passed away."

"Who are you talking about now?" Asks the commissioner.

"Solimena Senior. The founder. He died five years ago. A brain ischemia."

The commissioner writes it all down in his notebook.

"When he had the stroke, they took him to Switzerland for rehabilitation. Marzio and his wife went with him, and they stayed there for six months with little progress. Then one night, Solimena had another attack and died there in the clinic bed."

"And then what happened? How did the company handle it?"

"At first, we were all scared. Prosud was Michele Solimena. He was like a father to us all. He had brought us together, one by one, and led us along this dream of building a center of excellence here in Campania, something to be proud of worldwide. When he left us so suddenly, and we lost his guidance, I remember being completely lost."

Ventriglia sits down next to the commissioner.

"At the time, Marzio was still studying chemical engineering, and his brother Umberto worked in the purchasing department. All the duties passed to him, and gradually, Prosud continued. We had revenue drops, but mainly because the cement industry came to a halt due to the crisis. Then came the new superplasticizer, and we breathed a little easier for a while. So, here we are."

"And Marzio? What was his special relationship with Cardia?"

"It's easy to imagine. Michele Solimena practically had three children: Umberto, Marzio, and Prosud. And perhaps the one he was most attached to was Prosud. He spent most of his time here. The man closest to him inside was Cardia, and they were often together, walking around the plant, having lunch. They did everything friends and colleagues do. Everyone knew they worked well together, and together they built this. So for Marzio, that man must have seemed like an uncle, the person closest to his father. a surrogate."

Ventriglia pauses and finishes his coffee.

"And perhaps for Cardia, it was the same. It was like still having Michele Solimena around, giving him reassurance."

"And Umberto?"

Ventriglia laughs loudly.

"No, Cardia never had any respect for Umberto. They always got along poorly. He called him a 'salesman,' with disdain. But I think it was mutual."

"But with Marzio, it was different." Says the commissioner.

"Yes, it was different." Ventriglia says with a relaxed expression.

"So when Cardia died, how did Marzio react? I imagine he was shaken, losing two such figures in such a short time. How did you see him?" Asks the commissioner. Agnese lowers her gaze.

"When was it?" Asks Ventriglia.

"May 8." Replies Agnese.

"Right, May 8. Four months ago. Well, what can I say, commissioner? He didn't take it well, but no one did. We all felt like the future cracked after May 8."

"The truth is, we all hoped Marzio could take Cardia's place." Says Agnese, now looking at the ceiling."

"But it was too soon, and he knew it. He knew it well. For a few days after his death, he kept coming to work here."

"All through May." Agnese adds.

"All through May, yes. Then something strange happened."

"What?" Asks the commissioner.

"He went to work in engineering."

"What do you mean?"

"The engineering and maintenance department, the one that handles the plants, builds the new ones, and maintains the old ones. The people who finalize our work."

"That would be the burned building."

"Yes, that one."

They fall silent.

"Commissioner." Ventriglia says.

"Yes?"

"The boy was shaken, and he lost his bearings. I don't know if it was his choice to move to engineering. But sometimes, everything seems impossible, and there's no way out. And maybe, if he made that decision, it was to avoid destroying this place. The place where perhaps he left his heart and soul. That's the explanation I give myself."

Silence fills the room again.

"What do you think, commissioner?" The technician asks.

Ventriglia stands and walks to the snack machine, presses two buttons, and something falls into the slot below.

"I think it's too soon for me to say. But a lot of bad things have happened here. Things I didn't know about. What I can say is, if someone wants to end their life, they don't burn themselves alive in their office unless they're trying to send a clear message. There are many easier ways to take your own life."

"That's true too." Says Ventriglia.

Agnese remains silent, leaning against the wall, just as she had at the beginning of the conversation.

The commissioner stands, reaches into the inner pocket of his coat, pulls out business cards, and hands them to both.

"Here are my contacts." The commissioner hands his business cards. "If anything comes to mind that you think is relevant, don't hesitate to call. No problem at all. Thank you for the conversation. It's been very interesting. I'll head back to where I came from."

"Thank you, commissioner. Goodbye." says Ventriglia, taking the card from his hand, while Agnese simply nods her head.

The commissioner walks back down the corridor and toward the door. The path seems shorter now. He pushes the emergency exit bar and steps outside. The clouds are still low. The plants are to his left. Some chimneys are spewing out dense, colorless smoke, distorting the clouds behind them. He turns to the right and heads toward the burned office building.

On either side of the sidewalk, there's a strip of well—manicured grass. It's like this throughout the facility. If the weather wasn't so bad, if the biting wind didn't seep into every fold of his coat, it would be pleasant to walk here.

The burnt building is thirty meters long and fifteen meters wide. There are two full floors, and above them, an eight—meter—wide, twenty—meter—long extension. The rest is a flat roof. The windows are shattered, and the interior walls are completely blackened. Outside, soot clings to the openings where the flames roared through, leaving marks like congealed blood. It looks like a face screaming in terror with its eyes gouged out. Everything is frozen, except for the yellow tape fluttering in the wind.

The commissioner slips a hand into his pocket, feeling the cigarette pack and craving a smoke. With the other, he searches for his lighter in his coat pocket. He stops when he hears a powerful car approaching. Turning around, he sees a Mercedes S—Class emerging from behind the management building and heading down the main avenue. The officer crosses the street and positions himself on the lane leading to the guardhouse. The car approaches and tries to pass him, but a tanker truck is crawling along in the opposite lane, blocking the maneuver. The commissioner lights his cigarette and walks toward the car, waving his hand and leaning forward toward the darkened window, which remains closed.

He knocks twice on the glass.

The window lowers, revealing a man in his forties, wearing dark sunglasses. Wrinkles furrow his brows and forehead. His lips are tightly pressed, and his head is sunk into his neck.

"Good morning, Mr. Solimena."

"And you are?"

"Commissioner Cardona, Police."

"Smoking is not allowed inside the facility."

"It'll be out soon and will extinguish itself. When can I have a chat with you?"

"I was available a while ago, but you weren't around."

"You're right, I was here observing the wreck."

"Commissioner, we need to focus on moving forward here. Prosud is a large company, and it's my job to take it even further."

"You really are a business leader, Mr. Solimena. I just need ten minutes, no more, and then I won't bother you again."

The man looks at the commissioner coldly, his lips turned downward.

27

"Come by tomorrow after six, and I'll see if I can meet with you. Call Miss Schiavone."

"Thank you, Mr. Solimena. Tomorrow it is, then."

The window rolls up, and the car starts again. The engine growls deeply, and the barrier lifts long before the car reaches it. With a roar, it passes through the gate, and the sound fades into the distance.

The commissioner takes one last drag, drops the cigarette butt on the asphalt, and stomps it out.

"Very well."

4.

I grip the coffee maker, then take a cloth, wrap it around, and squeeze it again, turning it a little more. Then it's the turn of a napkin. I dampen it with some water and wrap it around the joint of the moka. I turn on the stove and place it on top.

"You know, Marzio, the thing is, none of this was supposed to happen."

I move to the table and sit down, resting my arms on it.

"You weren't supposed to die. And I wasn't supposed to be alone."

Marzio looks at me, standing in the kitchen doorway, one step inside and one out. He's wearing a white shirt and fitted black pants. His expression is sad, and he seems pale.

"Do you miss me, Marzio?"

His expression doesn't change.

"I've missed you so much, to death."

The water in the moka starts bubbling.

It feels as if someone is gripping my stomach and squeezing tightly. As if I have a million words to say, but they all pile up at that tiny doorway, pushing and pulling, each one wanting to come out first, and I remain silent, waiting for them. He's in front of me, watching, and for a moment, I calm down. I live in this anxiety that pulls me into this whirlpool, dreaming of waking up again like last Sunday, in your arms. And your voice whispering that everything's okay.

But is everything okay, Marzio? If everything is okay, why did you leave?

"Did you want to die, Marzio? Did you? I don't believe it. I don't believe it, not for a second."

I stand up, the coffee is rising, and I take a step toward him.

"Marzio, why won't you talk to me? Why won't you tell me what happened to you?"

I take another step. We're two meters apart now.

"...what really happened, my love."

I take another step, and he moves back, serene.

Maybe I could touch him if I threw myself at him. But I'm afraid.

What if I touch him? What happens if I touch him? I'm afraid he'll disappear.

It's an endless torture. A tear falls without me wanting it to. I feel like my life is fragile, like it doesn't make sense.

"It doesn't make sense without you, do you understand? It doesn't."

You filled it up.

I wipe my tears with my hands. He used to wipe them for me, with his fingers.

The coffee is ready.

I go to the cupboard and take two cups, putting a teaspoon of sugar in each, then pouring the coffee into two equal parts. I stir it well, and a strong aroma rises from the porcelain with a wisp of steam. I place both cups on the table.

"If you want, your coffee is here."

I haven't slept all night. Or at least, it feels that way. I don't remember well.

I don't know if God exists, or hell or heaven. If I'm going mad and seeing visions, but all of this feels so real. You feel so real, so now, so here. This feeling of truth. It's not possible to fool yourself like this with your mind.

Or is it?

Maybe.

Yes. I could be completely mad. I could be schizophrenic, and eventually, they'll lock me up. Lock me up and throw away the key.

In the meantime, I could believe. I could believe it's true and that you're here. Do you think I'm hurting myself by doing this? I could say that life moves on, that I'll suffer for a while over you, and then I'll forget you, and you'll disappear. But it's not like that. And even if it were, I don't want to be like that because, to me, you are everything. And I can't deny what everything means to me. I can be crazy then, yes, I can, I can accept that, and I want to believe you're here for a reason. And my madness will be confirmed or cured when I find out why you're here, haunting my soul. Inside my eyes.

You're so beautiful, Marzio. I almost forgot the color of your eyes, the length of your fingers, the shape of your shoulders. It seemed like you were slipping away from my mind, like a mark in the sand at the water's edge.

In the end, I'd still have the photos, but it wouldn't be the same. It would be remembering the memory of you. No longer knowing what was hidden in that tiny scrap of flesh so microscopic on paper or pixels that blur when I zoom in on the image, preserving you in something so meager for what you are, for what you are to me, Marzio. You are my champion.

My sign of victory.

The words of love die, suffocated in my throat.

"Drink your coffee, please."

I extend my hand to indicate it and smile. It feels sweet on my lips, and I remember the first time we met. The warmth in my heart. The bookstore, the lower floor, the coffee counter. The last slice of berry cheesecake, you asking for it while I was still standing there, not knowing what to choose, and when I heard your words, I let out a sharp little whine. I didn't even know why it came out of my mouth, I didn't mean to, I swear. It was automatic, maybe it was karma spilling from my lips. And you turned, looked at me, and said, 'If you want it, I can give it to you, and you can buy it, or I'll buy it and offer you half.' I remember laughing and blushing at the same time. I hated you for embarrassing me but adored you for the sweetness with which you did it. You were always so handsome. I would have taken my heart out of my chest and given it to you. It's yours, I would've said. Do with it what you want. And finding out that you, like me, were waiting until seven to go to an exhibition of an unknown artist in that nearby gallery, how could two people end up doing something like that in such a small space? It's a density of probability that makes no sense, you yelled, and laughed. 'You like berry cheesecake and neo–realist artists. You're someone worth knowing! Except in the morning at breakfast! Unless there's a sufficient supply of berry cheesecake!' Amen! My love.

Amen, my love. Let it be so, in your arms.

My coffee cup is empty. Yours is full.

It's time to do something.

I feel cold, it's the cold of the morning, of the sleep that's missing, of the new day arriving, of life and its breath tightening my skin. The sweater I'm wearing is loose and high–necked. I wrap my hands around my waist, my lips clench into a tight line until they disappear. I want to cry, but I can't.

"Now we're going to do something, Marzio."

As I say this, I'm looking at the ground, trying to convince myself I can move from here.

I can do it. I need the computer, and we'll start from there.

It's an irresistible force that keeps me still. If I stay here, it tells me, nothing will happen. If you move, you'll be attacked. The memories, the pain, the sorrow. What's better than this precarious balance, where you just breathe to live? You could forget everything and believe that time passes without purpose today, tomorrow, and beyond. In the meantime, you wouldn't suffer. The claws wouldn't tear at your flesh. Your gaze is cold, but at least you're looking at me, and I'm looking at you. It's not life, but it looks like it, and I'd be willing to accept it.

I don't think you could have tolerated this speech from me, you know? I think you would have taken me by the arm and pulled me out of the room, shouting in my face that action is what matters. That those who stand still die. Those who stay silent lose. Isn't that right? That's why you're here now, isn't it? Because you can't stay silent, because you can't help but act. Because there's something that needs to be done, and it has to be done so intensely that you're standing here in front of me, even though you're dead.

Why are you dead, Marzio?

I bite my lower lip. It's impossible that you wanted to die, love. It's impossible, you would never have done it, you wouldn't have left me like this, without a word, a sign, something. You were supposed to be happy. We were supposed to be happy together. A shiver shakes me, and it's warm. Anger rises inside me, boiling in my stomach. Someone did something to you; it can't be anything else.

I pull away from the counter where I was leaning and walk toward him. He steps back and to the right. I step out of the door and smile at him. He never looks at me. I walk toward the living room on the left. The laptop is on the two–seater couch. I sit, pulling my legs up to my chest, grab the computer, place it on my knees, and open it. I type the password, and it's on.

Where do we start?

From your personal email.

I go to Google and click on Gmail, account name marzio.solimena@gmail.com.

Password. I try the one for Facebook, I know that one. I type it in, my heart tightens as I do. I love you. But it's okay. I press enter, and from Google Accounts, a gray screen opens. The blue bar in the middle loads, and at the top, it says 'Loading marzio.solimena@gmail.com.' The inbox screen appears. There are 128 unread messages, and I start scrolling through the names. Some I recognize, scattered among the ads. Among the names I know, from Thursday until today, there are farewell messages. In the email headers, there are goodbyes, and in the body, small farewell phrases. I don't know what to think. Whether it disgusts me, saddens me, or if it's something beautiful.

How long has it been since I opened this computer? My hands tremble and feel like damp wood. I stop to read these words. I clench my teeth. I don't want to, but it happens.

How many people truly cared about you, and how many just wanted to take and use you? Keep you by their side like a trophy. I don't know, how many of these names seem like bearers of lies? I can't recognize them anymore.

Wednesday.

Wednesday. You were at work on Wednesday. Were we supposed to meet? No, we weren't. You were working. It was a long day. I reach into my pocket and grab my phone. I open WhatsApp and read our conversation. The last message received at 2:35 PM: I ate, you wrote. I miss you, I love you. We'll talk later.

We'll talk later.

Ads. Newsletter from the Teatro San Carlo, Art Market Insights. One of my emails, a photo taken with Instagram. There's so much stuff here. My eyes fall under the inbox, and I see 'Special' and below that, 'Important.'

I look at the 'Special' folder. There are sixteen emails, almost all from me. They're the love letters I used to write to him from time to time. Oh God, why am I doing this to myself? I cry, I cry, and I can't stop. I cry, and my mouth opens, frozen in a grimace of pain. I feel the muscles in my face tightening, the spasm locking up my body, the skin on my face becoming warm, burning, my temples, my eyelids. I clench my fists against my chest and collapse onto the cushions. A few seconds, just a few seconds.

It's okay, it's okay. Now it's okay. I continue.

I stay there for a moment with my face pressed into the cushions, breathing, arms stretched out. You need to stop crying. You need to do something. I sob. Unwillingly. It's as if my soul wants to escape from my chest.

I'm almost okay.

I'm almost okay, I would settle for being able to say that if someone asked me. I wipe my tears with my wrists. I take a deep breath. My cheeks are warm, and I take the computer in my hands again. 'Special.'

The first one's mine, the second one's mine. They're arranged from oldest to most recent. Each has a particular flavor, a vivid memory. My mind clouds over. There's Cardia. Dated April 25. And there's another, more recent, August 29. The sender is 'lili', lowercase. I open the one from Cardia.

It's brief.

Hi Marzio,

I've thought a lot about what you told me. I know your father relied on you a lot, as do I, and you've given me reason to believe that I'm right.

Just know that there are some things I need to tell you. You need to hear them from me, looking me in the eyes. You're young, and it's the young who have the strength to change things.

I'll be waiting for you at my place tomorrow evening after dinner.
AC

As I read it, I feel my heart pounding in my chest. I try to think back to Marzio during that time. Before Cardia's death, I remember our happiest time together. I remember him sweet and carefree, our trip to Paris, when we left without notice, and I had to ask for time off on the very night he came to pick me up from work with the suitcase ready.

"I packed everything you need." He said. "We'll get the rest there."
"You're crazy." I said.
"Let's go; the plane leaves soon. We might miss it."

The simplicity with which he faced obstacles made them insignificant, small bumps to glide over without breaking stride.

"How do you do it?" I would ask.

"If you stop to think about it, you'll only make it worse. Just act, do, and everything will follow. It's zen, my love!"

Zen, he always said it. Be natural, he'd say. Let things flow and act.

And I, stuck wondering why. Whether it was right or wrong. Whether the consequences would hurt or destroy me. And he, animated, would run, taking me with him, chasing his dreams and freedom. So much fear, so much joy in following him blindly. I, naturally still, could leave behind my anxieties of failure and fly on the wind he blew under my wings.

"You know what Cardia says? He says if you fall from a high peak into a bottomless ravine, just spread your wings, and you'll fly. Do you know Bernoulli's theorem? The stronger the wind that hits you, the more lift your wings will have. Don't hold yourself when you're scared, embrace the world. Keep your arms wide, and the wind will lift you. Because you are a wonderful person, and the world preserves wonderful things."

Does it preserve them, Marzio?

I look at him. He's there, watching me silently as I watch him.

Then why did you disappear?

Slowly, the urge to see those lips move slips away. They're livid, cold, and he's pale.

Rain begins to patter on the windows. The living room is dark, and the little light that enters casts long, blurred shadows.

How happy you were, how beautiful it was to be infected by your happiness, my love. My eyes fall back to the screen.

The email signed 'lili' is even shorter. It says only this:

I received the message. I know how to help you, and I want to do it.
Let's meet at Caffè Letterario at 10:00 PM
Tomorrow
Lili

These words swirl in my mind. There's a black hole in Marzio's life, and I know nothing about it. These are the milestones of his descent into the abyss. I look at my hands as if peeking into my soul. I didn't notice anything. What did you go through, Marzio, to reach this point?

It started with Cardia's death, and it led to this 'lili.' These four months flew by like the wind while my life flowed smoothly, easily, with thoughts of you. What did you live through? Why did you keep me out of it? Were you protecting me? Did you want to protect me, or did you not trust me?

I get up, leave the computer on the couch, and start pacing the living room. I try to think of Marzio, how he was in May after Cardia's death, the funeral, the black clothes, his somber expression for a few weeks. But he came back to me every night; we ate together, and eventually, we laughed again. If something was going on, and these are the signs, I didn't notice it. But could I have noticed it?

I turn to him.

"All of this, this thing that happened, led to your death. It was important. Why didn't you ever tell me?"

My voice trembles without my will. I don't know if I shouted or whispered.

The sound of the bells is sharp, crystalline. All my muscles lock up. I can feel him behind me.

His presence fills the room, as if an enormous shadow had snuffed out all the light, and only the flicker of a candle illuminates my heart, clenched tight in a vice.

It's heavy, oppressive. I don't want to turn around, I don't want to, but I have to. It's as if he grabs my shoulder and pushes me, forcing me to pivot on my legs. I do it.

I see his hands gripping the dresser to the right of the window. His fingers are wide, pressing hard on the white lacquered wood. Between his hands, in the middle, the hat with pointed tips and bells peeks out. He presses hard and pushes, shifting the dresser twenty centimeters forward from the wall. His face appears, and as he rises, the hat moves, and the bells jingle. It's an unpleasant sound. It fills me with anxiety. He laughs.

He's a strange creature. I don't know what he is, but his presence is unsettling. My mind howls, and my thoughts are confused. I'm frozen. Part of me screams, wishing he would disappear, while the other wants to sleep and wake up when all of this is over. But he rises, kneeling on the dresser and sitting. He looks at me with a defiant grin and laughs. His laugh is dry, raspy.

"So? How's our little adventure going? Have you two made any progress? Oh, you make such a perfect couple! No secrets between you, is that right, my dear?" He claps his hands in satisfaction, then assumes a startled expression. "What's that? Things have happened, and you haven't told her? Why didn't you, my boy?" He puts his hand to his ear, leaning forward. "Oh, but I don't know if that excuse will be enough to stop your girl from going mad with rage." He chuckles malevolently.

"You... are you talking to him?" I can't believe I managed to say anything.

"Oh, of course! But I could also say no, and that I'm deceiving you!" He laughs louder. "Do you think I'm talking to him? Let's play a game! Ask me a question, and I'll ask him for you! If he answers, I'll tell you his response, and then you can decide if I'm lying or telling the truth. But know this game comes at a price. Do you still want to play?"

"What's the price?" My heart trembles as I say it.

"If you choose to play, I'll take his eyes. They'll be mine." He jumps up excitedly. "Seems like a fair trade!"

"His eyes?" I don't understand.

He leaps down from the dresser and walks quickly toward Marzio, dragging his right leg slightly as he moves. He reaches him, grabs hold of his waist, clings to his shirt, and climbs up him, fast. He wraps his legs around Marzio's abdomen and his left hand around his neck. Perched on his shoulders, he looks at me, touching Marzio's eyelids with his right hand.

"See these?" He forces Marzio's eyes shut and then open again with those wretched, wrinkled hands, pushing hard as he does. Marzio remains impassive. 'I want them for myself. They'll be mine. Mine!"

He laughs. It disgusts me to see him touching Marzio's face like that. A terrible rage rises inside me, bubbling in my stomach and climbing to my throat.

"Stop touching him, damn you! Get off him! Enough!"

I scream and rush toward them, taking three heavy steps. It feels like the walls are shaking from the impact. I reach them; I can touch them. I extend my arms but stop, frozen by his icy eyes staring at me. I see joy and fury mixed together. His grin is exaggerated and cruel. The fury in me suddenly dissipates. It strips me, leaving me naked, covered only by fear.

"Go on, touch us." He says, his muscles tense with spasms in his demonic laughter.

"Touch us." He repeats, his voice sharp.

I don't do it. I know that if I do, something terrible will happen.

"Touch us!"

His voice thunders with an infernal roar. The room trembles, and objects fall from the shelves, porcelain shatters into pieces, and I'm thrown backward. I fly as if hit by the explosion of a bomb, my back slamming against the edge of the couch, and a dull pain spreads through my right side. I arch and moan in pain. My ears ring, and I see the walls spinning around me. Another sharp pain, I cough. I place my hands on the floor. Oh God, what's happening to me? I exhale and cough again. I'm lying on the floor, my right cheek and temple pressed against the ground. I can't focus on anything more than ten centimeters away. Everything is blurred and confused. I exhale in pain. Breathe. Exhale in pain. I'm still alive. I know I am. Exhale in pain. It's easier this time.

I bring my hand to my side, massaging it, and close my eyes. I reopen them. And he's still clinging to Marzio, holding him with his hands. Marzio looks like a helpless puppet. It hurts to see him like this.

"I haven't finished telling you the rules. I haven't finished, so I forgive you for this act of arrogance, you insignificant little being. Rotten flesh."

His face is twisted with rage. His eyes are sunken, his lips turned downward, and deep wrinkles carve into his sharp nose.

"You're a foolish and dangerous girl, and you don't understand the game. You want to break it, and you want to offend me. And if you continue, I'll devour your soul. I'll burn you, rip everything from you until you scream in pain forever. Through the infinite of time, and I'll take pleasure in it."

His voice is deep, dark, completely different from before.

"The third rule of the game is that once you're in, you can't leave without losing everything. You either play until the end and I'll give you the chance to save yourself and let your boy sleep, or accept the consequences, and become mine, like he is now."

He grips Marzio's neck, sliding his face against his cheeks. It's tormenting to watch.

"But you can do nothing but play."

His voice fades, leaving only a high-pitched ringing in my ears. I don't know what's happening to my life. I don't know what trick of fate has been laid before me.

The only sensation I have, deep in my heart and mind, is that if I fight against him, I won't win. I won't prevail and take back my life. I just have to go along with him. I have to flow with him. See where this river takes me.

I sit up. The pain is fading, but I can't breathe deeply without a stabbing pain in my ribs.

"You're here because he asked you to be."

He doesn't respond.

"He asked because there are things I need to know and things I need to do." I feel clear-headed as I speak these words. They come out of me on their own. "I've discovered there are things I don't know. Things that led Marzio to act, to say certain things. And then to burn inside his company, inside his office. Marzio is telling me that nothing is by chance. That something brought him there, that something brought him death."

His hands rest on Marzio's shoulders, and his face seems to be relaxing.

"I will. I'll find out what happened. And what you want me to discover.

The being climbs down from Marzio's shoulders, sliding down while keeping its hands on his waist. Then it walks toward me. It approaches until it's just centimeters from my face. It's terrifying. His eyes are deep, endless, his breath shallow, and his skin looks like rubber.

"Excellent." He says with his acidic voice.

He laughs, showing yellow, crooked, broken teeth. I shrink back, closing my eyes, still afraid.

Tears well up in my eyes, and I let out a small whimper. Then I open them again.

He's gone. He's disappeared. The room is back in order. Nothing happened.

Marzio is in the corner of the room, where he's always been.

5.

Cardona enters the room. The desks are empty, the window closed, and the neon lights are on. The light coming in is so dim it seems the sun has already set. He moves toward his desk, searching through the scattered papers.

"Cesarano!" He shouts.

He brushes aside the countless documents cluttering the surface, grabbing a few, but they seem to multiply, never revealing the gray laminate beneath.

"Commissioner, you're back?"

"Cesarà, why does it feel like no one ever works in this room except me?"

"Commissioner, they just went out."

"They're always out, aren't they, Cesarà?"

"Commissioner, what do you want me to say? When De Michele doesn't see you here, I say the same thing, but we've got to help each other out, right? How else do we get by?"

"You've got a point." He stops, walks around the desk, and sits down. "Have you seen my planner?"

"Commissioner, you ask too much."

The commissioner opens the first drawer, then the second, pulling out a pack of cards.

"But, Commissioner, I do have good news."

"Eh, Cesarà, you're going to make me a happy man today."

"Commissioner, I'm not joking. Look what I got for you at the hospital."

He waves a brown envelope, sealed and stamped.

The commissioner stops and looks up. He fixes his gaze on the envelope, then at the officer's face. Cesarano is smiling as he shakes the piece of paper.

"Good job, Cesarano." The commissioner says, satisfied. "The autopsy was exactly the second thing I was looking for."

"Thank you, Commissioner." Cesarano's face beams with pride as he gently places the report on the desk.

The commissioner picks up the envelope, reaches into his pocket, pulls out his house keys, and grabs the longest one. He slips it under the glued flap and begins to open it.

"Now, you need to do one more thing for me."

"Just tell me, Commissioner."

"I need you to pull everything you can find on the Solimena family, Michele, Umberto, and Marzio. Everything. Criminal records, residence, properties, university, all of it. And I need it faster than this autopsy. Oh, and Cardia, Augusto. He worked at Prosud. See what you can dig up."

"My dear soul! You want to bury me! How can I do all that? I'll need a month!" Cesarano throws himself back in his chair, arms spread wide.

"Cesarà, you know what the Americans say?"

"Oh, here we go! The Americans! You always bring those people up!"

"The Americans say eighty percent of crimes are solved in the first..."

"In the first fifteen days." Cesarano finishes.

"Twelve, Cesarà. Twelve days after the event."

"Oh, now it's twelve."

"And that's not all. Bring me everything you can find on Prosud too, articles of incorporation, shareholder meetings, and everything else from the founding to today."

"My goodness!"

"Go, Cesarano, let the wings of justice fly!" The commissioner exclaims with amusement.

The uniformed officer shakes his head and walks away, muttering something, hands on his hips.

"Cesarano." The commissioner's voice is serious.

Cesarano turns back, and the smile is gone from Cardona's face.

"Cesarà, don't leave me now. There's something I need to understand."

The man looks at him from near the door.

"Commissioner, he killed himself. A rich, spoiled kid who fell into depression."

"I wish it were that simple. If it is, I promise you I'll buy you a pizza. But until I can confirm it, you need to stay close."

Cesarano turns and leaves the room without saying anything.

The commissioner pulls the document from the envelope. Dr. Fabbri Luigi.

"Fabbri, Fabbri, you were quick this time. Who lit a fire under you?"

The first page says nothing, date, day, place, blah blah blah.

'Autopsy'. Let's see.

The autopsy was performed on the morning of Friday, September 8th, at 8:00 AM. The body is identified as Marzio Solimena, confirmed by dental records provided by the deceased's dentist. Both the maxillary and mandibular arches match. The body is completely carbonized and locked in the boxer's pose, with arms hyperflexed toward the chest and knees bent and drawn up to the abdomen. This suggests the person burned while collapsed on the ground. The muscles appear contracted and retracted. The skin is mottled with leopard spots, alternating between different degrees of lesions. The internal organs are visible from the outside. The mouth is half-open, with teeth fully exposed. All bodily fluids are evaporated or coagulated, indicating prolonged exposure to flames. In some areas, the tissues have fused with the body. The bone structure remains intact except for a cranial fracture.

The commissioner grumbles as he reads the last sentence, leaning forward over the paper.

However, it should be noted that this fracture does not appear to be caused by an impact with a blunt object but by overpressure from gases generated in the cranial cavity due to heat.

Analysis of the deep airways reveals soot accumulation in the main bronchial trunk, indicating respiratory activity during the fire. Bronchial and pulmonary edema are also present.

The heart has the consistency of boiled meat. A blood sample was taken from inside, and analysis shows a carboxyhemoglobin level of around 10%. This further suggests respiratory activity during the fire. It is reasonably assumed that the victim was alive but unconscious during the carbonization process.

The report continues with detailed descriptions of the internal organs, nothing too interesting.

The commissioner leans back in his chair, letting the papers fall from his hands. He was alive while he burned.

Cardona presses his lips together until they disappear, squinting. Then he suddenly lunges forward, reaching across the right side of the desk, pushing aside some folders, and grabbing a blue folder. He opens it, discards the first few sheets, grabs a thick stack, lifts it, and nods in satisfaction as he flips through it. He stops at a document, the cover labeled 'Interrogation Transcript.'

"There it is."

Antonio Lupi, employee of the Vigilanza e Protezione security company, stationed at Prosud S.p.A. as a night guard during the shift from 10:00 PM to 6:00 AM.

The commissioner delves into the report. Lupi was alone during his shift, and when asked why, he explained that his colleague, Francesco Acanfora, had felt unwell, nausea, diarrhea, and feverish chills. Acanfora called to be replaced and left, saying he hadn't felt well when he arrived at work. After half an hour, he called in to ask if he could go home. He took his car and left. Lupi remained alone from 10:30 PM. At that time, the plants were idle, as production wasn't running across three shifts, so the entire facility was shut down. He didn't notice anything strange or suspicious, and the night passed quietly until 12:15 AM, when a bright flash caught his attention. He turned and saw building 3, the one housing the engineering and administrative offices, engulfed in flames. The windows had exploded, and the flames were pouring out. He raised the fire alarm and called the fire department.

They asked him if anyone had entered the facility. He said that since he started his shift, he hadn't seen anyone enter.

The fire department arrived at 12:45 AM, but by that time, the fire had already consumed the entire building.

There's nothing else of relevance. The commissioner sets the paper down and takes out his notebook, writing, 'talk to afternoon shift guard.' He pauses with the pen in hand, then adds, 'badge entry list.'

He puts the notebook back in his pocket, picks up the phone, then takes out his cell phone. Flipping through his contacts, he dials the landline while reading from the screen.

The phone rings.

"Hello?"

"Vincenzo, hey, it's Cardona."

"Commissioner! How are you?"

"Doing well, Vincé. Am I bothering you?"

"Of course not, don't worry. What's going on?"

"Everything good at the fire department?"

"Not bad, we're getting by."

"Listen, Vincé, I'm doing some research on the incident at Prosud. You know the one, right?"

"Of course. What do you need?"

"I've been thinking because I read that the security guard noticed the fire at 12:15 AM and said the flames were already coming out of the windows, which had exploded."

"Uh–huh, and?"

"So, I wanted to ask you, based on your experience, how long does it take for windows to explode from fire?"

"That depends, Commissioner. It depends on the fire–resistance class."

"They were offices. What class do you think they had?"

"Off the top of my head, I'd say that unless they were archives, the offices probably weren't classified. So, I'd guess they were regular windows, maybe double–paned for thermal insulation."

"And how long would it take for those to break?"

"Commissioner, please take what I'm about to say with a grain of salt. Without knowing the specifics, I'm just throwing numbers out there."

"Don't worry, Vincenzo. I just need an idea of what we're talking about."

"Okay, well, let's say they were offices, so the fire load would mainly come from paper and scattered documents, which are easy to ignite and produce a lot of flames, meaning heat. Under those conditions, an untempered window would shatter about... let's say five minutes after the flash point."

"And what's the flash point?"

"It's the point at which there's enough heat in the room to ignite all combustible materials at once. Basically, a small flame starts, grows bigger and hotter, and then everything else catches fire. The flames become strong, enveloping everything, and in a closed space, the temperature quickly reaches around 600 degrees. Then, in at most five minutes, but often in just a couple, the windows explode."

"So it doesn't take long after the flash point. How long does it take to reach the flash point?"

"In a standard office room, like that, about twenty minutes."

"And once the room is fully ablaze, how long would it take for the whole building to burn down?"

"Give me some dimensions."

"Fifteen meters by thirty meters."

"The fire starts from the ground up, right?"

"Right."

"If there's no fire control, the whole thing would burn down in an hour, assuming the fire load is steady and evenly distributed."

"An hour from the flash point?"

"Yeah."

"And if the firefighters arrive?"

"They control and reduce the fire, but once the flames have engulfed the building, it's usually better to let it burn out and contain the area rather than try to save ten square meters of space. That's what they usually do."

"Got it."

"That's it."

"Alright, Vincé, you've been helpful as always."

"Commissioner, take my words with caution."

"Don't worry, Vincé. Thanks for everything."

"Goodbye, Commissioner."

"Bye."

Cardona hangs up the phone and looks at the interrogation transcript.

"Did they ask you if you knew Solimena was inside?"

The transcript remains silent, just paper. The commissioner flips through the file, stopping at the on–site inspection report. It's signed by Vasto.

"Well done. You sent someone who was transferring to Pisa two days later. Bravo, De Michele. I'll give you a round of applause when I see you."

The report is sloppy and incomplete, describing the site's state in barely two words. It doesn't mention the building or the room where the body was found, simply stating that everything was burned. What kind of report is this, the commissioner wonders, irritated.

He stops at one sentence.

Solimena's car, a gray Mercedes C–Class coupe, was parked behind the building. It was impounded and taken away.

The commissioner straightens up. He mentally reviews the facility's layout. The employee parking lot is to the left of the guardhouse. You enter, pass the guardhouse, and turn before building 3. The executive parking lot is behind the glass and aluminum building on the right. So that car is out of place.

They impounded it at the judicial depot. The commissioner opens the evidence sheet, scrolling through the list. He reaches the end and shakes his head. He starts again from the top and goes back down. The car key. It's not there. It's not among the evidence.

6.

The shower water makes me feel safe, falling on me like a gentle caress. I need to renew myself. Regenerate. Act. That's what you say, isn't it, my love? I look at myself, I observe my body. I've lost so much weight. I feel like a walking skeleton.

I step out of the shower, the air in the bathroom is warm, the fan heater works well. The layer of steam on the mirror is so thick that when I wipe my hand across it, it feels like I'm sinking into it.

I don't like what I see. The dark circles under my eyes are so deep they frighten me. I gently wrap the towel around my body and then my head, rubbing a bit harder. My underwear is in the sink. I pick it up and slip it on one leg at a time. I take out the hairdryer, plug it in, and turn it on. I aim it at my chest, moving it back and forth before drying my hair.

I looked up the address online. It was easy. But it's out of the way, in Torre del Greco, at the foot of Mount Vesuvius. I'll have to take the scooter, fill up the tank, and head out. I printed the route; it says the trip will take forty minutes.

Having done something makes me feel better for a while, I feel lighter. I know it's just a moment, fleeting, but I'll take this little bit and hold on to it.

I don't think much.

I watch my hair as the brush runs through it, following it centimeter by centimeter with the hairdryer's nozzle.

Stopping the questions is the right thing to do. Only looking ahead, for fear of falling backward.

I apply light makeup, primer, concealer, alternating powder and cream, a bit of eyeliner, mascara. I'm ready. I dress in layers: t–shirt, sweater, scarf, jacket, hat, leg warmers, and jeans. I grab my backpack, stuffing it with a raincoat, an umbrella, my wallet, and a folder with the printed emails.

I'm going.

I leave.

I insert the key in the door and unlock the two bolts that separate me from the outside world. The light outside irritates me, and I bury my face in my scarf, locking the door behind me with one turn of the key, and I rush away.

I run down the stairs and find myself in the building's lobby. I have the scooter keys in one hand, and I insert them into the lock. The compartment under the seat opens. I take out the helmet, take off my hat, and put it in its place, then close the seat. I insert the keys into the ignition, turn them, and press the start button. The scooter vibrates and starts up, the rear wheel begins to spin. I put the helmet on my head and fasten it. In my right pocket, I check that I have the itinerary.

The road is simple. I just need to get to Via Marina, and then it's a straight road for almost the entire trip. The name changes a thousand times, but I can tell it's always the same. Sometimes it's narrow, sometimes wide, the buildings around rise and fall, the traffic is dense, then sparse. But I can feel it, I can see that it's one continuous vein. It stretches long and uninterrupted along the coast. The lifeline where the consciousness of so many different lives flows.

I wonder if anyone else is suffering like I am right now.

It could be. I might not be the most miserable person in the world. Is that a comforting thought? I don't know why, but it doesn't satisfy me.

The wind is biting, cold, and damp. I pull my scarf up over my nose, lower the visor, but it still finds a way in, stabbing my eyes from every gap. It's a losing battle, and I grow irritated.

He once told me: 'When you're on a bike, you should never worry about the cold because if you do, it will take hold of you. You have to breathe deeply and square your shoulders. Challenge it, believe it doesn't exist, because it's just a creation of your senses, and your senses are flawed. If you don't believe in it, it doesn't exist.'

I feel like I see him among the people, behind cars or kiosks, as I speed through yellow lights.

I need to turn left. The road climbs steeply, and the buildings vanish, replaced by pastel–colored villas surrounded by gardens. Some are hidden, with only their roofs visible behind tall hedges marking their boundaries. Here, the dull roar of traffic gives way to a deep silence, broken only by my scooter. I almost feel ashamed to be riding it. If I had pedals, I would turn off the engine and pedal on. The summit of Vesuvius isn't visible; the gray clouds shroud it. I stop at number 56.

On the mailbox, the name 'Cardia' is written.

I press the intercom button. A short ring.

I wait for someone to answer. The gate is green, made of wrought iron, with vertical bars that curve away from the center, leaving space for an oval where the letters A and I are intertwined in a soft, cursive script.

No one answers. With some hesitation, I raise my finger to the intercom again, hoping I haven't come here for nothing.

I'm about to press the button when a female voice comes through the intercom.

"Who is it?" The voice is kind and elderly.

"Good evening, ma'am. You don't know me, but I'm here to talk to you." My heart pounds in my chest. "I'm Marzio's girlfriend."

No response from the intercom, but I can sense the woman is still there.

Seconds of silence pass. I'm unsure if I should say something or not. My arms are behind my back, hands clasped. I look at myself from the outside, I look like a schoolgirl.

"Come in."

A metallic click and buzz come from the gate. It opens. I push the scooter inside by hand. The path to the villa is about fifty meters long, lined with a well–kept lawn and a few scattered trees. The green foliage, heavy with rain, is neatly rounded from careful pruning. The grass is damp, cut short, and small yellow hedges guide the way along the basalt–paved path. I park the scooter a few meters after passing through the gate, leaving the helmet on the seat, and continue walking alone.

The house is an antique pink color and two stories tall, very high. There's a triangular pediment resting on two white columns. Beneath it, there's a space about two meters deep, leading to a solid wooden door. I approach, climb three steps, and stop in front of the entrance. I look for a doorbell.

The door opens, and an elderly woman with white hair peeks out through the crack.

"Are you Marzio's girlfriend?"

She looks me up and down, sizing me up.

"Yes." I say, bowing my head slightly as I speak.

We look into each other's eyes now. There's a moment of tension, then she softens her brows.

"Marzio spoke a lot about you. He cared about you very much." She says softly.

I exhale, my eyes filling with tears, and press my lips together.

"Come in, come in. I'll offer you something, and we can talk a little."

She extends an arm, stepping back to open the door fully. I wipe my eyes with the back of my hand and step inside.

"Thank you." I say in a faint voice. I turn to her and smile.

She closes the door, then gestures toward the living room.

She smiles at me, warmly. Her manner reassures me.

"You're very kind, ma'am."

"Please, call me by my name, Isabella."

I nod, embarrassed.

There are three white sofas arranged in a horseshoe around the fireplace. Two large windows with cream–colored curtains light the room. I sit on a two–seater sofa, near the armrest, my hands on my knees. He's there. Watching me. Standing behind the sofa across from me.

"Would you like some tea?"

I nod. Something warm sounds nice.

She walks away and disappears behind a door, then reappears and sits next to me on the sofa beside mine.

"Here we are. She says, smiling serenely. "Marzio talked about you a lot. He said you were beautiful, and he was right. He also said you were very intelligent. He was happy to be with you."

I shrug, unsure of what to say. I smile and stay silent.

"You came here for a reason, didn't you? Is there something you want me to tell you?"

I lower my gaze. My backpack is on the floor. I open the zipper and pull out the printed emails, handing her the one from her husband.

"This is an email your husband wrote to Marzio. It's dated April 25th."

Mrs. Cardia takes it and reads it. Then she hands it back to me.

"Augusto was a strict man, but he had very strong feelings deep inside." She says, looking at me with pride. "I know he loved Michele Solimena very much, and I could see that he loved Marzio in the same way. They worked together and formed a deep bond. Marzio needed a father, and Augusto needed a son, a son I was never able to give him."

She remains expressionless as she says it, but it's as if the room trembles with great energy for a brief moment.

"I can tell you that Michele Solimena had absolute trust in Augusto and his decisions."

She pauses.

"A trust that faded when Umberto took over from his father."

Her hands remain still as she speaks, one on the armrest and the other on her lap. She has a particular grace, and it's pleasant to watch her.

"Their relationship was never good and gradually deteriorated. Things left unsaid, small grudges, silly slights. I remember Augusto coming home nervous, often angry. More than once, he shouted in this house that he was going to quit and never set foot in that plant again. Augusto was like that, though he rarely reached such extremes, and he never threatened to leave Prosud, which was his whole life."

Her hair is tied in a chignon behind her neck. She's slender, her face marked by time, but her features remain fine and elegant. I wouldn't tire of watching her. I hope to be like that when I grow old.

"Marzio's arrival changed many things. They started working together, and Augusto calmed down. He found peace and creativity again. He started teaching Marzio a lot, and Marzio followed him, hanging on his every word. They often stayed late at work and came back here to eat together. It was always very late, and they would sit and talk on these very sofas."

I touch the leather beside me, caressing it, and look up at my Marzio.

"And I would have him stay the night here." She says with a smile. "I earned a few glares from his mother for that, you know. I think she thought I was trying to steal him away. I won't hide that I loved Marzio very much, as did Augusto, and it was nice to have him close. Did Marzio ever talk to you about his relationship with his mother?"

"No, never. He never talked about his family. It was like a dark side. Every time the subject came up, he would change it, and eventually, I stopped asking and avoided talking about it."

"Yes, that's how he was. Michele was never home, and Umberto and Marzio were raised almost entirely by their mother, which created two very different bonds." She says, her expression turning serious. "With the first, there was a visceral attachment. I believe it was because Umberto had a severe case of pneumonia as a child and almost died. I think that triggered something in Margherita that defined her relationship with her sons."

A woman in a white apron brings in a silver tray with a teapot, sugar bowl, and two white cups decorated with pink patterns. She places the tray on a stand between the two sofas. Isabella thanks her, picks up the teapot, and slowly, gracefully pours tea into my cup.

"How much sugar?" She asks sweetly.

"Two teaspoons, thank you."

She sets the teapot down and removes the sugar bowl lid with her thumb and forefinger, scooping sugar into the cup twice. Then she repeats the gesture for herself. She takes her cup and leans back against the leather of the sofa.

"In short, she always adopted a protective attitude toward Umberto, while Marzio took on a supportive role. He supported his brother from childhood through to his university years. I had seen Marzio silently accept this role, as if it were normal." She sips her tea. "I won't hide that Augusto played a fundamental role in rebuilding his self–esteem, helping him realize that he was talented and good not only at his job but in life and everything he decided to do on his own. Augusto jokingly called him a 'glorious head.' I could see the love in his eyes when he said those words to me about him."

She sighs, and for a moment, her shoulders slump.

"I believe Margherita never forgave us for pulling her son away from the role she had chosen for him. This idea had only grown stronger after Michele's death. Umberto had to become the head of Prosud, and failure wasn't an option. Everyone had to be sacrificed to make that happen. Even Augusto was questioned and could be discarded. What I call the 'Rebirth of Marzio' always disturbed her. I hope she only hated me and Augusto and never Marzio, but I can't say that for certain. All I know is that he was at peace when he slept here."

We drink our warm tea in silence. Outside, the rain falls heavier than it did this morning.

49

I feel good in this moment. Mrs. Cardia's words are soothing. It's nice to know there was someone who loved Marzio the way I do. I believe it was easy to love him.

"You don't know what your husband wanted to tell Marzio in that email?"

Isabella looks out the window, remaining silent for a few moments. Then she shakes her head.

"No, I don't know. Augusto was going through a tense time in his life, and although sharing it with Marzio lightened his burdens, there were heavy ones he carried. When the heart attack took him, he was here. I couldn't hear his last words. I only remember finding him in the bathroom, lying on the floor, his hands on his chest, with an expression of pain and worry. I'm convinced he died with a sense of incompleteness. And that he died sad."

"Marzio suffered greatly from his death." I say softly.

"I remember he spent the two days of the wake here and the day of the burial as well. We never touched or spoke about it, but he was the person closest to me during that time. We didn't even need to look at each other, just knowing he was there was enough."

"Yes, that's how he was. And from that moment, he became sad too."

Isabella runs her hand through her hair, gently stroking it.

"Yes, sad. But I can't help but remember him as worried, thoughtful, with a weight on his heart. Don't you remember him that way?"

I'm taken aback. It's true. I remember him that way, but I can't pinpoint the first time I saw it. The truth is, that dark shadow always accompanied him. And even when he smiled, it never seemed to leave his soft eyes. His gaze was like a warm caress, protecting me from the winter he carried inside.

"Maybe, in the end, Augusto told him everything he needed to say" I say, hoping.

"Maybe" Isabella smiles. She says nothing more.

We sit in silence. The sound of rain fills the room, and the light dims, the colors turning into shades of gray.

Isabella's eyes are lost in the void of the room, gently stroking her hair. I would have liked an aunt, maybe a mother, like her.

I rub my hands on my jeans. They feel damp, and the skin beneath them aches. I push myself up, ready to leave, feeling like I've already disturbed too much.

"In truth, there's something I'd like to show you." She says just before I fully stand.

Isabella rises from the sofa and gestures for me to follow her. She is long–limbed and elegant, walking as if she's floating. She leads me from the living room down a tall corridor. The walls are lined with old prints of Mount Vesuvius, almost all depicting it in eruption. She stops in front of a pair of sliding doors. The glass panels are frosted, and a large oval frames the intertwined cursive initials 'AC.' She opens the right door and slips into the room, and I follow her. It's a study, with a large inlaid wooden desk at its center. Bookshelves filled with eclectic volumes line the walls.

"I found this while tidying up and trying to remember him, when he would retreat to his study, and I'd bring him a cup of tea."

She hands me a photograph.

It's worn, with white creases running through it, the legacy of being folded and carried in someone's pocket without much care. The paper is thick, matte, and seems to have been printed in the 1980s, maybe the 1970s.

There's a boy and a girl in the picture, leaning against a wooden table. Behind them is a garden full of dark green leaves. The girl embraces him from the right, wearing a thick black wool sweater.

He's wearing a yellow–looking sweatshirt, and they're smiling serenely, happily.

His hands are clasped on the table, with an open piece of paper underneath them and a plastic ruler not far from his fingers. Her right hand is stretched over his, missing the last phalanx of her pinky, with a long white scar running lengthwise across the back of her hand, just at the base of the wrist.

"When was this taken?" I ask, not really wanting to know.

"I don't know. But I don't think it was too long ago." She says, turning the photo.

"L. and M." It says in writing.

"That's Augusto's handwriting. I've never seen this girl before. I don't know who she is".

"Where was it taken?"

"I think it's our house in Sorrento." She stands beside me, and as we both hold the photo, she leans her head so close it almost touches mine. "Yes, that's Sorrento, and this table… I bought it in the spring to use during the summer. This is a photo from this year."

"What's that paper in front of them?" I ask softly.

"I don't know." She pauses. "But it looks like a drawing, doesn't it? What's that ruler for?" She doesn't answer. I can hear her steady breath next to my ear. "Isabella, can we go to this house? I'd like to see if I can find anything."

We stay still, looking at the photo. She remains silent.

"Alright. Stay and eat with me, and then we'll take Augusto's car."

7.

"How much longer do I have to wait, Santopietro?"

Santopietro's curly, short hair clings tightly to his temples. His hands dart between the drawers, opening and closing them all, then repeating the sequence. He stops, glances at a paper, then resumes searching.

"Commissioner, I told you, I can't find the keys for the, um, what's it called."

"Santopié, are you kidding me? I told you they aren't here. They haven't been found."

Santopietro stops.

"And so, what do we do?"

"It's simple: you take me to the car, and we'll open it."

"Commissioner, are you serious? The car is impounded. What are you planning to open?"

"Santopié! Take me to the car!" The commissioner shouts and slams his fists on the desk. Someone peeks through the door with a worried expression, observing the scene before quickly disappearing.

"What kind of behavior is this?" Santopietro rises from his desk and walks over to the coat rack. "Every jerk who comes in here expects a show... Commissioner, who do you think you are?"

"Come on, Santopié, let's go see this car. When you retire, I'll open a bottle of sparkling wine for you."

Santopietro stares at Cardona, then sighs with frustration.

The commissioner stuffs his hands into his dark coat, watching the head of the impound yard rise from his chair and put on his blue jacket. Then he follows him as they head out of his office.

"Everyone wants it their way" Santopietro grumbles as he leaves the office.

They walk in silence for a while. The impound yard is packed with multicolored shapes, some dented and rusted, but the vast majority are new and shiny. Sports cars, German sedans, even a few trendy minicars.

"It's a sight that makes you think." The commissioner whispers. "Do you like cars, Santopié?"

Santopietro grumbles again, incomprehensibly, but from a few syllables, the commissioner gathers he's now cursing.

His phone buzzes in his pocket. Cardona pulls it out, checks the number, and answers.

"Yes."

"Hello, Cardona? Commissioner Cardona, right?"

"Yes, that's me. And you are?"

"Davide Simoni, from Mercedes Service."

"Ah, good. So, Simoni, your colleague mentioned that with some device you have, I can find out the last time the car was started and other things like that. Is that correct?"

"Yes, that's correct."

"And you've got this device with you?"

"Yes, I have it here."

"And where are you right now?"

"Outside the impound yard."

"Good. Santopié, there's someone outside who needs to work with us. Can you let him in?" Santopietro throws his hands in the air. "Simoni, do me a favor. Get out of your car and head to the front gate. Tell them you're my assistant, and they'll let you in. Just walk straight down the road, and you'll see me. I'm wearing a long black coat."

"Got it, Commissioner. See you soon."

The commissioner ends the call and pockets his phone. Then they stop.

They're standing in front of a blue Mercedes C–Class.

"Santopié, is this the one?"

"Yeah. So what do you want to do? Help me understand."

The commissioner looks at him, silent. Then he approaches the car. He touches the handle, but the door doesn't open. He walks along the side and leans against the window, bringing his hand to his temple to peer inside.

"I want to do my job."

The car is clean. Inside, the white leather seats are clear of clutter, with no signs of obvious wear. The commissioner takes a step and looks at the back seat. Empty, clean. He runs his hand along the frame, slowly following the contour as he walks beside it. He circles the car and repeats the motion along the passenger side. He stops at the side mirror and stands up, looking at Santopietro.

"We should open it."

"You're crazy!" Santopietro exclaims, overemphasizing the letter 'c,' which explodes under his tongue as the muscles in his face contract to their maximum.

The commissioner remains impassive as Santopietro's face sinks into itself. He watches him, biting the inside of his cheek, listening to the sound of his skin beneath his teeth. He nods slowly toward the curly–haired man.

A car pulls up behind Santopietro. The door opens, and a blonde guy in a red mechanic's suit steps out, looking sharp.

"Santopietro, why don't you go take a walk while I do my job?"

"You're out of your mind! You need to leave right now! You're going to get me in trouble!" Santopietro shouts, visibly upset.

"How about this, Santopietro? You leave now, I'll chat with the gentleman here about Napoli soccer team by this nice Mercedes, then I'll stop by your office to say goodbye and leave. We'll be friends as always. Or..."

"You really don't get it, do you? Now you..."

"Or," The commissioner raises his voice, cutting off Santopietro, who falls silent. "You keep making problems here and now, like you're doing. I'll still open the car, but I'll make sure you get burned, Santopié. We both know what happens around here when no one's watching, and I know exactly how to make your life miserable. So, what's it going to be, Santopié?"

They stand in silence, Santopietro muttering. His hands are stuffed into the pockets of his bomber jacket. He spits on the ground and turns toward the offices they came from. The commissioner watches him go, and when he's about ten meters away, he turns to the mechanic.

"Simoni?"

"Yes, that's me, sir." Simoni replies, a bit nervous.

"Very good. Now, I want to know a few things. Number one: when was this car last locked?"

"I can tell you everything you need to know. I just need to connect this to the control unit." He says, raising the aluminum case in his right hand.

"I don't have the keys."

"Oh." They exchange a silent glance. "Okay, I get it."

He turns and sets the case down on the car, then approaches the Mercedes, placing his hands on the hood. He presses a bit, feeling something beneath his palms.

"This one is new. We're in luck."

He goes back to the car and leans inside, emerging with a flathead screwdriver.

He kneels in front of the car's nose, slowly slipping the screwdriver under the hood. He sticks out his tongue and licks his upper lip. Moving his hand slowly as if searching for something, he finds it, stops, grimaces, and then pries with the tool. The hood makes a dull sound and lifts a few centimeters. He stands, pockets the screwdriver, and smiles at the commissioner, placing his hands under the hood and opening it.

"There you go. He says, satisfied "Just a moment while I check everything."

He grabs the case, sets it on the frame, opens it, and quickly connects a cable to the control unit. He looks at the monitor and types in some data using the keyboard.

"Here we are. What do you want to know?

The commissioner nods and steps closer.

"When was it last locked?"

"Okay" The young man taps at the touchpad. The device looks like a rugged laptop. "Here we are. The locking signal was sent at 11:47 PM on September 11, 2013."

The commissioner writes it down in his notebook.

"If you want, I have the history."

"Give me the last movements."

"Okay, we said it was locked at 11:47 PM, then unlocked at 11:44 PM. Locked again at 9:25 PM, engine off at 9:25 PM, a few seconds earlier."

"Wait, so you also have the engine start times?"

"I have everything you want, Commissioner."

"Well done, Mercedes. Read me the times."

"Engine on at 8:18 PM, doors opened at 8:12 PM, doors locked at 2:24 PM, engine off at 2:18 PM, engine on at…"

"Wait, wait. Can you print this or something?"

"I can email it to you."

The commissioner nods, slightly irritated.

"Listen, can we find out where the car has been? The last movements while it was being driven."

"Well, yes. If the GPS was on, we can see the last destinations entered. It could be helpful…"

"It is helpful. Let me hear it."

"Okay, give me a second. I'll export the history. How far back do you need?"

"As far as it goes."

"Alright, let me check." He fiddles with the terminal. "The last five months. From the last service to today."

"Good. Now read me the GPS data, then do the same for me, pull out the information."

"The GPS… just a second."

"Hey… Simone, right?" The commissioner asks, distracted.

"Simoni. That's my last name."

"Yes, Simoni. Can you unlock the car from there"

"Unlock it? Um." He scratches his head. "Yes, I mean, it's possible, but it's a bit complicated."

"But I need you to open it." The commissioner presses.

The young man looks at him, then approaches hesitantly, shrugging as if feeling a bit guilty. He has the look of someone unsure if he can say what he's about to say.

"Commissioner, there's a faster way to open the doors. But it's not exactly… I mean, you don't usually do it in front of the police."

Cardona stares at him, unfazed.

"I don't care. Just open the car."

The young man stands up, reassured. With a couple of quick steps, he returns to the car, pulling out a wire, which he twists into a hook shape. Then, he grabs pliers and cuts the wire to a length of about thirty centimeters. He approaches the driver's door, places his hands on the window seal, and swiftly removes it from its slot. He inserts the hook into the gap and moves it toward the edge of the door, glancing upward as he searches for something inside with the piece of wire. He touches it, feels it catch, pulls up, and with his other hand, pulls the handle. The door opens, and the young man smiles.

"Well done. Now read me the GPS."

"We can check it from inside."

"Check it from the outside. I'll go inside."

Simoni raises his hands and returns to his spot.

The commissioner walks around the car and slides into the driver's seat. He sits, looking around. The car's upholstery is white. Immaculate. He places his hand on the black leather steering wheel. He inspects the dashboard, then glances at the central LCD screen.

"Commissioner, don't touch anything electronic while I check the GPS history."

"Yes, sir." He mutters as he looks at the center console.

Coin holder, cup holder, all empty and clean. He places his hand on the armrest. The white leather here is a bit worn. He feels it for a moment, then opens it.

"Alright, Commissioner. I'm ready. There's a destination entry on September 7th, 11 AM. Let's see... the destination is Sorrento, Traversa Punta Capo. The starting point is the A3 Napoli Salerno highway, and it looks like an alternate route to the highway was selected."

"He took the back roads?" The commissioner looks up at the windshield, only able to see the raised blue hood.

"Seems like it."

"Maybe there was an accident or traffic."

"Could be. He canceled the navigation while on the SS145."

"The one that leads to Sorrento." He murmurs, Simoni's voice distant.

"Then I have other routes, but they're older. There's one to Rome..."

"Alright, do me a favor. Get me everything you've got and print it out."

"Roger that. I can print it out once I'm back at the shop."

The commissioner returns to the armrest. He opens it. Inside, there are keys, three sets. One is bulky, and the commissioner runs his fingers over it, seven standard keys attached to a white plastic keychain. The tag reads 'Marzio' in blocky handwriting. The other sets have fewer keys, each with a key for a security door. One has a metal keychain, a flat strip bent into an upside—

down 'N.' The right leg of the 'N' curves into a circle and ends with a horizontal tip pointing back toward the 'N.'

The commissioner runs his finger over it, tracing the symbol. The metal feels warm, scratched in places. He brings it closer to his eyes. The color is a deep yellow. Probably gold, he thinks. He clenches it in his palm, convinced. Among all the keys, one is flat, round, stubby, with a pattern of holes in three rows. In his other hand, he holds the last keyring. The security door key is longer, and attached to the ring holding the keys is a square metal tag engraved with the letter 'H.'

The commissioner stuffs the three keyrings into the inner pocket of his coat, then closes the armrest.

He moves to exit but stops. It's as if something has come to mind. He leans back into the seat and reopens the armrest, leaning over it. He grunts, as if to confirm something to himself. He reaches in and pulls out a photo. A boy and a girl, embracing. They're sitting at a table with a drawing in front of them, a blue ruler lying at an angle. She's hugging him, her hand resting on his.

They're smiling, serene.

The photo is new. It seems freshly printed; the paper is still slightly curved. The commissioner brings it to his nose and smells the ink.

He looks at it again.

They look happy.

8.

The wrought iron gate opens silently, and before me stretches a large garden, with patches of English lawn occasionally dotted with flowerbeds. The flowers are colorful but fragile, some petals scattered on the grass, slowly dying.

A paved path, about a meter wide, leads us toward a white two–story house, modestly decorated with plaster accents. Surrounding the house are low flowerbeds that outline a light terracotta walkway, running along the perimeter walls for as far as I can see from here.

Isabella walks ahead of me by a couple of steps. Her grace calms me. I glance at her often. It feels good.

As we near the front door, Isabella already has the set of keys in her hand.

"It's a beautiful house, Isabella."

"I'm glad you like it." She says as she takes the first key and inserts it into the lock.

"Although, I don't know, do you really feel the need to come here when summer arrives? The house in Torre del Greco is spectacular, I fell in love with it." I pause, almost cutting myself off. Maybe I've gotten too comfortable.

She smiles, pulling the key out of the lock and moving on to the second one.

"You're right." She says, looking at her hands as they work the lock. "If it were up to me, I'd never leave there. Here, there's so much chaos, traffic. In the summer, this city turns into hell." She pauses, pulls out the second key, and flips through the keyring to find the third. "But coming here in the summer was never, how should I say, up for negotiation with Augusto." She says, smiling sweetly. "He was born here. And this house was the first thing he bought with his savings. Even before the house in Torre, before anything else. Imagine, he used to drive around in an old Alfetta, which sometimes wouldn't even start when it was too cold. And in the summer, if we got stuck in traffic too long, the radiator would overheat." Her smile widens, and she pauses with her hands still. "He once told me something. He said a girl lived here. He was just a boy, and he fell in love with her. He told me she was sick, and her parents brought her here to breathe the sea air. He lived nearby, just a street kid having fun, but every day, he'd come here to watch this girl. He'd climb the wall, scramble up the trees, and sometimes even try to sneak in. He told me the servants would chase him away, but he always came back."

Isabella picks up the keyring again.

"And did he ever meet her? Did they become friends?"

"He never told me. He never told me how it ended." She pulls out another key. "I'm so sorry, but I can never remember which key opens which door. It drives me crazy every time. And there are so many keys on this keyring. I think there are about ten, there's one for the house, the guesthouse, the tool shed, the cellar, the two gates…" She shakes her head. I smile.

"Don't worry, Isabella. It's no problem." She continues and inserts the fourth key into the lock. "Maybe, in the end, he bought this house because they always tried to keep him out."

The lock clicks open.

"Yes, maybe that's it. Maybe it was his way of getting back at the world."

Isabella steps inside and makes room for me. The house is dark, damp. We're in a foyer with three doors, one on each wall.

In front of us, above the only closed door, there's a print of Mount Vesuvius, with the sun rising softly behind its curves.

"We should open the shutters a bit, let in some air and light." She says as she enters the door on the left.

Then she peeks back, motioning toward the other door, giving me a kind smile. I nod and step through it.

There's a wicker sitting area arranged around a rough stone fireplace. On the wall to my right are two windows. I walk over and open them one by one, leaving just one shutter open.

As I return toward Isabella, I notice a small table with four wide candles arranged in a diamond shape. They've all been lit and are burnt down. Three are almost the same height, while the fourth is taller, almost double the others.

The foyer is empty. Isabella is still in the other room. From here, I can hear the sound of running water and some dishes being moved. She's probably in the kitchen.

I turn toward the closed door. It's made of wood and divided into two quadrants, one at the top and one at the bottom. Each quadrant is further divided into four smaller squares. It looks like a chessboard. I step closer, and the handle is round, a knob. I wrap my hand around it; it's warm. I turn it, and the door opens, light flooding in like a diffuse glow.

It's a long room, with floor–to–ceiling bookshelves for the first three meters. The corridor formed by the shelves is just over a meter wide. My silhouette blocks the light from the doorway, and I can't see the end of the room. I turn sideways to let more light in, but it changes little. I step in, searching for a light switch. The walls are covered in books; the shelves are full. As I move forward, the room's outlines become clearer. I see a desk and the wall ahead with two French doors. The corridor ends, and I run my hand along the wall, looking for a switch. I'm not anxious, as I can now make out the room. I step fully out of the corridor, and there's enough light to see the entire space. The bookshelf actually continues, occupying the wall where the corridor opens out. The desk is placed at an angle in the room. On top of it, there's an inkwell, a letter opener, and a black stone holding down some scribbled papers.

I move toward the windows to open them and realize there's a painting hanging in the space between them.

The frame is classic but simple. The subject is a girl with light brown hair, smiling, her hair tied back in a long ponytail. Her big blue eyes have arched corners, and her nose is small. Her shoulders are bare, except for the thin strap of a white dress on her left shoulder. The strap on the right has slipped down, resting on her arm. She looks young, fresh, serene.

The room brightens. The warm light from the chandelier fills the space. I turn around, and Isabella has her hand resting to the left of the door, tucked into a gap between the wall and the bookshelf.

"Shall we open this up too?" She asks as she walks toward me.

"Who is this girl?. I ask, pointing to the painting.

"I don't know. It's a painting that's always been here. Since we bought the house." She replies, walking down the corridor without looking at where I'm pointing.

"Maybe it's the girl your husband wanted to meet" I say, looking at the painting again. I like it.

Isabella crosses the room, moving to the other side of the desk. She approaches the window and begins to open it.

"I wouldn't know."

"This is your husband's desk?"

"Yes, it is." She says as she opens the outer shutters, letting the daylight in.

"And he sat here, with this painting, maybe thinking it was her. Maybe he believed it."

"You know, if they left the painting here…" She pauses, and I move to the other window and open it. The handle makes a bit of noise.

"What?"

"The owners… if the parents left this painting behind, if it represents their daughter… If the mother didn't want to take it with her, maybe it means she doesn't have fond memories of it. Maybe it means the girl didn't make it in the end. Maybe leaving it here was the mother's way of leaving the pain behind. Of forgetting all this."

The blood freezes in my veins. I open the shutters, and my arms lock up. I lean inside. I can only see Isabella's back. She's looking outside. I look back at the painting. It doesn't seem possible that this girl died from an illness.

I turn away. The bookshelf is full. In the far left corner of the room, where the shelves end and the wall begins, I see Marzio, staring into space.

9.

The commissioner places the papers on the round table. A thin wisp of smoke rises from the hexagon–shaped plastic ashtray. He pulls his hands from his pockets, takes a cigarette from the pack, and brings it to his lips, lighting it. There are only a few left in the pack.

He moves the coffee cup to the other end of the table and leans forward. The papers are filled with records, numbers, names, dates, and times. A waiter arrives and places a yellow highlighter next to the ashtray.

"It's almost out." He says before walking away.

"Thanks." The commissioner mutters, the cigarette glowing red.

He rubs his temples. There's a muffled buzz around him, distant and muted. His eyes run over the paper. The numbers and words flow in a primordial chaos. The font is blocky, utilitarian, not pleasing to the eye. His gaze struggles over the lines, like walking along a cliffside. The bottom of the page is already in sight, and the only feeling left is frustration. A deep drag from the cigarette. He refocuses, exhales, and begins again.

The first number doesn't seem to make sense. Then there's the date, year, month, day, followed by the time, hours, minutes, seconds. A code: this means ignition. Then there are numbers and letters with hidden meanings, but he's not interested. This seems like the key. It repeats on every line. We've got it, he repeats in his head. He inhales again.

April 12th, 9:32 AM, ignition. Then it's off shortly after, then on again, off after half an hour. Just after 10 AM.

These are the first four lines. To his right is another, thinner stack of papers. He grabs it.

The first line mentions April 12th, 9:37 AM. There's an address. He recognizes it, it's Prosud. There are numbers next to it, latitude and longitude. Location data at the time of departure. The navigation was interrupted after ten minutes, the location had changed. But the numbers don't help. He needs a map to decipher this.

He shrugs and leans back in his chair. It's uncomfortable, pressing into his lower back. He grips the cigarette between his lips and takes a hard drag. The smoke turns hot and bitter. He pulls it from his mouth and looks at it. It's finished. He crushes it in the ashtray, and without thinking, another cigarette is already in his mouth, beginning its sacrifice.

He's more confident now, reading. His eyes start to find a rhythm. Yes, there's something different now. Suddenly, the numbers become familiar, there's a pattern, a near–constant ritual. He sees it. He exhales. He sees it.

We're almost there; it's getting easier. Everything is steady. A creature of habit. He takes a pen and draws lines along the weekdays on the left side of the page, covering mostly four lines per day. Departure at 8:00, 7:55, 8:03, 8:06, 7:53, 8:10, 7:55. We're there, it fluctuates, but it's consistent, nothing strange. The arrivals are nearly all thirty minutes after departure. The commissioner can picture him getting in the car, turning on the radio, shifting into first gear, and pulling away. Traffic, the speedometer needle. A sense of relief. It all seems simple. He leaves between 6:30 and 7:00 PM. The return trip takes as long as the departure.

The weekends show more variety. Saturdays have later departures, averaging around 9:30, with returns varying between noon and 1:00 PM. The afternoons and Sundays are irregular. There's no clear pattern. He circles the weekend lines with the pen.

He turns the page, stubs out the cigarette in the ashtray, and grabs the pen. He reaches the end of April. The 25th is a holiday, and there's a string of short trips, with two longer ones at the beginning and end. Perhaps a day trip. The next day is back to normal, fitting perfectly into the weekly routine, but there's an ignition at 9:20 PM that breaks the pattern. The car starts again just before 2 AM. The commissioner marks these lines with an asterisk. A wild night? He traces the morning departure lines with the pen, counting four days. It's Thursday. He writes the day's abbreviation at the end of the lines.

The morning departure is normal, 8:10 AM. No recovery of the lost sleep.

The commissioner grabs the other set of papers but finds no navigation data in the report.

May begins, everything steady until now.

May 8th.

10:17 AM, departure. Arrival after thirty–five minutes.

Then silence. The next line is just a few millimeters away, but in truth, it's light–years distant.

Cardona takes his notebook, flips a few pages.

Cardia's death. May 8th.

He leaves the next day, just after 11:30 AM. Stops after forty minutes. And stays there for three days. Another forty–minute trip. Calm resumes until May 14th, when the normal cycle begins again. Morning, evening. Morning, evening. He continues, steady, for a week.

Then something changes. There are trips. Frequent ones. Lasting just over an hour. Generally, he leaves around 11 AM and returns between 3:00 and 4:00 PM. One or two times a week in May. The day varies. The commissioner highlights these with yellow. The navigation system shows no data for these days. He writes 'known destination' in his notes and draws lines connecting all the highlighted entries to these words.

May ends. The commissioner looks up and signals the waiter. He waits to be noticed, then returns to his papers. In June, the trips repeat, but there's a small change, they're about fifteen to twenty minutes shorter. From the second week on, there's only one trip a week, every Thursday. Starts at 11:00 AM, stops at 3:30 PM. Steady.

"Yes?" The waiter looks somber.

"Another espresso." He says, reaching for his cigarette pack.

"Shall I change the ashtray?" It's overflowing with cigarette butts.

The commissioner looks at it, nods, and lights another cigarette. He shakes the pack. There's only one left inside. The waiter, a young man in his twenties with dark hair and a bored expression, clears the used cup and ashtray, turning and walking away.

The commissioner doesn't watch as the table is cleared. He draws a straight line across the page, marking the first short trip. Then he counts them and highlights them.

He draws more lines toward a common point and writes again, in block letters, 'unknown destination.'

He flips his notebook to a blank page and writes down a question: 'Where does he go every week?'

The pages fill with lines and circles, asterisks next to some movements that need further investigation. He continues like this until July, when the coffee arrives at the table.

"With sugar." The waiter says before leaving.

Cardona stirs the thick liquid with a spoon. He's just begun July. He flips the pages; there aren't many left. He checks his watch, it's nearly 4:30 PM. He feels the urgency and gulps the coffee down in one go. There's no new ashtray. He lights the last cigarette and flips through the stack. The smoke spreads blue through the room as he breathes it in, acrid, until he reaches September. Monday the 3rd. The usual four lines marking a workday.

On the 4th, he leaves in the morning on time, turns off the car after twenty minutes. The commissioner checks the navigation report, no navigation on September 4th, only one on August 29th to Rome and another on September 7th. He leaves again after two hours, turns off the car after thirty minutes. Six hours pass, then he leaves again, stopping after half an hour. It's September 6th when he starts the car an hour earlier than usual, drives for fifteen minutes. He stops for forty minutes, then leaves again. Stops at 8:33 AM. The car stays off until 8:10 PM, then runs for twenty–six minutes. Another departure at 11:24 PM, sixteen minutes, then off again. Four minutes later, he starts the car again, drives for ten minutes, then stops. It's nearly midnight now, and three hours pass before the car starts again. Ten minutes later, it stops again. It's Thursday morning, and the routine is broken, he leaves at 10:20 AM. Stops around noon. Leaves again at 8:18 PM. Stops at 9:25 PM.

The page ends there.

The lines take up only the first quarter of the space. There's nothing after.

The commissioner brings his hand to his mouth, inhales, but feels nothing, the cigarette has gone out, the ash fallen onto the table.

He picks up the pen. At the line where the car stopped at noon, he writes 'Sorrento', underlining it with a firm stroke. He drops the cigarette butt into the cup. With the back of his hand, he brushes away the ash that fell onto the plastic surface. He gathers the papers, neatly fastening them with a clip. He places them in front of him, neatly organized. With his right hand, he pulls back the sleeve of his coat to check his watch. Almost 4:50 PM.

He stands, gathers the papers, and walks toward the register.

10.

I realize my hands are aching. I clench them into fists, and the sore muscles respond by squeezing less tightly than they could. The pain is dull, and I focus on it until it becomes almost pleasant. I modulate the pressure of my fingers against my palms, exhaling softly through my lips, my eyes half–closed.

Isabella places a cup of hot coffee in front of me, the sound of porcelain against porcelain as the cup meets the saucer. Both are white, with a delicate floral symphony of pink, orange, and blue that spreads gently across the surfaces. I nod my head in thanks. The pain disappears as soon as I open my hands and reach for my coffee. I lift the saucer to avoid scraping it against the table. It's new, clean. I like it. The wood is walnut, rich and deep, the grain like dark, mysterious caverns, and the patterns they create resemble flames, flowing left, stretched and sinuous, disappearing beyond the rounded edge of the table.

I think I'm sitting exactly where Marzio was in that photo. I'm not sure if I did it on purpose.

I feel the warmth of the cup in my hands and take a sip. It's sweet and warm. My eyelids burn, and they droop over my eyes. Isabella sits to my left, placing her small tray on the table. She takes her cup with two fingers and inhales the aroma rising from it. Behind me is an ivy plant climbing a light wrought–iron structure. It climbs between two pillars and continues on a frame, covering the space between the table and the house. The vine blocks much of the light above us. I look up, and through the dark green leaves, I see a few spots of gray belonging to the clouds.

"Where do you want to start?" Isabella sets her cup down on the saucer. I open my mouth, but no sound comes out.

"What are we looking for?" She prompts.

Answering that is even harder.

I search inside myself, but I find only darkness, not a path, not a direction. I don't even know why I'm here, in Sorrento, sitting at this table. I feel as though someone has taken me by the arms and spun me around in a long whirlwind. And here I am, lying here, breathing and trying to understand.

He's there. His hair is neatly combed, short, dark, brushed to the left, falling slightly over his forehead.

"It would be simple if it were just you and me, only you and me."

"What?"

"In the world, just you and me. Nothing else, no one else around. I'd stay by your side, wake you up, cook for you, build our house, and we'd live there. Imagine a beach, maybe with a small hill nearby, and our house perched on top so we wouldn't be afraid of the storm. Wouldn't that be perfect?"

"Yes, it would be perfect." He hugs me tightly. The television crackles with something unclear in the distance. I feel his skin against mine. The windows are open, and the lingering summer heat in the city is starting to fade.

"Wouldn't it be the best world?"

"Any world where we're together would be the best world." I think. There's nowhere better than where I am right now. There's peace here in this room. I haven't felt this good in a long time. He strokes my hair. I think I'm happy.

"I have to go now."

"Go where?"

"Just nearby. I have to take care of something, meet someone."

"Why?" I sit up. "Why do you have to leave now? So late at night?"

He smiles at me. Sadly. His eyes are sunken into their sockets. Distant.

"It's work. I need to talk to someone. I'd rather do it outside of office hours. I'll hear what they have to say and come back."

"How long will you be?"

"I don't know. Not long. It won't take long. I'll be right back."

I look at him. He smiles at me. But he's already far away. Light–years away.

"Hey." Isabella takes my shoulder and shakes me gently. I turn my gaze away from Marzio and look at her, shaking my head.

"Sorry, I got lost in my thoughts. I suddenly remembered Marzio, our last night. He was tense. He left to talk about work with someone. He didn't tell me who. I woke up the next morning in his arms. He went to work later that day. We had breakfast together, stayed in bed late." My eyes fill with tears. "We talked about vacations, he asked me where I wanted to go, we talked a lot." My voice cracks. It rises to the surface in fragments through my throat, choked by spasms. "He was happy, he was normal. It can't have ended like this."

I repeat it like a mantra, my arms wrapped around my knees, my feet resting on the chair. I try to speak, but I can only manage broken syllables between sobs.

Isabella moves closer, stroking my shoulders and head. I just need a moment of peace. Marzio watches me, both in reality and in my memories. It can't be, I scream silently. It can't be that you're here, unable to do anything while this happens to me. I don't know if I said it out loud. Who took you away from me, throwing me into this abyss? His soft skin, I lower my head and inhale his scent, resting my head in the crook of his neck. He holds me, keeps me in his arms, whispers words, any word would be fine, as long as I can hear the soft sound of his voice in my ears, keeping me away from that morning. I pray. I pray for strength. Just a little more.

My face feels like it's on fire, my eyes burn. I pull away from her, not sure how long I've been there. I can't look her in the eyes.

"Sorry."

"Don't worry."

"Really, I'm sorry."

"I think what you're doing is important. And I think it's normal for it to hurt. You're brave for doing all of this, and you have to keep going. Search and find the answers you deserve. You have to do it for yourself and for him. For all of us, even for Augusto and me." She strokes my shoulders gently. It's comforting. "If you feel like this is all wrong, we need to figure out why."

She looks at me without saying anything. She looks me straight in the eyes. I nod. I feel like screaming. Why, why me, why us?

But these are questions I don't know how to answer. I'm here, now. That matters. I'm here for him too. I place my feet on the floor, stand up, and look ahead, nodding, trying to clear my blocked nose. Isabella watches me, then gathers the cups and saucers. She places them on the tray and takes them away. I watch her leave and am left alone with the silence around me. I press down on my legs and stand. I walk toward the windows in the study, right in front of the table.

I step inside. I move the chair and sit down. The desk is solid wood, and in the center is a brown leather document holder. I flip open the flap. Inside are handwritten notes. I take them and examine them one by one. There are various notes, names, some formulas, diagrams, sequences. Codes I don't understand. One page shows a calculation, a sum, and a difference, it looks like money movements. I don't see Marzio in these papers. I move a few centimeters back from the edge of the desk. There are three drawers on the left and three on the right.

I reach out and touch the first drawer on the left. It has a small handle in the center. I slip two fingers underneath it and pull. The drawer slides out with difficulty; the wooden track isn't well–aligned. I give it a little shake. It slides about thirty centimeters out. Inside are blank A4 sheets, perfectly clean. There's a stack about a centimeter thick. I slip my thumb underneath the stack, lift it, and flip through it. No pen marks, no print. I close the drawer and open the second. Inside is a black notebook, covered in textured leather. It's closed with a small gold–tone buckle. I take it and open it on the desk. More notes, numbers, names, and phone numbers written haphazardly on the pages. The last entry is from last September. The rest of the pages are blank. I leave it on the desk. It might contain some useful information; I could read it with Isabella. I open the third drawer. Inside is a phone charger, a couple of screwdrivers, and some AA batteries, one has leaked some fluid. Nothing interesting here either.

I close it and move to the right side. I open the first drawer. There's a business card holder, a professional association stamp made of wood and rubber, an ink pad, and some ballpoint pens in different colors, black, red, and blue. There's also a white ruler, which seems to be made of bone, with black, engraved numbers. They're lying on some bound papers, three or four folders. They seem to be scientific articles, with titles in English. The first is authored by Augusto Cardia. I move the ink pad aside. The second name is Marzio's.

I close the drawer and move to the second. I pull the handle, but it doesn't move. I try again, thinking it might be stuck. I pull again, but nothing. I bend down. There's a small gap under the handle, a keyhole. I hadn't noticed, but all six drawers have them.

"Isabella!" My voice comes out weak. "Isabella!" I repeat more firmly.

I lean back in the chair and look at the drawer. My heart races a little. Maybe I've found something. I'm not sure what I'm feeling relief, maybe? I'm anxious. I open the third drawer. Inside are legal–sized papers, typewritten, dated 1998. It's a document. I take it. I realize it's a copy. It's old, yellowed. It's a Prosud shareholder meeting report. Present were Michele Solimena and Augusto Cardia. I start reading what it's about.

"Did you call me? Did you find something?" I look up and see Isabella between the two bookshelves.

"Yes, come here. I found this drawer. It's locked."

"Locked?" She asks, surprised.

She approaches, walking around the desk. I watch her and, when she's close, point to the drawer.

"All the others open."

"I didn't even know these drawers could be locked."

"Do you know where the key is?"

"No, I don't. Really, I don't." We stand in silence for a moment, thinking. "Wait, I'll check in the bedroom."

She walks away quickly. I watch her leave the room again.

I'm left alone again. Every time it feels like the ground is slipping out from under me. I wish I could be surprised by how fragile I am. But I'm getting used to it. My eyes settle on the books lining the room. I stand and walk toward the bookshelf on the left. Almost all the books are hardbound, with their titles stamped on the spines in austere fonts. This section is filled with technical and scientific literature. Names of professors from the past. Physics, mechanics, thermodynamics, hydraulics, construction science, electronics, many of the titles are in English. Some are in French. I rest my fingers on the spines, letting them glide over each one without stopping, feeling the rough texture of the fabric beneath my fingertips. I wonder if Cardia had read all these books or simply collected them. I wonder if Marzio had ever opened or read them. If they had ever been here together to study, to talk about science, about research. I move on to the right side. Here the themes are different. There's the History of Italy by Montanelli, with all its volumes, Ovid, Pliny, Dante with The Divine Comedy, Boccaccio, Italian Renaissance literature, Goethe, Hugo, the Russians, philosophy, Aristotle, Plato, the Enlightenment thinkers, Kant, Hegel. A string of names I don't know. Lofty titles. The Encyclopaedia Britannica.

An unsettling feeling, the air seems thick here, suffocating, as though every breath I take fights through the weight of dust and the memories it hold. The low light from the desk lamp cast long, eerie shadows that crawls along the walls, stretching like claws. I sift through the old papers, feeling the familiar twinge of frustration creeping up my spine. The key to the drawer has to be here somewhere. I know it. But everything feels like a maze, endless and winding.

I brush my fingers over the worn edges of the hardcover books, binded with leather. The next breath stops in the middle, feels like chocking. Cold, the unmistakable chill of dread creeping over my skin. The hair on the back of my neck stending up.

A low, rasping laugh. My hand frozen mid—air.

"Ah, there you are." Comes the voice I had hoped to never hear.

I turn, my breath shallow, and there he stands, leaning casually against the far bookshelf, his bell—tipped hat jingling lightly as he moves. His crooked grin gleamed in the dim light, and his eyes dark, mocking, glinted with malicious amusement.

"Making progress, in our game are we? But not fast enough." His voice slithers through the room like smoke, filling every corner. "I must say, I'm rather enjoying this… watching you struggle. It's delightful, really"

I take a step back, my body tense, but I can't move far enough away. His presence clings to the air, inescapable. The light flickers as his shadow stretches longer, darker.

"I watched Marzio, too." He continues, his tone almost gleeful. "Poor, sweet Marzio… so filled with love, with hope. But his anger? His grief? They were mine. I devoured them. And I took his voice as well, the token to play the game. So delicious, so delicious." His skinny hands touching Marzio's face in blissful delight, it disgusts me, it makes me want to throw up.

"But not enough. I can't be satisfied of only this. I need more. More time and more I crave. You refused my offer, I could have helped. I could have gave you something. And take more from him. You didn't want me to take his eyes, you silly you. But time passes. Passes inexorably. And if I can't touch him, because you will not allow it. Then…" He steps forward, his smile widening. "Then soon I'll take yours."

"No." I whisper, my throat tight. I try to will myself to move, to fight, but my legs felt like lead. "No!"

He laughs again, sharp and cruel.

"You'll try to hide, won't you? Just as he did. You close your eyes and pretend it's all just a nightmare. But it's not. I'll crawl into you, just as I did with him. I'll claim you, body and soul. His anger, his grief, his torment they will be yours." He reaches toward me, his gnarled hand stretching through the dimness.

"And you will be mine." A dark growl.

I can't breathe. My heart pounding in my chest as the Jester's hand move closer. My eyes squeezed shut, tears welling up despite myself. I back into the library wall, my hands gripping the edge with desperate force. Nowhere to go. His fingers graze my arm cold, sharp, like ice and I recoil, trembling.

And then, nothing.

I open my eyes, blinking rapidly. The room empty. The Jester gone.

I swallow hard, forcing myself to breathe again. Slowly, I back away from the desk, my pulse still racing. My hands shake as they released their grip on the wooden edge.

I turn, ready to flee. I turn and I see Marzio by my side. I am in the corner where he stands, staring into the distance. A step away from him is a tall book. I focus it's an atlas. I touch it, my cheeks flush, and the urge to cry rises sharply.

"How could have you took a deal with such a monster, Marzio." I control the urge to cry. Exhale. "But I guess if you are ready to go to such an extent then I have to follow your path because where you want to bring me is important."

The book is blue, with gold lettering. I pull it out with one hand, but it's heavy, and as soon as it's fully off the shelf, it tilts downward. I grip it tightly, managing not to drop it, and quickly grab it with my other hand. I hear a metallic sound, something has fallen. I look at the floor. A small, single–tooth key lies on the white floor. My heart races. Maybe it's the key to the drawer. I bend down to pick it up. It's small and brown. I walk quickly toward the desk, placing the atlas on the surface. I take a step back and pause. The atlas is closed, but there's a bulge between the pages a mark left by the key that was stored inside. I open it, flipping through the pages until I reach the spot where it had been. It's a map of Rome, and the key has left an indentation where it had been pressed. I run my finger over the groove. It says Via Balduina.

I still have the key in my other hand. I have to open the drawer, I tell myself. I walk around the desk and sit down. I insert the key into the lock and turn it. I hear the lock click. I exhale and pull the handle.

There's a set square inside, made of transparent plastic, shaped like an isosceles triangle. It's resting on some papers. I close the leather document holder, reach into the drawer, and pull out its contents. I move the set square aside. The papers are enclosed in an A3 sheet folded in half. I open it, and on the left side, there are numbers stacked to form a sum. They're written in pencil, it's not Marzio's handwriting. The letters are soft, slightly slanted to the right, with a sense of urgency repeated in each line. Inside the A3 sheet is a file. It's a financial report, written in English. It's about ten pages thick, and the paper is crinkled, making a noise between my fingers, like it had been soaked in water and then dried. I move it aside. What I see next unsettles me. A blank sheet of paper. There are three lines written in block letters, spaced five or six centimeters apart. The first line was written by Marzio, I recognize it. It says,

We are here, brothers.

Below that, someone else writing.

We are one today, wind, a living family.

The third line contains stranger words, ones I don't understand. Or maybe I don't want to understand.

My breath in your throat,

It is written by Marzio, followed by another hand that wrote,

My shoulders in yours.

The last part is written twice, pressed down by two different hands.

For eternity, I recognize nothing but you in me.

At the bottom of the page, there's a brown stain. Jagged. I touch it with my right index finger, it's blood. Dry and clumped. I don't know how many drops were spilled. A shiver runs down my spine. I feel cold and tremble like a twig. With whom did he swear this oath?

"I didn't find anything..." Isabella's voice trails off when she sees me bent over the desk, my hand touching the paper. "You managed to open it?"

I don't respond. I don't even hear her. She walks around the desk, leaning over.

"What is it?"

I handle the paper as if it were made of the thinnest glass, afraid it might shatter into a thousand pieces.

"Is this Augusto's handwriting?"

She takes it from my hands and reads it. Seconds feel like hours. She shakes her head and hands it back to me.

"I've never seen anything like this." She says, her face pale and growing paler as she speaks.

"Isabella, what does it mean?"

"I don't know. It seems like a ritual formula, an oath."

"With whom did he swear this brotherhood?"

She shakes her head. She doesn't know. A shadow of fear crosses her face.

We stare at each other in silence. I search her eyes for comfort, but I've lost faith in her grace. Isabella seems tired, aged. The wrinkles that once gently marked her face now look like deep ravines. I clench my teeth. I'm more alone than ever now. I lower my head. I return to the papers. There's only one left. It's been folded into four parts and then unfolded again. The creases remain. In the first quadrant, it says, Sept. 7. Assembly, and beneath it, there's a phone number. A cell number.

11.

The commissioner grabs the badge and slips it into his pocket.

"The administration building is over there. You can walk the rest of the way."

"Walk? Come on, it's pouring rain, and I don't have an umbrella. How am I supposed to get there?"

"I'm sorry, but we can't let unauthorized cars in."

"Listen, I'll drive slowly, at a walking pace, and park behind the administration building. No one gets wet, and everyone's happy." The guard hesitates, unsure of how to respond. "What's your name?" the commissioner presses.

"Look, it's not up to me."

"It's simple, just press that button there." He says, leaning over the counter and pointing to the button. "Open the gate, and I'll drive through."

"Alright, Commissioner, just this once, it's not a problem."

The commissioner turns towards the voice. The guard has a strong local accent. He's a stocky man, with a large round belly that hides his belt. He has extra stripes on his shoulders, a white goatee, and small eyes.

"And you are?" The commissioner asks.

"Pragliola Antonio. We'll let you through, Commissioner, you can drive in."

"Mr. Pragliola, are you in charge here?"

"Yes, I am."

"So, to get a printout of the badge entries, do I ask you?"

He raises his hands.

"Commissioner, we just raise the barriers here. Our job is simple. For anything else, you'll have to ask someone inside." He smiles with a hint of poorly hidden sarcasm on his face. The commissioner watches him carefully. "Ask Miss Schiavone. She'll know how to help you."

"Thanks, Pragliola." The commissioner says, turning toward the door.

"Vicié, raise the barrier for the commissioner. His car is the Alfa outside." Pragliola calls out loudly as he returns to his seat in a separate cubicle.

The commissioner walks quickly through the downpour, unlocking his car, which responds with a few flashes of the hazard lights. He slips inside, pulls out his notebook, and writes 'Pragliola in charge' at the bottom of his notes. He tucks it into his pocket, inserts the key, and turns it. The car starts, and he points it toward the white and red striped barrier. The windshield wipers are at full speed, but it's raining so hard they can barely clear the water from the windshield. The Alfa rumbles at idle speed along the main road of the facility. The sound of the rain on the roof is so loud it drowns out the rough growl of the diesel engine. He turns right at the first crossroad and follows the path leading to the back of the administration building. Solimena's Mercedes S–Class is parked there, along with a few other smaller German cars, about ten in total. He pulls up to the left of the Mercedes, stopping just a few centimeters from the driver's door. He turns off the car. As soon as the wipers stop, a misty layer clouds his view. He pulls out the keys, runs his hand through his hair, shaking off droplets of water, then quickly opens the door and heads toward the canopy in front. He reaches it in just a few steps but already feels soaked to the bone. He looks to his right, where three steps lead up to a glass door. Schiavone is waiting for him behind it. She adjusts her glasses as soon as their eyes meet.

He moves forward, staring at her. She meets his gaze. As soon as he steps onto the first stair, she opens the door and makes room for him to enter.

"Good evening, Commissioner."

"Good evening, ma'am. Thank you for seeing me."

"It's always a pleasure to see you. Thank you for being punctual. Mr. Solimena is very busy these days."

"I don't want to waste anyone's time." He says with a smile. It's not his best expression.

"This way, please." Schiavone's smile, on the other hand, is something else entirely.

She walks ahead of him. He keeps shaking his hair trying to dry it.

"A very rainy autumn." She says.

"It's still summer."

"Yes, you're right. You're very precise, Commissioner."

"It's part of my job."

"But it's also a matter of personality, isn't it?"

"I often think I couldn't do anything but this job, really."

The girl laughs politely.

"And what does your wife say about your zeal, Commissioner?"

"I wouldn't know." I'm not married.

"No one to take care of you?" She asks curiously. "A woman is a source of balance for a man, don't you think?"

"For the sake of that woman, I haven't found anyone yet who's willing to take care of me."

"I'm sure you'll find her. You're an interesting man."

"Thank you, Miss." He pauses. "And you?"

They walk down a wide corridor, the walls made of wood.

"Oh, well... you're not my ideal type of man, Commissioner."

She speaks without ever looking at him, always half a step ahead, holding a dark leather folder in her left hand.

"Of course, I never doubted it, but I wasn't suggesting anything. I was just wondering if there's anyone here who inspires you."

"There are many interesting people here, but none like my boyfriend, Commissioner."

"Ah! So there's a lucky one!"

They stop in front of an elevator. She presses the call button and turns toward the commissioner.

"I'm the lucky one to have him."

"Well, it sounds like a couple destined for happiness." He spreads his hands and smiles. "Tell me, is he happy with your work?"

"Yes, just as much as I am."

"I really can't imagine a future that isn't bright for you two." The officer's hands return to his trouser pockets.

"Thank you, Commissioner. I really wouldn't want a life where..." The elevator chimes with the sound of its arrival, and the doors open.

"Please." Schiavone gestures for the commissioner to enter with her right hand. He steps into the elevator and leans back against the mirror at the rear.

"You were saying?"Cardona prompts.

The woman presses the button for the second floor, then leans against the left side of the elevator, clutching the folder to her chest.

"I was saying that I can't imagine a life without him waiting for me at home, just as I can't imagine not being able to wait for him when he comes home late."

"Very romantic."

"I'm lucky."

They remain silent until the elevator reaches the floor. When the doors open, the woman exits first, followed by the commissioner. Another long corridor stretches ahead. At the end is a wooden double door. They walk until they reach it. On the left side of the corridor is a recess with a desk and some cabinets, an LCD computer monitor, two phones, a keyboard, and a mouse. Beyond the desk, a rain–blurred window overlooks the plant.

"This is your office?"

The woman circles her workstation, dials a number on one of the phones, and lifts the receiver.

"The commissioner is here." She nods "Alright she sets the receiver down and turns to Cardona. "Mr. Solimena is waiting for you inside."

"Thank you." The commissioner replies, stepping toward the door. He places his hand on the brass knob, but before turning it, he lowers his head.

"The last time, you didn't take me up the elevator to get to Mr. Solimena's office."

Schiavone remains silent, taking a seat behind her desk.

"This is Mr. Solimena's main office. Last time, I took you to where Mr. Solimena was meeting with his staff."

"Of course."

Cardona turns the knob and opens the door.

The room is spacious, with a large floor–to–ceiling window at the far end, offering a view of the plant's facilities, all blurred by a veil of rain that makes everything appear hazy. The cold lighting makes the room feel sterile. He sees Solimena seated behind the steel and glass desk, a polished, curved panel hides his legs. Raised on the panel is the stylized blue logo of the company. The commissioner moves forward, a large rectangular rug extends to the desk, two chairs in front rest on it. The dominant colors in the office are blue and gray. On either side of the room, there are photos of the plant. Light–colored wooden sideboards are placed at regular intervals along the walls, with one beneath each picture. On the last one before the desk are several photos of two children, along with a larger frame on the left. Inside is a por-trait of a younger Solimena, likely in his thirties, smiling and wearing a light–colored shirt. On the other side is another photo, where he is embracing a woman, presumably his wife.

The commissioner approaches the desk. It's clear, with a stack of papers neatly piled on the right, and two blue–covered ledgers stacked nearby. The words 'for signature' are written in gold cursive. The commissioner leans for-ward and extends his hand to Solimena, who grasps it firmly, perhaps too firmly.

"Thank you for seeing me, Dr. Solimena. I promise I won't take up too much of your time."

"Don't worry about it. How can I help you?"

The commissioner sits down and takes out his cigarettes.

"May I smoke in here?"

"No, you may not. It's company policy."

"I figured." The commissioner smiles, setting the pack upright on the desk. "Doctor of what, if I may ask?"

Solimena looks at him, a hint of doubt in his eyes. He remains silent, una-ble to shake it.

"I'm not a doctor, Commissioner."

"Oh, excuse me, I didn't realize."

"I earned my degree here, in this company. You could say I graduated as an entrepreneur."

"Oh, well, of course." The commissioner turns the cigarette pack ninety degrees, resting it on its side. "So, Mr. Solimena. How are you?"

"Commissioner, I'm not sure exactly what you want to know from me. If we're here for a friendly chat, I'm afraid I won't be able to stay."

"By no means, Mr. Solimena. It's not my intention to waste your time. I'm just interested in knowing how the victim's brother is feeling."

"Victim?" Solimena's forehead is marked by two parallel wrinkles. Since the commissioner entered, he hasn't seen them relax, and now they're even deeper.

"The victim of the incident. Your brother."

"How do you think I feel? This is not an easy time for any of us. We never expected this... act."

He places his hands on the table, fingertips lightly touching the surface.

"I imagine."

The commissioner, is sitting at an angle to the desk, his right arm resting on the glass surface. "It's tough losing a family member and a close colleague. And, well, Cardia's death doesn't make things easier." He says.

"But we are a strong company and a strong family. We'll get through this too."

"Of course, you're leading on your own now. Without experienced advisors or the trust of a family member in the field. It must be even harder, no offense."

Solimena leans back against the desk, resting his elbows on the armrests of his chair and bringing his fingertips together.

"Look, Commissioner, I've been sitting in this chair since my father passed away. Everyone's words are important, but in the end, you have to run the company according to your convictions, your ideas. If I had done what my father did, we would have shut down in two months."

"Well, of course, you're the boss, right? You set the course, and everyone follows." Solimena spreads his hands, then brings them together again.

"I see. So, you didn't talk much with Marzio."

"What makes you think that?" He pauses, but before Cardona can respond, he continues. "I talked with Marzio a lot. He often had interesting things to say. Many of his ideas became valuable advice. He was a good advisor and a good brother."

"But?"

"But he was very immature. He was hardworking, had good intentions, but he was also quite capricious. Many times, he avoided his responsibilities. I never blamed him, after all, he was still a kid when my father died, so I couldn't rely on him much. But he could have gone far."

"Yes, but he didn't. Did you expect it? I mean, this act." The commissioner presses.

Solimena swivels his chair to face Cardona.

"I'll be honest with you, Commissioner."

"Please."

"Marzio was always, how should I say... like a reed in the wind, you know? He always needed a figure to guide him. He had my father at first. A great man. And like all great men, he had great virtues and great flaws. Marzio idolized him, even more so after his passing. When he lost our father, he sought in Cardia what he no longer had. And, well, I'm sure you've heard about Cardia. That man could be many things, but a father figure wasn't one of them. And when Marzio found himself without him as well... what can I say? It seems he couldn't bear it."

"But did you notice any strange behavior?" The commissioner pauses briefly.

"What do you mean?" Solimena asks, perplexed.

"Look, Mr. Solimena, people who are considering suicide usually give off signals before the final act. They're often looking for help, wanting to be saved by someone. Do you understand?"

Solimena continues to stare at him, remaining silent for a few seconds.

"Well, the Monday before his death, he knocked on my door." He says, looking directly into the officer's eyes. "He came by to visit my kids, for no particular reason. He brought them a small gift. I asked if we could have a drink together. He hesitated for a moment, then declined and left. I think it was the first time since I've been married that he came to my house without an invitation."

"Ah, that's important, you see?" The commissioner opens his notebook and takes notes. "Monday, you say. Monday was September third. Got it." He closes the notebook and places the pen on top. "These details are important. You said it was around the time for an aperitif?"

"Around eight in the evening."

"Okay. And I've heard Marzio was working in engineering before this? He used to be with Cardia, doing..." He flips through his notebook.

"He was doing research."

"Research, right. Do you know why he changed?"

"He never told me. In fact, he justified his request by saying he wanted a more hands–on approach." He clenches his fist and squeezes it a couple of times. "But the truth is, he was looking for a new role model, and, unfortunately, he wasn't well, he didn't feel capable of filling Cardia's shoes. He was still too inexperienced to even imagine it."

The commissioner nods and closes the notebook.

"And why didn't he look to you as a role model?"

Solimena spreads his hands and smiles.

"What can I say, Commissioner? I tried to teach him something, but he never had the humility to listen."

"Humility is an important quality."

"Essential."

"Are you humble, Mr. Solimena?"

"I know my limits, unlike some."

"You're a decisive man."

"Thank you."

"You have clear ideas." Solimena nods in acknowledgment.

The commissioner glances toward the photos.

"Is that your family?"

"Yes, my children and my wife."

"And that's you in the shirt?"

"Yes, that's me a few years ago."

"It's a bit egocentric, isn't it, to have a photo of yourself like that among the others?"

"My wife gave it to me as a gift."

"You were in great shape."

"Yes, now I've put on a few pounds and lost some hair."

"Well, for the weight, there's the gym, and for the hair, there are transplants in Turkey, right?"

Solimena smiles coldly.

"I'm fine as I am, thanks."

They remain silent for a while, staring at each other.

"Very well." The commissioner stands. "Thank you for your time, I hope I didn't take too much of it." He extends his hand to Solimena, who stands and shakes it.

"It's no problem, Commissioner. If you need anything, you can contact Miss Schiavone. She'll provide all the support you need."

"Thank you, really. I won't hesitate if I need anything."

The commissioner raises his hand in a farewell gesture, turns, and walks briskly toward the door. He opens it and finds Schiavone standing, waiting for him with her folder in hand. She smiles. Together, they head toward the elevator. The doors open as soon as she presses the call button, and they step inside. She selects the ground floor.

"Miss, can I ask you for the log of entries and exits from the facility?"

"Of course. I'd need a written request, though. You know, sensitive data, for privacy reasons."

"No doubt, but if you make a copy now, I'll send you an email as soon as I'm back at the office."

"I'm serious. We need to log the request officially, and extracting the data from the servers takes some time. It's already almost 7:00 PM. There's no one left in IT by now."

The commissioner checks his watch.

"You're right. I'll come by tomorrow morning."

"Around noon would be best."

The doors open. The commissioner steps out before Schiavone and raises his hand.

"No need, I remember the way. I'll stop by tomorrow morning, then. Good evening."

"Good evening." the woman replies curtly.

The commissioner walks briskly to the glass door and opens it. The rain has eased. He pulls out his car keys and unlocks the doors, walking under the canopy until he reaches the front of his Alfa. He turns and climbs inside.

He starts the car and turns on the headlights, the twilight is nearly gone. He pulls out his notebook and flips through it, reading a page carefully, then turns back to the last one, where he noted Marzio's visit to his brother's house on Monday evening. He underlines it twice and writes beside it, 'Car not started during this time.' He tosses the notebook onto the passenger seat, starts the engine, and reverses. He's about to turn onto the main road when he glances toward the R&D building, some lights are on on the first floor. He stops and grabs his phone. He selects a number from his contacts.

It rings.

"Hello?"

"Ventriglia, hi. It's Cardona."

"Ah, hello, Commissioner."

"You're still at the plant?"

"Yes, Commissioner."

"Still? How much are they making you work?"

Ventriglia laughs.

"What can I do for you?"

"I'm at the plant. How about grabbing a coffee together?"

"Why not?"

"I'll be at the department door in a minute. If you come down, we can chat".

"Alright, I'm coming."

"Thanks.

The commissioner ends the call.

12.

Isabella insisted the entire drive that I stay with her for dinner and the night. It's raining heavily now, and I don't feel up to riding the scooter all the way home.

So, I find myself here on the couch, waiting for dinner to be ready. On the coffee table are the papers I found in Cardia's drawer, folded exactly as they were. My head rests against the back of the couch, my body stretched out as I sit, my arms hanging weightlessly at my sides, my fingertips brushing the soft fabric. You wanted to take me far away, travel away from here, free for a few days. I feel sad because the tenderness I feel when I think of you is fading slowly, replaced by a liquid unease that makes it hard to breathe. It makes me want to kick, to shake it off like a too–tight shirt. But it's here, immovable, like a tattoo on my skin.

There's a vague feeling, creeping in like a worm. It started. I remember when I saw you for the last time, motionless in that wooden casket. Standing in front of those wet steps. There's something wrong with all of this. I repeat it to myself in whispers in my mind every minute. Something bigger than me, perhaps bigger than you. That took you and brought you here.

There's a hidden message in these papers. You've left me the task of deciphering it. I don't know where this path will lead us. I only feel afraid to walk it. There are too many questions I can't answer. It unnerves me to know that the hidden answers are dark, and I know many of them won't be pleasant and will bring me more pain.

Are we atoning for our sins, Marzio?

My eyes are half–closed, the scent of dinner fills the air, it's almost ready. Isabella is in the kitchen with the housemaid, preparing. I should go help. I take a deep breath. I sit up, reaching an upright position, but pause before pushing myself up.

The white papers.

A flash of lightning illuminates the room. I count. I reach four, and then comes the rumble of thunder, powerful and near. The rain falls in heavy drops.

I open the folder. I take out the last page and unfold it. From my pocket, I pull out my phone. I unlock it and dial the number on the paper.

I watch it glow on the display. My thumb hovers just millimeters above the green button. I hold my breath. I wonder if I'll ever have the courage to hear the voice on the other end. I close my eyes. I press the screen and bring the phone to my ear. My heart pounds in my chest. I hear static, the call has been sent. The circuits are active, the phone is searching for the connection, building the bridges to my recipient. It hasn't started ringing yet.

"This is a free message: the number you have dialed is unavailable or does not exist."

The voice is automated. It repeats the message in English. I end the call before the sentence finishes. The tension drains from me. I'm relieved no one answered. Only moments pass before guilt washes over me.

I shouldn't be happy about this. I should be devastated.

Yet I feel better than before. I tried, but it didn't work. But I tried. That's something.

Yes, it's only a consolation. The excuse I'm trying to give myself to justify my actions, to convince myself I've done well, that I couldn't have done more.

I drop the phone onto the table, almost tossing it. I hate myself for being so weak. A warm shiver runs up my spine. It's the frustration. I don't want to be myself. I don't want to do any of this.

I could just watch.

I could help someone else take this path, make this journey, do this search. I don't have the strength for it, see? It's stronger than me. Bigger than me.

I put the page back in the folder, take the stapled document, and place it on top. I don't want to see that number anymore. I bury my face in my hands and exhale forcefully. I truly hate myself.

I'm waiting for dinner. I'm waiting anxiously. I'm waiting for the night, I'm waiting for tomorrow. Tomorrow something will happen, tomorrow everything will change, tomorrow will be salvation. It will all be over.

Concrete Works Ltd.

That's the name of the company in the financial report under my eyes. Located in London, England.

Annual Report is the title of the document. Inside, there's a long description in English, filled with numbers and graphs. It's an accounting document. I think it's a company report with commentary. I pick it up and flip through it. Some sentences are highlighted by hand in yellow. At the end of the descriptive section, there's a name, Adam Langley, Chief Financial Officer, and below it, a phone number. I look at the number. It starts with +44, the UK dialing code.

The UK dialing code, I repeat in my head.

I grab the phone, dial +44. I pull out the folded paper. Maybe I'm being foolish. I copy the number and press the green button.

My heart leaps to my throat. But the call has been made. It's traveling north. I don't know what I'll say when someone answers, I don't even know if someone will answer. I don't know if I'm doing the right thing.

It rings, the sharp tone of the call sounds slightly hoarse.

It rings again, and again.

Someone answers.

There's background noise. For a moment, I think I hear breathing.

"Hello? – I say timidly."

No one responds.

But they're still there. On the other end of the line.

They exist. They're alive.

"Hello?" I repeat, trying to sound more confident.

My left hand presses against my temple, while my right holds the phone tightly to my ear.

"Hello?" Why aren't they answering? My heart pounds. "Why aren't you answering?" I say aloud.

Still nothing.

I can feel our time running out. I know I'm wasting it. I need to say something before it's too late.

The paper under my eyes vibrates. I focus and read.

"What assembly was scheduled for September seventh?"

I've said it.

I feel I hear a tremor on the other end. The wet sound of lips parting. It lasts for just a moment. Then a soft click and silence.

The phone is silent. I pull it away from my ear and look at it.

The screen reads call ended.

I don't know what to think.

"Dinner is ready."

It's the housemaid calling me from the door of the living room.

I get up, my legs springing up like loaded coils. I'm on my feet before I realize it.

Whoever answered knows something. I'm sure of it.

I'm sure of it.

13.

The machine hums and vibrates, and the blonde man pulls out the key that activates it. The cup drops into place, and the cycle begins.

"So, Ventriglia, now in all honesty, you need to tell me something."

"What's that?"

"Do you love your boss?"

"Who, Solimena?"

The commissioner grunts in agreement.

"Commissioner, bosses aren't made to be loved."

"But you cared about Marzio. So, he wasn't a boss to you."

Ventriglia thinks about it for a moment.

"It's different."

"What's different?"

"It's a matter of behavior, really."

"Explain."

"One of them always seemed to be saying, 'I'm the boss,' repeating it every time you saw him, every time you spoke to him. The other never said it. Not once. But when he said something... let's just say, you did it, no questions asked. It was a natural response. There was no need to emphasize anything."

"Yes, I think I understand."

The coffee is ready. Ventriglia grabs it and hands it to the commissioner.

"Thanks."

"So, Commissioner, why the question, and why at this hour, if I may ask?"

Cardona stirs his coffee with the transparent plastic stick.

"I just came out of Solimena's office. Had a chat."

"And?"

"Nothing much. I got more or less the same impression you just shared. I was just curious to hear your thoughts about Marzio."

He takes a sip of his coffee.

"Did you see him the Wednesday of the incident?"

"No, I didn't see him. Not all week."

"What time did you leave the plant on Wednesday?"

"Not too late, I think. Definitely before 7. That was his routine." Ventriglia pauses and looks at the commissioner. "But that's just my guess." He says gravely.

Cardona moves closer to the trash can and tosses the disposable cup inside.

"So, Commissioner, you don't believe Marzio killed himself."

The commissioner shakes his head, then looks Ventriglia in the eye.

"Not even a little." He pulls out a cigarette from the pack and puts it between his lips. "Not at all." He takes out his lighter "Can we smoke in here?"

Ventriglia laughs softly.

"Just open the window, and we can do whatever we want."

"Good, good." The commissioner lights his cigarette. Ventriglia climbs onto a chair and stretches to open the small rectangular window high on the right wall. It takes him a moment the handle is high, and he can barely reach it. With a firm twist, the window tilts open to about a 15–degree angle.

The commissioner watches him.

"Since we're at it, mind if I have a cigarette too? Can I borrow one?" Says Ventriglia.

The commissioner offers him the pack. Ventriglia pulls one out and steps closer to light it.

Cardona lights it, then puts the lighter back into the pack.

They smoke in silence. A few drops of rain come through the window, though the rain is less intense now.

"Ventriglia, before we leave, there's something we need to do."

"Tell me, Commissioner."

"I need you to show me Marzio Solimena's office."

"I can show you the door. It's locked."

"Seeing the door will do."

"It's upstairs, on the second floor." He points upward.

"Let's go."

Ventriglia is only halfway through his cigarette. He walks over to the trash can, raises his shoe, and crushes it against the sole. Then he tosses the butt into the bin. Cardona follows suit. They exchange glances.

"Follow me." Says the technician.

They walk quickly down the corridor. It's already dark outside. After about fifteen meters, they turn left and climb a wide staircase, large enough for two people to walk side by side. They reach the second floor and turn left again. They pass two brown wooden doors on the right. At the third door, Ventriglia extends his arm and points to it.

"That was Cardia's office."

He continues for another four meters and stops, turning to look at the commissioner.

"This was Marzio's office." He looks at the nameplate on the door. "It still is Marzio's, actually."

"Has anyone been inside? Since he's been gone, I mean."

"Commissioner, it's the boss's office. You don't go into the boss's office without permission."

"You called him the boss."

Ventriglia smiles but doesn't respond. He nods.

"Well, let's see."

The commissioner pulls out the three sets of keys he found in Marzio's car. He approaches the door and begins testing the various keys.

"And where did you get these keys?"

"The mighty power of the police, leaves you speechless, doesn't it?"

The first key doesn't fit. He tries the second one. It slides in smoothly. He turns it. The lock clicks, the mechanism moves, and the spring latch releases. He pushes. The door opens.

"Very good."

The commissioner enters and feels along the right wall for the light switch. He finds it and presses it.

The room is simple. Rectangular, stretching toward the back where there's a window, directly opposite the door. It's covered by a lowered gray roller blind. The wood–veneer desk is positioned lengthwise along the room's axis. On the side facing the door, there's a large PC monitor. In front of it is a bookcase, while behind it, there's a sideboard with some folders on top. On the desk are two picture frames, both facing the chair, which is sleek and looks comfortable. From here, the commissioner can't see who's in the photos.

"No one's been in here for a while." Says Ventriglia.

The commissioner approaches the desk, running a finger over it, then looks at his hand. There isn't much dust. From here, he can see the photos in the frames. He leans forward to peek. In each Marzio is with a different men beside him. In one the plant is behind them, the other is in the interior of an elegant house.

"I imagine one is the father and one is Cardia?" Asks the commissioner.

"Yes, the one with Mr.Solimena is the one taken in the plant."

Cardona exhales deeply, letting out a low sound.

The desk is tidy, no papers scattered about. The pen holders are in order, with a red pen, a blue one, a black one, and a mechanical pencil.

"Ventriglia. Did you see Marzio during his last week? Did he behave strangely? Anything out of the ordinary?"

"I didn't see him much. Caught a glimpse of him in the cafeteria once or twice, but I'm not even sure about that. He was in engineering, didn't come here anymore."

"Who should I talk to in engineering? Someone who knew him well."

"I'm not sure. I don't know them well, but I'll think about it. I can give you a name tomorrow."

The commissioner still has the set of keys in his hand. He looks at them and selects the smallest one. He inserts it into the desk drawer and turns the lock, then opens the drawers.

"Ventriglia, can I borrow your bag?"

"Commissioner, isn't this illegal?"

"I'll bring them back tomorrow. They'll be right where I found them."

Ventriglia thinks for a moment, standing still, then steps back.

"I'll go lock up my office and be right back."

He leaves the room quickly.

Cardona remains in the room. He's sitting in Marzio's chair. His hands rest on his knees. Something is eluding him.

In here.

"Something's not right."

But he can't say what.

14.

The bed is cold. I'm tucked under the sheets and a thick white blanket. Darkness surrounds me; the shutters are closed, not letting a single sliver of light through.

Marzio has slept here a few times. At night. In this bed. In this room with its bare walls. I feel my feet, distant and cold. A separate part of my body. Shivers run through me. My eyes burn, and a weight presses down on my chest, making it hard to breathe.

Another thought adds itself to the others tonight. I'm really afraid. Afraid of seeing him. Of seeing his eyes glow in the dark. His voice. His sounds.

What demon he is, what spell summoned him, what he ultimately wants, what twisted game I'm playing, I don't know any of it.

My forearm presses against my forehead. I know I shouldn't ask, I shouldn't think, that if I stop, I'll go mad. But I don't sleep, I haven't slept in a long time. I don't sleep. Sleep doesn't come. I give in to exhaustion, maybe a couple of hours a night. Then I wake up like this, as if struck by lightning. My mind and body disconnected, my strength leaving me. And I'm left alone with my thoughts. Tonight, Marzio isn't here. I don't see him. I used to feel you, your warmth, your breath, even in the pure silence of the night, even on the other side of the bed, the room, the world. You were there.

Now you're not here. In this room. Hidden from my sight. You've disappeared. For the first time, I truly feel that you're dead. That you're a corpse. That what I see isn't even your soul, but the lifeless remains of a corpse.

The sound of this thought tears my heart apart. I feel the need to tear my skin away, to feel pain, something to distract me, to absorb my fury, this unease that slithers through my body, into my throat, down to my stomach, twisting around my esophagus. It dries my mouth, makes my eyes a desert. Burning, burning. Cold flames.

I get up. I can't tolerate this darkness. I need to open the shutters. I need to see light.

The phone vibrates, and the room lights up. The cold glow of the screen casts gothic shadows on the walls. In the opposite corner of my room, there's Marzio. I can't see his eyes, they're lost in the darkness. My breath lasts an eternity, the sound filling my ears. I hold it in so it doesn't deafen me, but it presses against my chest, and I let it out through my mouth. The cough catches in my throat. The phone goes dark. And I'm back in the comforting darkness.

I reach for the nightstand, groping around.

With my fingertips, I tap the wooden surface in different spots. I find the outline of the phone, grip it, and bring it to my face. I click and check the notifications on the lock screen.

1 unread email.

I press the phone to my chest. It could be anything, ads, spam, newsletters, or random notifications. It could mean nothing.

I unlock the phone. Open the email app.

In the inbox is an unread email.

No sender. No subject.

I tap it with my finger, and it opens.

I know it was you who called today. If that happened, it means something has gone wrong. I don't want to imagine what, but the fact that you called and not him makes me fear the worst.

There's a chance for both of us to escape this vortex before it takes hold and crushes us. But for that to happen, you must be ready to believe my words and do what I say.

The first thing you must do is delete the phone number you used to call me. I've already destroyed my SIM card and phone, and you should also erase all traces of that call from your phone's log.

They don't know about you. That gives us an advantage, but when things get serious, it won't take them long to figure out who you are and find you. And from you, it won't take much to reach me.

All of this will be terrifying, just as it was for me, but He made sure there would be a way out. It will work if you believe, just as I did.

One last link in this chain is holding all of this together: you. You must be strong and believe. He believed in you and knew you could save us, which is why he saw you as his anchor in this storm.

And if he believed in you, then so do I.

The first rule is silence. Don't talk to anyone about this. Every word is sacred and must be kept.

The second rule is action, you must move, act, do. Many times, you won't know what you're doing. It's a matter of trust. If you trusted him, you must do the same with me. Without this bond, we are both lost.

The third rule is speed. Everything you do must be done immediately, like lightning striking the earth.

I can't believe I'm writing these words to you. They're the same ones he said to me. On a night like this.

The first task is this: at your house, in your closet, search through his coats for a beige trench coat. In one of the inner pockets is a piece of paper with notes.

I'll be waiting for your contact. In the meantime, be strong and good luck.

It's unsigned.

I'm breathless.

My eyes burn as if I'd poured salt into them. I look again at the blank header. The email was sent at 3:13 AM. My heart pounds violently against my chest, then stops. I hold my breath. A cold shiver runs down my neck, making my hair quiver in pain. It's as if I'm submerged in water; my ears press against my brain. There's a weight on my ankles. I tilt the phone to light up my legs.

There's a shape under the sheets, the same sheets covering me now. It moves slowly, rising. It grabs my ankles and squeezes. I gasp in a strangled sob of terror, scrambling up the bed, curling against the headboard, kicking to free myself. The sheets fall away. It doesn't let go. It squeezes even harder.

There it is.

Small and wicked. At the foot of my bed, it grins. Silently, with its grotesque smile. The walls are gone. There's only an infernal darkness here, and me and it, staring at each other.

I gasp again in terror. My throat is a knot of flesh. A hiss of warm air escapes, instantly condensing in the cold now that I'm free of its grip.

I reach for the nightstand, groping for salvation, for the light, for the switch, desperately panting. My hand slams against the wood. Nothing. There's nothing.

Its hands move up, rough against my skin, grabbing one knee, then the other, squeezing and pushing down, then sideways. I have no strength, and my breaths become sharp, my heart exhausted. My fingers touch something square, and I grip it in my palm with all my might. I feel a button pressing against my skin, squeezing tightly, opening and closing my hand again. I can't feel my fingertips. I'm so scared I wish I were dead.

With its cold hands, it moves up further, clawing at my skin, with disdain, with hatred. It climbs over me. It wants me tonight, to tear me apart with all its malice, the taste of evil wetting its lips.

I scream, I scream loud, I scream until the light floods my face. I open my eyes to see an undefined white screen. I have to shield myself with my hands. There's a figure at the door. It speaks. It asks how I am. It moves toward me, toward my bed. I can see its outline.

"You had a nightmare. It's just a nightmare."

She reaches out to touch my face. But I jerk toward the wall, not meaning to. I look at her. It's Isabella, in her dressing gown. I look at my legs. Covered by pajama pants. There's no one else in the bed but me.

15.

It's dawn. He notices from the light seeping through the windows. The shutters are wide open. Cardona's head rests against the pillow, propped almost vertically against the wall. On the floor are crumpled greasy papers, an empty beer bottle, and a pair of inside—out dark socks.

He hasn't slept much, but he wanted to wake up exactly now. He grabs his watch from the nightstand, puts it on, and tightens the steel clasp. He pats his legs, throws off the scratchy blanket that covered him, and sits at the edge of the bed. He runs his hand over his face, feeling his beard beginning to grow excessively. It's so early that the offices would still be closed. Fine, he thinks, now's a good time to shave. He gets up and heads toward the bathroom. The tiles are cold; he feels the dust under his feet. Just a few steps, from the hallway to the bathroom. The walls are bare, the house old, with cracks running through the walls. The bathroom light is cold, and opposite the door is an oval mirror with a white frame, chipped in places, revealing the layers of plywood beneath.

Cardona looks at himself. He's a bit surprised. He turns on the water, which splashes into the limescale—stained sink. He runs his hand under the flow.

He has deep bags under his eyes. But his eyes are alert, and beneath the stubble of his beard, a mocking smile is hidden. The corners of his lips are imperceptibly turned upward.

"What's up, Commissioner? Did you sleep well?" He says to himself, looking into his eyes.

"We've got work to do, huh?" He nods after saying it.

He grabs the shaving foam and sprays a puff into his left palm, massaging it onto his face, whistling. Then he laughs. When was the last time he woke up in a good mood?

He can hardly believe his ears, or his eyes.

The foam spreads evenly across his face, forming a thin layer from his sideburns to his chin. He feels like a cigarette. He returns to the bedroom and pulls one from the pack on the nightstand, lighting it and taking a long drag. He's genuinely happy.

There's a contradiction, something that doesn't add up in Solimena's words. It was just a feeling until yesterday afternoon, but now it's a certainty. Something is going on, and he's getting into it. He's getting into it with relish. He heads back to the bathroom, breathing in the smoke, holding it in his lungs, then exhaling it against the mirror. He feels a path beneath his feet. He feels the strength in his legs. He grabs the razor, the blades are worn, and the moisturizing strip is completely used up. He presses it against his skin and begins to shave.

The air is fresh. Full of moisture. The clouds are still low, gray, and heavy. Cardona bites down on a cigarette before unlocking the car and getting inside. The aroma of coffee mingles with the smoke, and he enjoys it. He starts the car, and after some reluctance, the old four–cylinder engine roars to life. It's a bit rough, but it's never missed a day of work. He lowers the window and heads toward the station. The road is clear; only a few fortunate souls are heading to work with him. Soon, the madness will begin on this asphalt, hoping it won't rain and that no poltergeist will emerge from the city's bowels.

He selects Cesarano from his phone contacts and presses the call button.

It rings. He automatically turns into the priority lane, even though there's no need, then glances to the side, relieved that at least this part of the road has fewer potholes. The documents he pulled from Marzio Solimena's office rest on the passenger seat.

No one answers.

"What the hell, Cesarano! What time do you get up in the morning?"

The sun begins to rise in the sky, evidenced by the gradually intensifying light. He tries to remember the last time he saw the sun's disc. Before he finds the answer, his phone vibrates. He grabs it. Cesarano's name is on the display.

"Cesarà! Good morning."

"Hello?" Cesarano's voice is thick with sleep.

"Cesarà, are you still in bed?"

"Commissioner, I just woke up. I'm making coffee. What's up? Were you looking for me?"

"Cesarà, did you find the papers I asked for?"

"Commissioner, you only asked for them the day before yesterday."

"Yes, I remember. So, do you have them or not?"

"Yes, Commissioner. Not all of them, but I've started working on it."

"Good job, Cesarà. What do you have for me?"

"I've got the reports, certificates, and a few other things. Before heading to the office, I'll stop by the chamber of commerce and get the filed minutes. If they're ready."

"They'd better be ready, Cesarà."

"Commissioner, that's not up to me."

"I don't want to hear excuses. See you at the office."

The commissioner hangs up without listening to what Cesarano says next.

He tosses the phone onto the passenger seat. He accelerates and turns. The street is empty, the yellow lines to his right are clear, and a sign indicates a no–parking zone, reserved for law enforcement. He parallel parks in one of the first available spots. He turns off the car, grabs the documents and his phone, and steps out.

He heads toward the entrance with his head down. The papers tucked under his arm. If Solimena is lying, it's because he wants to make it appear that his brother committed suicide. So, he's interested in pushing the suicide narrative. If he wants the suicide version to stick, there's another version he doesn't want to be known. If it wasn't suicide, it was an accident or, a drum-roll sounds in his head, it was murder.

"Good morning, murder." The commissioner greets the thought with a bow. And if he's lying about the version, why would he lie if it were an accident? He's lying because he doesn't want the incident version to be seen as murder.

"But it is murder." The commissioner whispers, then raises his head and nods to the guard at the entrance.

"You're up early today, Commissioner!" The guard greets him cheerfully.

The commissioner waves and mumbles something, not stopping as he heads quickly toward the stairs.

So, if he doesn't want it to be seen as murder, that means he's involved. And if he's involved, there's only one question left to ask. The main one. The one that drives this investigation.

"Why did Marzio Solimena die?"

He enters the office and stops. His feet planted on the floor. The room is empty. The window is closed.

"That's it." He says.

He moves forward and drops the papers onto his desk. He walks over to the window and opens it. Then he returns to his seat. There's a folder on the desk labeled 'Cardona' in Cesarano's handwriting.

The commissioner lines up the two folders in front of him. On the left is Cesarano's, and on the right is the one found in Solimena's office.

He thinks for a moment, resting his hand on the folder on the right, tapping it with his fingers. Then he decides, grabs the folder on the right, and places it in a blue file. He opens the third drawer of his desk, pulls out a couple of folders, and slides this one inside. He drops the other folders on the floor and returns to the one from Cesarano.

He opens it. Inside are reports, criminal records, and birth certificates there are three Solimenas and Cardia at the end.

He takes Umberto's first and opens his notebook. There are notes on the company shares he joined Prosud S.p.A. with ten percent ownership eight years ago, then rose to forty–five percent after his father's death. It says 'inheritance' in the note. The commissioner also takes Marzio's report. It says the exact same thing. The commissioner writes everything down in his notebook. There are two other shares, one in a company called Sol Immobiliare and another in Sol Finanziaria. Both are at twenty–five percent.

Only one property. The commissioner writes down the address, feeling the keys found in the Mercedes in his pocket. He checks Marzio's report. Only one property here as well. Via Carducci 10. He notes it in his notebook and underlines it. It could be interesting to take a walk there. It says it was transferred through inheritance. Marzio also holds shares in the same three companies with the same percentages. The commissioner grabs the landline phone and automatically dials Cesarano's number.

"Cesarano."

"Commissioner, tell me."

"Where are you?"

"I'm outside the chamber of commerce. I'm parking."

"Listen carefully, and take note. I need you to find all the documents for Sol Immobiliare and Sol Finanziaria." The commissioner enunciates the names slowly.

"Oh, Commissioner, I know you too well. I already asked for them. I knew you'd be looking for these two as well. I'll grab everything and bring it to you."

"Cesarano, I'd say I'm impressed, but really, you just confirmed what I already thought of you." Says Cardona, beaming.

"Flattery, flattery!" Cesarano exclaims, amused.

The commissioner hangs up, slams the phone down with some force, and dives back into the papers.

The criminal records are empty. No outstanding charges. He circles Umberto's name with the red pen.

"Not for long."

The report also lists the positions held in the company. Umberto's first role was ten years ago, as a member of Prosud's board of directors. He became CEO when his father died, and he remains in that position today. Around the same time, he became the managing director of Sol Immobiliare and Sol Finanziaria, where he was previously a board member. Marzio's story is different, he joined as a board member at Prosud seven years ago. According to the report, he still holds the position, as they haven't recorded his death yet. He joined the other two companies late, in May, after Cardia's death.

There's a historical record of shareholdings. Umberto had more than a few, with companies bearing exotic names: Copacabana Srl, Groove Fitness Srl, Indigo & Co Spa, and others. All shares have been sold or transferred, and he never held an administrative role. All sales and transfers occurred before his father's death.

Marzio, on the other hand, was never involved in any other companies besides Prosud and the two Sol companies.

The commissioner writes down the names and dates, creating a diagram of names and connections. So far, it seems simple.

He opens Cardia's file. The first document is the family record, married to Isabella, no children. Next are the property records. They own several homes; one is in Torre del Greco, which matches his wife's residence. There's no mention of a divorce; his wife was widowed, and they were still legally married when he died. There's another house that catches the commissioner's attention, Sorrento, Traversa Punta Capo. The commissioner taps his pen three times on the desk, flipping through his notebook, though he doesn't really need to. He grabs the page listing destinations from the Mercedes' GPS.

"There you are." He folds a corner of Cardia's report and marks the address in his notebook with an asterisk.

Cardia's story is complicated. There are shares, positions held, and many companies he was involved with some seem to be linked to Prosud. Around ten years ago, everything narrows down to just Prosud S.p.A., and the other shares are dissolved. Notably, he remained in his role as technical director from the company's founding until his death.

Cardona strokes his freshly shaven chin. He searches for Prosud's documents. He wants to know who the current technical director is. He flips through the file but finds nothing. He'll have to wait for Cesarano. He needs an organizational chart.

His phone vibrates. The number on the display isn't saved in his contacts it's a landline. The area code is local, and he recognizes the first three digits, it's the prosecutor's office.

"Hello?"

"Cardona?"

"Yes, that's me."

"Hello, Cardona, this is Prisco." The voice is young, bright, and detached.

"Ah, good morning, prosecutor." In the commissioner's mind, he pictures the public prosecutor at his desk, phone in hand, wearing a brown tie.

"Good morning, Cardona. I see you have the file in hand."

"Yes, Doctor."

"Well, Cardona, it seems to me that much has already been said. I've also read the autopsy report. There doesn't seem to be much more to add."

"Well, actually, Doctor…"

"The father died a few months ago. Clearly, the boy fell into depression and killed himself." The prosecutor continues without allowing the commissioner to interrupt. "These spoiled kids today are crushed by the first difficulty in life. There's not much more to say about it, and the newspapers have already had their fun dredging up filth, so we'll…"

"Doctor, if I may." Cardona cuts in, and for a few words, their voices overlap, but the commissioner presses on. "Doctor, I took a walk around the scene of the incident, and I have a couple of observations."

"Oh, you took a walk there." The prosecutor repeats.

"Yes, I went there, and, Doctor, with all due respect, there are a few things that don't quite make sense to me."

"Cardona, didn't we work together a few years ago on that Leggiero case, right?"

"Yes, Doctor, but this is different."

"Alright, let's hear it." The prosecutor says, irritated. "No, because I'm listening, Cardona, but I remember that investigation well and all the drama that came from your... let's say, unique way of interpreting State Police work."

"Look, Doctor, this is a completely different situation, and we're different people now."

"I hope so, Cardona. I really hope so. The prosecutor makes no effort to hide his annoyance." So, what do you have to say?

The commissioner grits his teeth and swallows a lump of cement–like saliva that slides down his esophagus, pushed by all the anger in his body.

"There are a couple of things that, in my opinion, deserve further investigation. First, you don't kill yourself by burning yourself alive. Honestly, that's the last method anyone would choose."

"Look, Cardona, that's not entirely true. Despair often manifests as suicide through fire. There are many cases, truly many, and the fact that he did it at his father's company also speaks volumes. He clearly had unresolved issues with his father and wanted to destroy what his father had built. You see a lot of these types of conflicted relationships."

"Sure, but..." Cardona raises his voice. "But he did it in a new office, in a new department where he had only recently started working. He spent years working in a different building at the plant."

"I don't see the connection. It's the symbolic act that matters. Do you have anything beyond psychological deductions?"

"Yes, I do. Have you seen the list of reports?"

"I've looked through them."

"Well, the key to Solimena's car is missing and..."

"And so?"

"Well, one moment, Doctor, the car was found parked behind the building that burned down. It wasn't in a designated parking area. The car was locked."

"And?"

"So, someone probably took those keys."

"And left the car where it was? What sense does that make?"

"Maybe that someone was interested in something inside the car."

"Speculation."

"It's a lead. And there's something else."

"Go on." The prosecutor is clearly tired of hearing all this.

"Umberto contradicted himself." The commissioner pauses. There's silence on the other end. "Doctor?"

"Go on, Commissioner, go on."

"I was saying that he contradicted himself."

"About what?"

"About what Marzio Solimena did on Monday evening before he died. He said Marzio stopped by to say goodbye to his kids around dinner time, but that's not true."

"And how do you know that?"

The commissioner pauses. He's unsure if he can say this. Then he convinces himself. He can't.

"I managed to reconstruct Marzio Solimena's movements in his final days."

"And how did you do that?" The prosecutor asks suspiciously.

"I spoke with some people, saw a few things. Anyway, if you'll meet with me, we can discuss it in person.

"Listen, Commissioner, I don't like where this is going. You're taking initiatives that are not your place and, in my opinion, outside of procedure. Listen, Cardona, if you pull any more stunts like this, I'll make sure you're out of a job. And I don't mean a transfer, I'll send you to hand out parking tickets." Prisco raises his voice. "Because with your career, you can do whatever you want, but I won't let you mess up another case and jeopardize my career. So be very careful, Commissioner, I mean it."

"Look, Doctor, you can say what you want, threaten me, yell at me, but if your intention is to close this case without looking into these things, then I'm the one who's going to get angry." The commissioner raises his voice as well.

"Cardona! Who do you think you are? Raising your voice on the phone, insinuating things that have no basis, and then expecting to teach me how to do my job? Are we joking or are we serious? We started off on the wrong foot... No, worse even, on both wrong feet. Cardona, this is going to end badly for you. I'm telling you honestly. I won't allow your delusions of grandeur, your American sci–fi mind, to create problems for the prosecution and cause pain to the family of someone who made such a terrible choice. The culprit is in your head, projected onto others because you're trying to escape your own problems. And I'm not here to be your therapist. We're done with this conversation. I don't want to hear any more about it. The files will go through the usual process, and I'll make my decision in due time. He pauses. Understand?"

The commissioner says nothing.

"In due time." The prosecutor enunciates each syllable slowly. "Goodbye, Commissioner. Take care."

The call ends.

"Go to hell." The commissioner mutters, throwing the phone onto the table. "What an idiot."

He pulls out a cigarette and lights it. He stretches out on the desk, legs extended, hands in his pockets.

He tries to clear his mind of thoughts, but only anger remains. He inhales deeply, harder. The guilt returns for opening the car, for talking to Ventriglia and that other girl, for speaking with Solimena Sr., for everything. Leggiero comes to mind again, the mistakes, the recklessness, the case melting like snow, the procedural errors. A case closed that turned into a disaster.

"Damn it." He says aloud. "Damn, damn, damn."

He repeats it a thousand times in his head.

Only the word remains. His mind goes blank.

The image of Prisco on the phone expands. There's someone at his desk.

Doubt rises.

Whether he's truly an idiot, or just playing the part.

Now, at this moment, the commissioner exhales, letting the smoke out in a thin cloud.

A fleeting thought crosses his mind, that he might be paranoid, but it passes. He'll keep going, one way or another, with or without Prisco.

"Go to hell."

16.

I'm standing outside my front door. The helmet is brushing against my right leg, held by its strap. I can hardly remember how I got here. I don't recall whether I took the stairs or the elevator. I don't remember the traffic; I don't remember if I was cold during the trip. I pat the left pocket of my jeans but can't find the keys. What if I left them at Isabella's? I panic, patting my other pocket empty. Then I reach inside my jacket, trembling, checking the inner pockets, then the outer ones. I don't want to go back there. There finally I feel them. I exhale. How is it possible that everything causes me this much suffering?

I take the longest key and insert it into the lock. I turn it twice, then a little more. It feels like an enormous effort, but the door opens. I push it with my shoulder and step inside, tossing the helmet onto the floor.

The wardrobe. I shove the door closed with enough force to make sure it stays shut. I take a step, hearing the loud clatter of the metal. Too loud. I'm looking for the wardrobe. I enter the bedroom. In that corner, Marzio watches me. His figure. It almost annoys me to see him now. It causes me pain, but now it's worse. More unbearable. I feel the hurt envelop me when he's near. Am I freeing him or myself from this curse? It feels like I'm only imprisoning myself. This isn't what I wanted. I move closer to the wardrobe, to Marzio's side. I open it. There are classic suits, two black, one gray, ties on a hanger, some shirts. I never learned how to fold them. 'Be thankful I iron them', I used to say. Then there are the jackets and coats, four of them, still light, summery. Here's the beige trench coat. I pull it from the wardrobe and lay it on the bed. I open it and search the inner pockets, nothing. Nothing. Wait, here's a smaller pocket, with a button. I open it, and it's so narrow I can only slip in my index and ring fingers. I feel a piece of paper. I grasp it and pull it out. Here it is.

It's a piece of graph paper, torn on all four sides, folded in half. I sit on the bed, or rather, collapse onto it, and open the paper.

It's Marzio's handwriting. Block letters.

lili is the key.

0611910757201002072012

There's nothing else written. Just this. Lili is the key. The same name from the August 29th email.

I'm too tired to think. I lie down on the bed. I've found the note he told me about. Now, what do I do?

I'm awakened by the sound of my phone. A call. I pull it from my jacket pocket, my mouth dry and sticky from sleep. The number is private. The clock shows it's nearly noon, how long have I slept? The phone keeps ringing. I press the screen over the green icon and bring the phone to my ear.

A recorded voice responds, it's in English, but I can't understand what it's saying, even though it's speaking slowly. There's a pause, then a ringing tone, like a call. A woman's voice answers, a recording.

"Access to node thirteen forty–six. Please insert the access code. Please hit the hash key at the end of your access code."

Silence.

It's asking for the key.

The key.

I grab Marzio's note. I put the phone on speaker and click the 'show keyboard' button on the screen.

I slowly type all the numbers in the code, moving my thumb after each digit to avoid mistakes, one by one.

There, I'm done. Nothing happens. I wait a bit longer. I must have made a mistake. Wait. The hash key is the pound symbol. I press the pound key.

"Your access code is incorrect. Access to node thirteen forty–six. Please insert the access code. Please hit the hash key at the end of your access code. You have two remaining attempts"

I made a mistake. I'm still half asleep. I sit up on the bed. Okay, I'll try again. The keyboard is still on the phone's display. Maybe I mistyped it. I try again from scratch, more carefully, one number at a time. Slowly, I keep my eyes fixed on the numbers in the squares. There, I've finished. Pound key. Silence.

"Your access code is incorrect. Access to node thirteen forty–six. Please insert the access code. Please hit the hash key at the end of your access code. You have one remaining attempt. The node data will be deleted after three failed attempts."

It added a sentence at the end. It says all data will be deleted if I make another mistake. I look again at the numbers on the display, comparing them with the ones on the paper. They're the same. Exactly the same. I didn't make a mistake. He's the one who put the wrong code in this system. I stomp my foot on the floor and let out a high–pitched cry. Now what? What do I do? Hang up? I don't want to delete anything. I don't know what to enter, I don't know the key.

I look at the note.

lili is the key.

0611910757201002072012

Lili is the key.

It's the key.

Under the numbers, there are letters. Lili is the key. Under five, there are I, J, and K. Under four, there's G, H, and I.

Lili is the key, the note says. To Marzio, it's the key.

I enter three fives, then three fours, then three fives, then three fours.

My heart races.

I press the pound key.

Silence.

"Access to node thirteen forty–six granted. Please wait, the data is load- ing."

There's more silence. Then I hear a distant click.

"Livio Ligresti was born in Rome in 1975. He studied at Liceo Scientifico Majorana." A mechanical female voice. It sounds like Google Translate. I tap my phone until I open the recorder app. I hit the red button, and the timer starts. It's recording everything. "He graduated with top honors in 1993. That same year, he enrolled at LUISS University, majoring in economics. He grad- uated in 1998 with a perfect score, earning a special mention and honors. His thesis was in finance, titled 'The International Financial Transaction: An In- novative Application. Regulatory and Jurisdictional Aspects in Global Macro- economics.'

In his thesis, Ligresti explored the topic of international corporate transac- tions, focusing particularly on South American tax havens. He examined their advantages and presented innovative accounting methods. The thesis was published in the Journal of Economics. It sparked a heated debate over the morality of its contents, which continued for months, with no resolution after four months of replies and counter–replies. The academic debate ended in- conclusively. During this time, Ligresti moved from Price Waterhouse Cooper, where he was a trainee, to McKinsey & Co as a junior consultant.

In 2000, he was admitted to the Wharton School of Economics to pursue an MBA. After completing the eighteen–month program, he returned to McKinsey & Co, staying until 2005. He then became the CFO of Krugel Schneider, a Swiss fund manager. His tenure lasted three years, during which he implemented his ideas on international transactions, refined during his years at McKinsey. Krugel's fund performance was exceptional, outperform- ing all benchmarks. In the summer of 2008, he resigned. Ligresti disappeared from public view, and the international financial community wondered about his fate. Months passed, and curiosity waned. The global financial crisis took over, and the subprime mortgage crisis erupted. Ligresti reappeared in 2009 as CEO of Lunar Finance, a Luxembourg–based company overseeing several commodity and semi–finished goods brokerage firms. Since then, he has remained in that role without change. He has consistently declined requests for interviews or comments and has made no public appearances since 2008."

There's a brief silence.

"End of recorded data. If you want to hear the data again, press one. If you want to delete the data, press nine. If you want to add a new record, press five."

I think about it. Then I return to the recorder app on my phone and hit stop. I go back to the phone keypad and press nine.

"The data has been successfully deleted. If you want to..."

I don't care anymore. I hang up.

I sit there, phone in hand, staring at it. Who is Livio Ligresti? What does he have to do with Marzio?

The feeling of confusion is lighter, at least I have some questions to answer now.

I get up and go to my desk. I open my laptop, and the screen comes to life. It's still on standby, asking for the password. I type Marzio's name and the date we met. As the computer wakes up, I reflect on how it's not the best password I could have chosen. She said no one knows about me, though he never talked about me to anyone. That stings a little. Maybe he was ashamed of me. Yes. That thought lingers. It makes me sad. Maybe this password isn't so insecure after all. If no one knows I exist. But Isabella knew. And maybe Cardia did too. And her. Who is she? What does she want is she the girl in the photo? The one embracing him, resting her hand on his?

I open the browser. I type Livio Ligresti into the search bar. The results page loads, Wikipedia, followed by English newspaper articles from economic outlets. I click on the encyclopedia entry. It opens, and there's a photo he's in a suit and tie, smiling. He's a handsome man, with wavy, slightly long hair, and his arms crossed. The Wikipedia entry matches exactly what I heard in the recording. Among the relevant links is one leading to the Lunar Finance website. I click. The site opens, with blue and gray as the dominant colors. 'Welcome to Lunar Finance' is written in French I can only understand that much, as my French is poor. The various sections offer only brief information, accompanied by generic photos of skyscrapers, smiling people, and workers. I open another tab with Google Translate and copy the descriptions from the site. As expected, they're just generic statements that reveal nothing about what the company actually does. They talk about increasing profitability, enhancing value, and suggesting growth strategies. Lots of words, little substance. I click on the last menu item. It says 'Contacts.' No translator is needed for that. I grab my phone. I set it to private number and dial. The international code suggests it's Luxembourg. I call. My heart races. My English isn't great.

After one ring, there's music in the background, and words in French. The music is classical, but I don't recognize the piece. A female voice answers.

"Hello?"

"Yes, good morning." I stop, trying to form the sentence in my head.

"Good morning." She replies.

"Yes, I am the secretary of Mr. Solimena. Is Mr. Ligresti available?"

"Oh hey, Francesca, is that you?"

I'm taken aback. Who's Francesca? Marzio had a secretary?

"No, I am Francesca's substitute. Sorry for my bad English."

"Oh, I see, it's okay. So you want to talk to Mr. Ligresti?"

"Yes, Mr. Solimena wants to speak to him."

"Okay, I'm sorry to say that Mr. Ligresti is out of the office right now. He's on a business trip." She speaks slowly, thankfully.

"Okay, okay. When will he be back?"

"I'm afraid I can't answer that question since he hasn't left any information about when he'll return."

"Can you please give me his cell phone number? Mr. Solimena really wants to hear from him."

"Sure, no problem. I think you should have it, but here it is: plus three five two, three three two, seven six, three, one, zero, twelve." I follow her voice, typing it into the browser's address bar. "Do you need me to repeat it?"

"No, it's okay. I've got it. Thank you very much."

"Thank you! And please pass my regards to Miss Schiavone."

"Okay, no problem. Thank you."

"Thank you! Bye–bye!"

"Bye–bye."

I end the call. I can't believe it. I called Luxembourg, pretended to be someone else, and managed to get Ligresti's phone number. I smile, proud of myself! I feel like continuing. I copy the number from the screen to my phone's keypad. I call. The phone starts dialing, and I hold it to my ear. I wait. A French voice answers immediately, without ringing, probably saying the phone is off or unreachable. I end the call.

I stare out the window in front of me. The city is alive outside. It's cloudy, but it's Friday. Someone out there is happy. The week is ending. I stay here. I feel like I've done something important today. Ligresti is connected. Ligresti knows. The only question is whether he wants to talk to me. A strange sense of self–confidence washes over me.

How strange I am.

17.

Cardona has the car keys in hand. Plays with them, spinning them and thrn tapping them on the glass of water on the bar counter.

The bartender approaches from the other side of the counter.

"Sweet." he says.

The bartender places the small cup on the saucer in front of him, rotating it so the handle is on his right.

The commissioner puts the keys on the counter, gulps down the glass of water, and turns the cup so the handle is on the opposite side. He picks it up with his left hand and drinks the coffee in one go.

"I'll stop by later."

The bartender nods.

"Put a coffee on the commissioner's tab!" He says loudly to the cashier.

A middle–aged woman with a few extra pounds and curls that are far too blonde waves at the commissioner while punching the receipt with the other. The commissioner returns the wave and steps out, hands in his pockets.

He walks to the left, heading toward his car. He's thinking about Sorrento as he looks for the nose of his 155. On his right, he sees a police car drive by. A familiar figure catches his eye, he looks more closely. It's Cesarano at the wheel. He reaches his Alfa and reconsiders, deciding to return to the station. He turns the corner and sees Cesarano's car pulling into the courtyard through the reserved entrance. The commissioner heads for the pedestrian entrance to cut through, walking across the high archway and into the court-yard. Cesarano has parked, stepped out of the car, and is opening the back door. The commissioner approaches him from behind.

"Well?"

"Who's there?" Cesarano exclaims, jumping in surprise.

"It's me, Cesarà. Who else would it be?"

"Ah, Commissioner, my goodness! You scared me!" Cesarano says, turn-ing and placing a hand on his chest.

"Come on, Cesarà, what've you brought me?"

"Almost everything, Commissioner. I turned the registry offices upside down for you."

"Well, that's good work. Let's bring it all up."

"Commissioner, do me a favor, give me a hand. I've got tons of paper-work here."

"Alright, give me something." The commissioner responds, kindly.

Cesarano leans into the car and pulls out several files crammed into a bulging gray binder tied with strings. It's about twenty centimeters thick. He sets it in the commissioner's arms, who feels the weight strain him.

"Wait." The officer warns. "I've got more."

He pulls out another equally full binder and places it on top of the first, stacked in the commissioner's arms. He pats the stack.

"Alright, Commissioner, you head on up. I'll take care of the rest here."

Cardona heads toward the first–floor office. He sees the elevator and the people waiting but makes his way to the stairs. He walks up the steps diagonally to see where he's going, as the binders are so tall they make it difficult to see in front of him.

He reaches the first floor and heads for his office.

Inside, no one is there. He places the binders on his desk, then takes the taller one and sets it aside. He sits down in his chair, turns the first binder around, and unties the knots, opening it. Inside are the meeting minutes from Prosud. He flips through the papers. Below are financial statements and explanatory notes. He feels satisfied, pulling out the first few centimeters of documents and laying them in front of him. He reclines in his chair, putting his feet up on the desk. He begins to read. This meeting is from 2009. The agenda includes approving the budget for 2010, the investment plan, the strategic plan, and miscellaneous items. No attachments.

Present at the meeting are shareholders Umberto Solimena, Marzio Solimena, Augusto Cardia. Margherita Vetere is absent.

Augusto Cardia is present. But according to the earlier records, he has no shares in Prosud. His reason for attending is explained later. It says Augusto Cardia present as a representative of the rights held by the Golden Share.

Golden Share.

The commissioner writes 'Golden Share' in his notebook.

The weight of the binders shakes the desk. Cesarano has brought two more.

"Here you go, Commissioner, this is everything."

"How far back do we go, Cesarà?"

"In what sense?"

"The date, the date."

"I didn't check, Commissioner, but I asked for at least ten years"

"Well done, Cesarà. There's a lot of interesting stuff here." The commissioner pats the binders, a mix of affection and interest.

"Commissioner, have you spoken to Prisco?"

"And how do you know that?" Cardona stares at him, intensely, as if trying to pierce him.

"Word gets around. Commissioner, I'm serious be careful. This could get you in trouble. Half the people here are waiting for that."

"Cesarano, I don't care about threats from nobodies. I have the facts on my side."

"I know you're acting in good faith, Commissioner, but I'm telling you as a friend." He leans forward, placing his hands on the desk. "Everyone's trying to bring you down, and you're giving them the excuse to do it. I know, I know there's something, I believe you when you say it. But, for God's sake, you need to be a bit more careful." Cesarano lowers his voice. "Don't do anything rash. If you need to wait a day longer, wait. But why are you risking everything over Solimena? Is it worth burning yourself for someone you don't even know?"

Cardona opens his mouth to respond, then stops and leans back in his chair. His throat fills with anger, but he knows Cesarano cares about him. He knows he's saying this for his sake.

"I can't help but do what I have to, Cesarano. This thing... this job, it's the only way I know how to do it. If this isn't the right way, then I'll walk away, no hard feelings or regrets. I do things my way. It's the only way I know. And I don't like that because I'm not well–liked, people use the one mistake I made as a crowbar to scare me. If it happens, it happens. Good night to everyone."

"Let's try to make sure it doesn't happen, though." Cesarano's face is close, genuinely concerned. "Just a little." He holds his thumb and forefinger a few millimeters apart. "Just a little caution."

Cardona looks at him and smiles, feeling a bit tender toward him.

"Alright, Cesarà. I'll take a little caution. I'll keep it right here. And he touches his chest."

Cesarano nods. He straightens up and steps back.

"I'm going to grab something to eat, Commissioner. I'm starving."

"Enjoy your meal."

Cardona watches him leave the room. He touches his chest, scratches it, sighs, and returns to the papers.

18.

The phone is still unreachable.

I put the phone down, a bit annoyed. I've been trying for a while with no success. Ligresti is still out of reach. But there's something strange, I mean, Marzio never had a secretary; he always did things himself. He used to tell me how much he hated making photocopies and how the research department needed a secretary to manage the paperwork that came out of those offices, but one never arrived. He said he asked for one, even though Cardia didn't care much about it. Anyway, this Schiavone is certainly not Marzio's secretary, and if she's not his, then she must be his brother's. So, is it Umberto who's connected with Ligresti? I wonder, then, if Ligresti is good or bad.

The Lunar Finance website is still up on the screen, frozen on the Contact page. The design is simple, pleasant elegant, even, if it weren't so anonymous. I can't tell if they tried to make something nice but failed, or if they deliberately aimed for this bland look.

Everything is smooth, polished. There's just one odd spot a small imperfection in the lower left corner of the page. I hover over it with the mouse. The icon doesn't change, and the arrow cursor stays. I move closer to the screen. It's square, like a stylized key. Maybe it's the signature of the site's creator, someone who wanted to leave a little mark of themselves for posterity. No link. I place the tip of the cursor over it. My cheek rests in my hand. I click.

The screen turns white. A pop–up appears. It's gray, with basic graphics. Two white fields with a blinking cursor. To the left of the fields are the words 'UserID' and 'Password.'

I lift my head from my hand. This is new. I stretch out my hands, grab the note, and look at the numbers.

The karma is good today, I feel it.

In the UserID field, I type lili, and in the password field, I enter the numbers from the note. Proud of my discovery, I press enter. The window turns white, then clicks back to the way it was before. The fields are blank again. At the bottom, in maroon letters, it says, Incorrect credentials.

Karma is good today, I believe it. I type 555444555444 in the UserID field and repeat the numbers in the password field. I carefully read them from the note and compare them to what I've typed. I press enter again.

The window blinks.

The fields are blank again. The maroon message remains at the bottom.

It's better to stop here.

Unpleasant things could happen. The feeling presses against the back of my neck.

But there must be a key. This path Marzio has laid out for me has to make sense. I twist my torso and stretch. I look at the wardrobe, the doors are still open. His clothes are hanging on the hangers. Without realizing it, I'm standing, my hands inside, feeling the fabric. I slip my fingers into every pocket, searching for something, a second clue, a signal for me. Coins, a business card, it's his, Marzio Solimena, with no title beneath. His phone numbers are written on it. I recognize the first, it's his cell phone. He only had one, for both work and personal life. One day, he would have had to get two. He was always being called, even late, even on weekends. What patience you had, Marzio.

I reach into a jacket pocket and feel a piece of paper, an envelope. I hear the rustling of transparent plastic that covers the window through which the recipient's name and address are visible. I pull it from the inside pocket.

It's a letter from the bank, opened on one side. I pull out the letter and open it. It's the statement for his credit card. The month is July. He spent €679.55 various items, books from Feltrinelli, a two–piece swimsuit for me. I remember that. Dinner on the Amalfi Coast on July 15th. Massa Lubrense. You were so sweet. A surprise, just like that. We picked up and went, blindly, up the coast, all the way to the end, and watched the sunset together on the terrace, sitting, eating everything, letting time slip by so fast, why does it happen?

Mr. Marzio Solimena.
Via Carducci, 10.

That's the address on the letter.
It's Marzio's residence. He lived there, on Via Carducci.
I sit on the bed, holding the paper between my thumb and forefinger.
He never brought me there. He never talked about it. He always spoke of home, of family. Via Posillipo.
Never mentioned Via Carducci.
I place the statement on the computer keyboard.
When I think about it, how many things don't I know about you?
I feel him take my hands, then my shoulders, my neck. This sense of confinement squeezes the breath from me. The walls seem to stretch for kilometers as they press down on my arms. I try to shake them off, to open my lungs to the relief I seek in vain. Was I just on the sidelines of your life?
The answer blazes in my mind. It flashes like acidic white light, pulsing inside me, pressing against my temples. I feel each heartbeat in my ears, my veins are too small for all this blood. It's a huge yes. A transparent, three–

dimensional laminate laid on the floor of an infinite room. Empty. It glows until it heats my face, burning it. I'm alone in this room. It feels like I'm falling into the chair, into a black hole that sucks away every trace of my soul, leaving me naked, cold. My hands grip my arms, shivering from the cold, like snakes slowly squeezing me. How small and insignificant I am now. So small I could disappear. This is a cage, this world around me, this story etched into my skin, the chapters sinking in, poisoning me, roots growing deep, the tight weave that blinds me from even seeing into my own eyes.

I'm hungry. And the nausea hits me the moment the thought occurs.

I stand up, my gaze fixed on the floor. I don't want to see him. Maybe if I don't look long enough, he'll disappear. He'll leave. He'll free me.

I lift my eyes and see him.

He's there, in the room with me.

We're alone, like we were so many times. We were happy in here. I remember. It rushes up with force, bursting forth. They're my tears. I promised I wouldn't cry anymore.

I don't know if I was marginal to you, Marzio. I don't know if I believe this thing I'm telling myself. I don't know if I just want to hurt myself. I only know that when I was in your arms, I was happy.

Yes.

In the end, the fact that you're here, even if it's terrible, it makes me feel less alone. At least I remember your face. I cry, I cry hard. All this pain will be worth it, Marzio. I know it. And maybe not. But either way, for the love you gave me, for the love I feel, it won't end here. It won't end until I reach where you want to take me.

"I'm hungry."

My hand rests against the doorframe.

I head to the kitchen.

One last glance at him, looking toward the window.

19.

"And this is interesting!"

Cardona raises the paper and waves it in front of an imaginary audience. Only the sound of the paper fluttering against the air can be heard.

He brings it back under his eyes, resting his legs on the desk, the chair creaking as he crosses his right leg over the left.

It's a public document, notarized by Molella, the notary who appears in most of the Solimena family and Prosud records. Present are Michele Solimena and Cardia.

He rests the papers on his thighs and reaches for a pen on the desk.

Solimena is granting Cardia a right. The commissioner skips over the formalities of identifying the attendees and opens his notebook.

Golden Share, he writes. Then notes the date of the document, six years ago.

Lower down, it explains what this right entails:

The holder of the right obtains a seat as an observer on the board of directors, has veto power over majority decisions of the Prosud board of directors, has veto power over the approval of Prosud's expenditure budgets, has the right to remove the CEO of Prosud if they fail to convene the holder of the right, and has the right to a private meeting with the company's auditors.

That's enough. There's the signature of Michele Solimena and that of Augusto Cardia.

The commissioner grimaces.

"All this power to Cardia, why?"

No one answers him. He writes down the rights in his notebook. The commissioner thinks about Michele Solimena, he must have trusted Cardia greatly to give him all this power. He practically tied his own hands unless there was unanimous agreement on the board.

He rewrites the last few words in his notebook.

Straightening up, he grabs Cardia's personal file from the many crowding his desk. He opens it and flips through it eagerly. He skips the first part and focuses on the second and last section. As he approaches the final pages, he slows down, reading the titles of the documents and records, turning them over and setting them aside, they don't interest him. He's looking for one, just one.

Only one.

His eyes light up. He chuckles to himself.

"There you are."

It's the will of Augusto Cardia.

It's short, handwritten, just one page on a lined sheet. There are the customary formalities at the beginning, the ritual formula, and then the serious stuff brief and to the point. He runs his finger down the lines, houses, money, and then a simple phrase:

I leave the right known as the Golden Share, transferred to me by public deed from Michele Solimena, to his son Marzio Solimena.

The commissioner runs his hand through his hair.

"This is a good one."

He tears the page from the stapled file it belongs to, folds it into four parts, and tucks it into his notebook. He shakes his head, smiling. He can feel himself smiling. He grabs the stack of meeting minutes. It's on the desk, on the right–hand side. Neatly organized now, in chronological order from oldest to newest. It's easy to check.

He pulls out the last stapled file.

Meeting minutes of the board of directors, dated April 17th, with Umberto Solimena, Marzio Solimena, and Augusto Cardia present.

This is the last meeting.

There haven't been any since then.

Typically, they occur every three or four months. In any case, there's always a meeting in June to close the fiscal year and approve the spending budgets. But not in the last year, nothing since April.

The commissioner bites his lip. He feels the heat rising to his temples, his hands trembling, his fingers drumming on the desk. He flips through Marzio Solimena's file, searching for his will. He goes through the papers but finds nothing. He tries again, more carefully, reading the headers, starting from the beginning and working his way to the last page. Nothing. No will.

Cardona brings a cigarette to his lips, it's one of the most satisfying cigarettes he's ever smoked. The tobacco feels heavy between his fingers, turning into a puff of colored air, spreading through the room, filling his lungs with pride. A flood of insults begins to form in his mind, directed at the faces of people materializing in his thoughts. The words land on their faces, disfiguring them. They bring their hands to their faces and flee, but there's no escape. Each word is a boulder, crushing them, one by one. Only the smoke remains.

The cigarette is already finished. He lights another and grabs the papers he took from Marzio's office.

The first documents are technical standards, written in English, dealing with chemistry, followed by scientific articles, photocopies from textbooks, and treatises on viscosity and non–Newtonian fluids, difficult to understand. Then there's a red folder. He opens it. Inside are pencil–written notes, flow diagrams, with weights, volumes, and times scribbled. There are several corrections; the numbers change once, twice, more. The central pages are the most confusing. Some are crossed out with a large, heavily marked X; others have the word surpassed written diagonally between two parallel lines. Then everything begins to fall into place, the numbers stop fluctuating, the diagram takes on an orderly tree structure, and arrows are added, indicating additives or raw materials being poured into containers. Each container lists the pressure, temperature, and sometimes heat.

The last two pages are immaculate, with no corrections. The first is a calculation sheet with a list of substances and reference data. The rows are color–coded, and the substances are named in English. The other page is a flow diagram drawn with a ruler and a template, with UF–10 written in large block letters at the top, and below it, in smaller letters, process flow diagram. At the bottom left is what appears to be Marzio's signature, and on the right, there's a dedication:

'From the seed of talent, ideas are born; from the persistence of work, structure emerges; from the purity of simplicity, its fruits are harvested.
Guard your talent, cultivate persistence, and remain pure forever.'

The signature belongs to Augusto Cardia.

This is the story of UF–10, the last product of Cardia's research, though it seems the idea came from Marzio Solimena. But that's irrelevant for now. He closes the folder.

The rest of the papers are a partially filled, slightly wrinkled notepad with sketches, scribbles, phone numbers, and brief drafts of technical reports, nothing truly interesting. He sets the notepad on top of the red folder. Beneath it is a business card holder made of transparent plastic, the size of an A4 sheet. Each page holds six cards in their respective slots, arranged alphabetically by company name. The commissioner flips through it distractedly, tapping his finger on a few names, but they're all unfamiliar.

His phone vibrates. He reaches into his trouser pocket, pulls it out, and brings it to his ear.

"Hello."

"Commissioner, how are you?"

"Who's this?"

"I'm calling from Il Mattino di Napoli. It's Olivieri. How are you?"

"Oh, great. What a pleasure." The commissioner replies, clearly annoyed.

"Commissioner, you're investigating the incident at Prosud, right? Do you have any updates to share?"

"No comment."

"Are you confirming the suicide theory? Any findings from the scene investigation?"

"Olivieri, I'm not telling you anything."

"Well, when you put it like that, it means you don't want to tell me anything".

"Yes, exactly."

"So, there's something you could tell me, you just don't want to." The journalist presses.

"Olivieri, you're annoying me." But Cardona is smiling.

"Come on, Commissioner, an anonymous statement, something, give me a direction."

"No, Olivieri, it's not happening."

"Are there any suspects?"

"There are no suspects." The temptation is too strong. "Not yet." Too strong.

"Commissioner, you're getting me excited!" Olivieri exclaims enthusiastically. "So, the police are considering the possibility of arson? Motive? Any ideas?"

"Olivieri, those are your own speculations. Your fantasies. If you write that nonsense, I'll come down to your office and give you a hard time." Cardona raises his voice. There's no criminal suspicion. You can write that.

"Of course, Commissioner. For now, right?"

"There's no criminal suspicion."

"Thanks, Commissioner."

The call ends before the commissioner can press the red button. He sets the phone on the desk.

Too tempting to resist.

He's not sure if he did the right thing by giving in. A shiver of anxiety runs through him. He thinks of Prisco. Then of some time ago. He rubs his forehead and stands up from his desk, pulling out a cigarette and lighting it. He walks toward the open window overlooking the street.

There's still traffic, but it's easing. He hears the noise coming from farther away. He leans out, resting on the windowsill, smoking his cigarette, trying to let go of the tension. In front of him is the narrow street where he parked his car. He cranes his neck to the left and sees the remnants of cars and honking horns clogging the exhausted road. The faces of the people walking by are focused, many are heading home. He checks his watch, it's past six–thirty. The time to leave has long since passed. He runs his tongue along his palate and then his cheeks. They're dry and warm, the smoke seeming to harden them into a tar–like coating. He hasn't eaten anything. Maybe it's time to go.

Time to grab something to eat. It's Friday night. The weekend is here. Rest is what people expect, tonight, the kids go out, drink, have fun. They forget everything until Monday.

That's one option. So the commissioner repeats to himself, it's one option, doing everything by the book, by procedure, by what they say. But if the papers, if your instincts lead you further, if there's a primordial call, if there's a force pulling you toward the answers, if they're here, just millimeters away from your nose, your ears, your fingers. If that force grabs you by the waist and pulls you away, all you can do is go along with it. And if you tell something like that to a journalist, it's because that journalist needed to hear it. And to hell with the rest, the thoughts, the calls, the provocations, and everything else.

He tosses the cigarette butt, returns inside, stops by his desk, grabs his notebook, his cigarettes, and the folder he hasn't yet read with the attention it deserves. He tucks it under his arm and heads out of the office.

"Let's get something to eat, then we'll see."

20.

The sun is setting.

I'm lying on the bed, listening to the sounds of the house. I'm tired. I haven't done anything since lunch. The dishes are still dirty on the table. My head rests on the pillow. I take deep breaths at regular intervals. The window is closed, through which the muffled sounds of the city below filter in. The high walls are draped in slowly creeping shadows. There's no direct light, only the cold beam of a distant streetlamp pointing somewhere else, but not here. Not where we are.

I'm waiting. Waiting for the night to come. For the day to pass. I glance at the time on the alarm clock sitting on the nightstand. It's pink, with a liquid crystal display and solar sensors on top. A little cat sits on top, white and round, with its right paw raised as if waving to me. If there were enough light or sun, it would rock back and forth, cheerfully greeting me, its smile painted on the plastic, its eyes large and black. He gave it to me, as a gift, after a trip to Japan. 'It's beautiful', I said. 'It's so sweet. Thank you.' I hugged him and held him close. We stayed on the bed, talking for hours.

A wave of warmth washes over my chest, and once again, I find myself in love with you. That sweet feeling again, the tenderness of your skin when I touched it. The thought, the sense of belonging that kept us silently together during the night. Eyes closed and hands clasped under the same blankets. Sharing breaths without even thinking about it anymore.

The twilight is colorless tonight. I realize there's no more light in the room. My eyes have drifted deep into memories, and now I'm back here.

It hits me like a flash.

It's his face that appears before my eyes and then disappears. The memory of last night. His cruel hands on me. His malicious intent to invade me, possess me, infest me.

My chest feels heavy, and I don't want to sleep here tonight. I don't want to sleep at all tonight. I can't stand the thought of being alone here in this bed tonight. To be a helpless prey. He wants me, trying to sneak in and conquer me. Marzio is his Trojan horse. I don't know what his goal is, if it's simply evil creeping in, if it's a restless spirit, or if it's a demon that latched onto Marzio's soul and, after consuming it, still wants more. And Marzio. You. What pact did you make with this demon? How much did it cost you to return here?

This process must be completed. The ritual must be fulfilled. We must be diligent. That's what she told me over the phone. I want to understand who she is, what ties she has to you. Why you were with her, with Cardia. At her house. Her hand on yours.

How many things did you hide from me? How many things are you revealing to me now? I want to believe that you had a plan and that it all went wrong. That you really wanted to live your life with me. And that you're here to help me understand that it's true.

Don't leave me now, Marzio. I depend on you at this moment. I chose to be yours even after you were gone. I could have tried to forget you. To be myself, alone, in the world, and find my own path. But we're together. Even now. I'm trusting you just as you chose to trust me.

It's truly dark now. The glow from the streetlights filters into the room. The orange tint casts a halo on the ceiling.

I can't stay here. No, I really can't. Forgive me, but I can't. I rub my hands on my legs; I'm still wearing jeans. I get up. I'll go out to eat, go be somewhere else for a while. I grab the scooter keys from the desk and head for the front door. Everything feels so fast. I'm in a rush, anxious. I grab the waterproof jacket from the back of the chair, put it on, zip it up to my neck, then grab my helmet, open the door, and slip my hands into the jacket pockets to find my house keys. They're not there. Where did I put them? I exhale a sigh of frustration. I just want to leave. I retrace my steps, back into the bedroom. The keys aren't on the desk. I move the laptop, still no keys. I check the bed, thinking they might have fallen out of my pocket while I slept, but they're not there. I head to the kitchen, walking faster and faster. I'm overwhelmed by the feeling that if I don't leave now, something bad will happen. I look on the kitchen counters, the shelves, the stovetop, the table with the dishes. No keys. I could leave the door ajar and just go. I just need to get out now. I'm back in the bedroom. I scan it carefully. There's the bed. The slippers on the floor at its foot. I should look under the bed. There could be anything under there. I can't form the thought. I collapse under the weight of my own body. I put my hand on the floor. Close my eyes. And lower my head.

Please let them be here.

Alone.

I exhale.

The floor is covered in a layer of dust.

There are some crumpled pieces of paper.

A pen.

I see the feet of the nightstand to the right.

The keys are right next to it.

I pick them up.

There, done. I have them, and I'm leaving.

I walk quickly to the door.

The white stairs are lit by a neon light at the bottom of the rectangular landing. The other two doors facing the landing are closed. I step out and pull the door shut. I keep my head down, not looking inside, I don't want to. I just want to get out. As the door closes, I catch a glimpse inside.

The demon is there. His left hand is raised, and his malicious grin is fixed on his face. He's waving with those thin fingers. His head is tilted, and his wide eyes watch me.

I yank the door shut with force and gasp loudly. The sound of the door closing blends with my gasp, creating a noise that echoes like thunder up the stairs.

It's as if I can hear his footsteps approaching the door.

"Are you leaving?" The voice from the door sounds like it's right in my ears, hammering against my eardrums. "Don't you want to play with me? I want to play with you." He continues in his shrill voice. "It's nice here. It's warm. Comfortable. We don't want to leave. We want to stay here with you."

I run away from the door. I run away from my house. The stairs are steep, and my legs feel like melted wax. I slam into the aluminum door that leads to the street. I open it and step outside to breathe. Four floors in, I don't know how long, but not long. Not long at all. That demon is stealing my life. He's tearing it from my hands. I feel the urge to cry. I lean against a linden tree growing out of a small square of dirt between asphalt and basalt. Its trunk is soft and flexible, welcoming my despair. I give myself ten seconds. I count them slowly. I force my heart to slow down, my breathing to become steady. My scooter is there. I even forgot to lock it to the pole with the chain. I insert the key and start it. I put on my helmet and mount the scooter. I start driving, feeling the wind on my face. It's better now. The traffic is gone. There are only a few cars left. This Friday night hasn't started yet. I find myself floating in the limbo of rest, just entering the dinner hours. If I look up, I see the windows glowing like incandescent lightbulbs, decorating the concrete facades. They're like fireflies in the night. So many homes, so many tables. So many families. I don't know where I'm going, but I'm going, not here. I don't want to stay here. The asphalt is wet, and it won't dry overnight. I feel the moisture in the air slapping my face, cold. It feels good, distracting me, almost invigorating me. I think. Little by little, my mind clears of all the useless thoughts. There's an automatic feeling that takes me away from myself and onto the road, a liberating sensation. The road rolls beneath the wheels on its own. Light.

I'm already downtown. A sandwich, a slice of pizza, anything will do. I stop in front of a diner. From the illuminated counter, trays of pizza with colorful, imaginative toppings emerge, thick and enticing. I take off my helmet and hang it on the hook under the handlebars. I step off and prop the scooter on its stand. I grab a slice of margherita, two euros, and a bottle of water. The napkin is greasy with oil. I take it and head to a nearby bench. I bite into it. It's warm and soft. Good. How will I spend the evening? I could call someone, hang out, spend some time at a bar, something like that. I could. There aren't many cars around, and they're driving fast. The sound of tires on the cobblestones is louder than the engines hidden under the hoods. I hear them coming from far away, before the curve that leads down here. Across the street is a low wall, beyond which you can see the sea and the gulf. I feel like looking at it. Ten steps, and I'm there. I cross the street without looking. I sit on the black, rounded stone that forms the edge of the wall. I cross my legs and take another bite of pizza. Below me is a drop of about fifty meters, I think. Then there are some apartment buildings further down as the hill slopes away. Beyond that, the slope becomes gentler, and at the bottom is the sea, with the lights along the shore encircling it like a crown of pearls. I watch it, and I see the peace of the sea. I feel calm. I breathe slowly. I imagine the sound of the waves crashing on the shore, breaking against the rocks. I follow the rhythm, and my eyes almost close, and I smile.

The clouds above me have a reddish tint from the city lights. I don't know if it will rain again.

The pizza is finished. I wipe my mouth with the greasy napkin I was holding, crumple it up, and toss it into the void. It falls in an arc, disappearing into the darkness. I follow it with my eyes as long as I can, then just sit there. Your name comes to mind. Never has a name been less appropriate for a person. You're probably with me now, too. If I turned around, I'd find you behind me. Maybe you're right in the center of my gaze now, in the heart of Piazza Vittoria. Down there. A microscopic dot in my eyes. Piazza Vittoria. The Riviera di Chiaia. Wherever I look in the city, you're there. You're there. And I know it. Piazza San Pasquale. Via Carducci.

Via Carducci.

I open the bottle and take a sip. My eyes are fixed on the street where you live. Number 10. I feel the urge to see your building. Your home. I want to understand where it is, what it looks like, what color it is. I want to do it. I want to understand why you never took me there.

I hop on the scooter, fasten my helmet, and start. The road slopes downhill, full of curves. It's paved now, making it easier to drive. I think maybe I shouldn't rush. Time always passes at the same speed, and the night will have to go by entirely. But the scooter descends, taking the curves, leaning into each turn. Thinking too much leads to the same end as thinking too little. That was one of your sayings. It came back to me silently, but I remember your lips saying it. I've reached Piazza Amedeo. Almost there. I round the circle and turn left onto Via Vittoria Colonna. I go straight, passing Via San Pasquale. There's a bus lane, but I don't care. I take it and turn right. This is Via Carducci. I slow down and look at the house numbers. On the right, I see

126

45, then 43, all odd numbers. The number I'm looking for is even. I look to the left, 24. I keep going, pass the Umberto high school. Sixteen. There it is, I see it. Number 10. I squeeze between two cars parked in a herringbone pattern, leaving just enough space for my scooter. I climb onto the sidewalk and turn off the engine. I take off my helmet and place it under the seat. I approach the door. There's a wide, well–lit entrance hall, empty. At the back are the stairs and the elevator. To the right is the intercom panel. I scan the names, looking for Marzio's. They're divided into two columns, one on each side of the keypad. There's no Solimena in either column. But on the right, there's a listing with just the initials S.M., and the number 510. I try the intercom. I push the button. No one answers.

The door opens behind me. I jump but try to hide my surprise as I turn around. A guy with a helmet in hand is rushing out.

"Should I leave it open?"

"Yes." I nod, embarrassed.

He doesn't even notice and is already off to his night out. I hold the door open with my hand. I step inside. To my left are the mailboxes, there are ten of them. I search for the one labeled 'S.M.' It's the last one. There are letters inside. I pull them out. Ads, bank letters, more ads. I hold onto them and head for the elevator. It's already on the ground floor. I step in and press the button for the fifth floor, the last one. The elevator moves swiftly, reaching normal speed quickly. The ride is short, the elevator slows, and a bell announces the stop at the floor. The sliding doors open, and I step onto the landing. To my right is apartment number nine. The number is written above the door frame. I turn left and find number ten. No nameplate. Nothing. I stop in front of the oak–paneled door.

"Here I am, Marzio." I say, addressing him.

21.

The beer mug is empty, with just a bit of foam clinging to the inside of the glass. The waiter has just cleared away the pizza plate. The restaurant is slowly starting to fill up. Cardona takes out his notebook and flips through it, retracing the key points in reverse order. The will, the Golden Share, the car, the movements.

He circles the movements from the last two days before the death twice, those in the early morning and late evening of the day before the death, and the trip to Sorrento on the morning of September 6th.

He knows that what happened during those times is the key. It's all that matters in this investigation.

"Anything else, sir?"

"No, thank you." He replies without looking up from his notes.

"A dessert, an amaro, a limoncello?"

"Nothing, thank you."

"Coffee?"

"Just bring me the bill." He says, looking up and glaring at the waiter.

"As you wish."

The waiter walks away, and Cardona returns to his notes. There's still a lot of material to go through. The plan is this: two days to pull together a detailed report on the situation, highlighting all the questions and underlining the inconsistencies. There's a structure of events forming in his mind. He just needs to fill it with facts, the substance to support the framework. Only a few more pieces are missing.

He has an idea. Since the night has to pass somehow, and he's already eaten, the thought of reopening the files doesn't appeal to him at all. This thing has been on his mind since the early stages of the investigation, and now he knows where to go. He puts his hand in his pocket and pulls out the three sets of keys he recovered. He sets aside the first one, the one used to open his office. The other two remain.

"Excuse me, I need the bill. I'm leaving." He says annoyed as the waiter passes by again.

"I'll bring it right away." The waiter responds without stopping.

Cardona collects his notebook and tucks it into his pocket. Then he takes a twenty–euro note from his wallet. The waiter places a metal plate with a non–fiscal receipt for eighteen euros on the table and starts to walk away. The commissioner stops him with an arm and hands him the note.

"Bring me the change and the receipt." He says, pulling a cigarette from the inside pocket of his coat. "Hurry, I'm leaving."

The waiter walks away without speaking, and Cardona heads toward the exit. The place is small, with three rows of square tables filling the room. Many are still empty. The commissioner pushes the door open with his shoulder and lights his cigarette while still on the threshold. A light, cold wind blows outside. His car is parked just a little further on. Via Carducci is only a few minutes' walk away. On a Friday night, there's no chance of finding parking closer than this, and he has no intention of leaving the car in a garage.

"Here you go, sir." The waiter says, handing him a two–euro coin placed on top of the receipt.

The commissioner pockets the change and heads toward his destination.

The street is pedestrian–only and not very crowded. He walks quickly, hands in his pockets and head down. The basalt slabs pass quickly beneath his feet. He wonders why. Why would Umberto Solimena lie? He tries to find a justification, a reason for which this statement could be in good faith. He imagines a taxi. Yes. Or a bicycle, a motorcycle. There could be anything, a second car.

He grinds his teeth and clenches his jaw. An eventuality he hadn't considered. He's falling in love with his hypothesis again, just like before, and he still hasn't shaken this flaw. He scratches his chin and grimaces. Maybe he really did go to see him that night. He pulls out his notebook and checks the page dedicated to Umberto Solimena. He lives in Posillipo, on Via Pacuvio, far from here, not an easy trip to make by bicycle. Maybe it was a scooter. He takes a pen from the notebook pocket and writes, 'check motor vehicle registry.' He could have taken a taxi, so he adds 'taxi cooperatives.' It's already Friday night, and the offices are closed tomorrow, but maybe he can find something online for the cars, and the taxi drivers work every day, he'll call tomorrow anyway. It's not even certain they keep records of the calls, assuming he called one. He could have just flagged one down on the street. Maybe he was walking here, on Via Chiaia, thinking of his nephews, suddenly deciding to go see them as he pondered his life, his fate, walking over these dark basalt slabs, under these trees. The commissioner lifts his head. On either side of the street, young trees cover the view of the buildings with their foliage. Around him, there are few people, and the light weakly penetrates through the forty meters of trees that lead down to a small paved square. To the left, there's a neat row of white taxis.

There. He comes here, takes the first taxi, gets in, and says, 'Via Pacuvio' to the driver. No second thoughts.

It's possible.

Cardona lets his gaze drift away from the taxi stand and pays attention to the sparse traffic continuing toward Via Filangieri. He puts the notebook and pen back in his pocket, turns right, and enters a narrow alley. The basalt is wet and shiny.

He could have really gone there. He can't find a reason to deny it. There's nothing, the elements he has can't refute it, and it remains just a contestable reconstruction.

He feels the tension in his neck. In his pocket, he grips the two sets of keys he still hasn't used and from which he expects some answers. He rubs his fingertips against them, wishing they'd turn to gold.

His soles thud against the uneven pavement in a steady rhythm, each step marking his thoughts at a precise, constant pace. One after another, he unravels his frustration until he admits that this shouldn't be a problem. He shouldn't worry about justifying what he thinks but rather focus on building his certainty. Just like he's doing now, walking down this street. A few days ago, it was all little more than a feeling, newspaper articles, the colors of that plant, the face of that boy, the silence of the office while he thought it over. And now that what he instinctively guessed has been confirmed, he just has to clear the dust from the picture, reveal the details, one by one. The pieces that will complete the puzzle. There are some clear areas and others that are still dark. Walking, he'll find the pieces. They'll appear right under his nose, just like everything else so far. He just has to keep walking down this path. He feels it in his gut. He repeats these words to himself, and the sense of unease fades. He's here on this street for more answers, he's not walking in circles but toward a destination he knows. It might take months, or it might take hours. But he knows where he's going. He's reaching his destination, and with him, he carries the experiences, the information, the words of those orbiting this story, planets or comets, polar stars or just dust and debris. Right now, he feels like a great magnet, and it makes him feel good.

He's on Via Carducci. On the left is the large building of Liceo Umberto. He turns left until he sees the building's number and continues down, following the sequence.

He feels lighter.

It's going to be an interesting evening. He can feel it.

He look up, the marble plaque of the building to his right.

Number ten.

He stops. He opens his notebook and checks the address. Then he closes it.

He approaches the intercom and looks for his name. He doesn't find it. There are many surnames stacked one above the other, the sequence flowing uniformly from the first column on the left to the second, where there's a break in the pattern. Two letters, an 'S' and an 'M', printed in black on a strip of white paper that's yellowing with age. The intercom number is 510.

He pulls the keys from his pocket and moves closer to the door. Two of them are the right size to fit the aluminum door lock. He inserts the first one and turns it; the door opens, and he steps inside. On the right is the doorman's booth, and to the left are the mailboxes. He walks over to peek inside the box labeled with the two letters. It's empty. He stares at it for a moment, then heads toward the elevator and presses the button.

The display shows that the elevator was parked on the fifth floor. The number disappears and reappears each time the elevator passes through the other four floors. It's a fleeting flash. The light in the hall is cold, coming from a neon lamp placed in the center of the lobby, covered by a round glass lampshade. Simple, cheap, not very appealing in design. The doorman's booth is made of brown anodized aluminum profiles. It's less than a meter wide and two meters deep. From here, he can see the thin desk and the sliding window that opens onto the lobby. It's dark, and not much can be seen inside, just a small TV with two crooked antennas, the outline of a dark chair back, and various papers and documents in disarray.

The doors open behind him, casting his long shadow on the floor, betraying the white light that pressed it to the ground under his feet.

The commissioner steps back into the elevator. He continues to look at the lobby, as if trying to memorize it. Then he glances to his right at the control panel and presses the button for the fifth floor.

The doors close, and the elevator begins its ascent. Inside the cabin, there's a sweet smell. The walls are made of smooth aluminum sheets, with scratches about a meter from the ground running around the perimeter. The floor is worn black linoleum, scuffed by countless feet. The light is warm, coming from two lamps placed in a recess in the white ceiling. On one wall, there's a message written in black marker. The writing is stylized, hard to read. It starts with an 'A', but Cardona can't make out the other letters. He reaches into his pocket, pulls out a cigarette, and puts it in his mouth.

The elevator arrives at the floor and stops with a jolt. The doors open, and once again, the warm light of the elevator clashes unpleasantly with the cold lighting of the building.

The commissioner steps out of the cabin. He brings the lighter to the tip of his cigarette and flicks the wheel. The spark catches, and a small flame lights the tobacco. That's when he notices a shadow to his left. He takes a drag and turns.

On the stairs leading up, a girl is sitting. Her hair is tied in a ponytail. She looks tired, with deep circles under her eyes. She stares at him silently, her legs pulled up, her arms wrapped around her knees, hugging them to her chest. Her thin shoulders are covered by a green raincoat.

The commissioner glances at the apartment number above the door she's sitting next to. It's 510. He takes another drag and takes a step toward her. She pulls back slightly, her back pressing against the wall.

The commissioner removes the cigarette from his mouth and looks at her. "And you."

He stops, locking eyes with her.

"Who are you?"

22.

The phone vibrates on the table. He flips through a page of the newspaper, skimming over the local news section. No crime stories today. He picks up the phone. The number isn't saved in his contacts, but he knows it.

"Hello."

"I'm doing what you told me."

"So why are you calling me?"

He's moving on foot, spent the whole day in the office, then went out. He had dinner at a restaurant and then continued on foot. He entered a building, but it's not the home address you gave me."

"Hmm." He pulls a pen from his pocket. "What's the address?"

"Via Carducci, number 10."

He writes down the first three letters of the street, then stops.

"And then?" He says aggressively.

"Nothing, I'm still here. I'll keep following him until further notice, but this seemed strange to me. I thought I should tell you."

"Alright."

He ends the call. With a snap, he clicks the pen shut and puts it back in his pocket. With his arms crossed and elbows resting on his wooden desk, he leans forward, reading the headlines. The office is dark, with only the light from the lamp illuminating the desk. There's nothing in the paper that interests him.

He knows that street well. He knows that building well. He knows everything about it. Perhaps he should have done more, should have made sure it wasn't dangerous, that it wasn't reachable.

He exhales forcefully through his nose.

He thinks there's already been one mistake on this job, and now it's dangerous. One more misstep, and it's over. He's taking a risk, he knows that. He feels it in his breath, something could go wrong. His lips press into a grimace of anger. He flips the page. It's the entertainment section.

Everything that needed to be taken has been taken. Nothing was left behind. Everything that was collected. Maybe something was left at the house. Maybe, but he never went there. Never, really.

And the fact that the guy is going there now means nothing. He's just a workaholic. It's Friday night, he doesn't have a social life, doesn't have a family, and wastes time thinking about work because if he thinks about himself, he'll just get depressed.

That's how it is. But people like that are dangerous because they think, they think about one thing all the time. He's exactly like that. Precisely like that.

He calms down. For a brief moment. He imagines him standing in front of the door. Sad. A useless portion of a man. Defeated by life. Standing still in front of that piece of wood.

That piece of wood.

How did he open that piece of wood?

He picks up the phone again and dials the number he called earlier.

It rings.

"Hello?"

"How did he get into the building?"

"What do you mean?"

"Did he ring the doorbell? Did he have keys, what?"

There's a brief pause.

"Uh, I didn't see clearly. I saw him approach the intercom, then go inside, but I think he had keys."

He sets the phone on the table. The conversation is over.

"Idiot." He mutters to himself.

He clenches his fists on the table, then slams them down hard on the wood. He grabs the newspaper, crumples it, and throws it away.

How did he get the keys? What did he have access to? What else could he have had with him?

"Idiot!" He shouts, his voice scraping his throat.

23.

I've been watching him for a while. He asked me who I am. He's wearing a long, worn black coat. His expression is tired, his eyes small but deep. They scrutinize me carefully. I don't really know if I should respond or leave. Coming here suddenly no longer feels like a smart idea. This person who just got off the elevator and came here for a reason, who is he? But more importantly, why is he here now? On a Friday night. So late.

I'm scared of the situation. I feel the urge to leave. As my muscles respond to the impulse to move, I realize he's gotten closer and placed his hand on the railing of the stairs. He leans slightly toward me, still watching. I press myself against the wall, unable to meet his gaze. I stretch out my legs, press my knees, and stand.

"Wait, wait. Where are you going?"

With one arm, he stops me from leaving.

"I'm leaving." I say, keeping my head down.

"Wait. You're right. Let's say I was rude. Let me introduce myself, okay?"

His voice is gentler now but still carries a firm tone. With his hand, he gestures for me to sit back down on the stairs without touching me. I sit again, I have no choice, curling up against the wall. I wish I could have your embrace right now.

"So, my name is Cardona. I'm with the police." He pulls out a badge with his photo and shows it to me. "See?"

I nod, glancing at the photo. It's him. It looks real, worn. He's with the police.

"Now, do you want to tell me who you are?"

"First, tell me something else." I search his eyes. "Why are you here?"

He looks at me. I think he's smiling. He straightens up.

"I'm here because someone used to live here. And since I need to figure some things out, I came to check it out."

"You're investigating Marzio?"

"Yes." He nods, deeply and slowly.

My heart races. His face seems to soften. I turn toward Marzio, who stands behind me, in the corner of the landing where the stairs end. He's looking down at the door.

"I'm his girlfriend. We were together."

"I see." He nods. "And why are you here now?" His tone is gentle.

"I don't know. I knew I didn't want to be home tonight. I didn't want to be alone, and I ended up here. I didn't know he lived here." I say, lowering my gaze slowly to the white marble of the stairs.

"You were never at his place?" He asks incredulously.

I shake my head.

"He never brought me here. He never even mentioned it. I found out today, by chance, that he lived here. I wanted to come, to see it. Then something would happen."

"And here we are."

"Yes, and then you came out of the elevator."

"So, let's say you're interested in knowing what the house is like, what's inside. And all the rest, right?"

"Yes."

"Why?"

"Because…" I hesitate, unsure if I should say it. But I need to. "Because I need to understand why things turned out this way. I need to understand Marzio and the message he left."

"He left you a message?" He asks, curious.

"Yes, I mean, no. "I lower my head, avoiding his gaze. "It's complicated, really."

"Explain it to me."

"It's long."

"I'm in no rush." He pauses, takes a drag from his cigarette. "Mind if I sit next to you? Does the smoke bother you?"

I shake my head. He sits down on the same step. His shoulders are broad, and his coat is bulky. The stairs are wide enough for both of us, but we're close. Our shoulders are only separated by about ten centimeters, and I press myself against the wall.

"So, tell me. I'm listening."

I stay silent. She told me not to trust anyone. She said everyone is dangerous.

"It's strange. It's a strange thing. Hard to explain." I pause, realizing I don't even know where to start.

"How long were you two together?"

"A year and five months."

"That's a while, huh? So, a serious thing."

"Serious… yes, serious. It was beautiful, it was something very beautiful."

"What was he like?" The question makes me remember him smiling. I turn and see him standing in the corner. "What are you thinking about?" he asks again.

"I'm remembering him. Sometimes I imagine seeing him. He was very sweet. He loved me. It's hard to let go of him. I feel like the bond is too strong. Too much." My eyes fill with tears, and I lower my gaze again.

"I'm sorry."

"Yes, sorry for me, for you, for everyone."

"How did he seem to you? I mean, in the last days? Did he seem like he wanted to hurt himself?"

I can't believe what I'm hearing. No. These words are like sharp knives in my eyes. What does this man want? What is he saying? And yet he's supposed to be with the police, supposed to be working to uncover the truth. He should be.

He looks at me, intensely, directly in the eyes.

"Marzio didn't kill himself." I say in a whisper. All the anger inside me freezes my vocal cords.

"And how do you know?"

"He didn't die. Someone took him. They took him away from me. He would never have left me like that. Never left me alone like this."

"Tell me something that would make me believe you."

The anger surges inside me, shaking me. I grip my knees, wishing I could dig my nails into his chest to make him stop talking. I stay silent, unable to form a thought. I just stare at his eyes, wanting to claw them out.

"How did he seem in the last days?"

"Before he died?"

"Yes, before he died."

"He was very tired. He'd fall asleep immediately. We'd lie on the bed together, and then he'd just crash."

"You slept together, but you didn't know this place. Where did you stay?"

"At my place. He started sleeping over more and more often."

"Since when?"

"Shortly after Cardia's death."

"And where do you live, exactly?

"In Vomero."

He pulls out a little notebook and jots something down. I see him smile but quickly mask it and turn serious again.

"It was a time of big changes for him."

"Yes. We started talking about the future more often. For him, it was important. We imagined being together. In so many places around the world. Happy." I recall his words, one by one.

"How long did you talk about the future?"

"Until the end. We were planning a trip."

"To where?"

"Lots of places. He loved the East, Japan, China." I remember the colors in his words when he talked about it. "Even though he'd already been there. India. I wanted to go to America, to see the United States."

"Well, that doesn't sound like someone who wants to die, does it?"

"He didn't want to die."

"Exactly." He writes something else in the black notebook. "But you're sure about this?"

"Yes, I am."

"Tell me, on Monday, the one before the incident. Was he with you?"

"Yes." I don't even need to think about it.

"What time did he get home?"

"He always arrived around the same time, give or take. Just enough time to come back from the office."

"Do you remember exactly?"

"Around seven."

"And he didn't go out, didn't go anywhere?"

"No, he came home and stayed there. We had dinner, watched some TV, then went to bed. Normal."

"So, he didn't leave the house." He repeats, making two quick, straight lines in his notebook, like crossing something off.

"No."

"Listen, earlier you mentioned something. A message he left. What's that about?"

I rest my head against the wall. There's not much I can do in this situation.

"I feel like something of him is still here. Something unfinished. Something that needs to be fixed. I feel like he…"

"Like he what?"

"Like he deserves it."

"You loved him a lot."

"I love him a lot." I exhale, then inhale. "I love him."

We stay silent for a few seconds. He writes again. My eyes are full of tears. It's impossible, every time I think of you, you choke me so hard. You exhaust me.

"Let's do this." He starts talking again. "There are still a few things I'd like to discuss with you. But for now, let's take a break." He stands up, putting his leather–bound notebook back into his pocket. "Would you like to come inside with me?" He points to the door.

I nod.

"Okay. Let's go in together. But one thing, we're about to do something that isn't exactly, how should I say, by the book. I know I can trust you, but you have to promise me you won't touch anything. And everything you see, you keep to yourself. "He puts his finger to his lips, signaling me to stay silent."

I nod again and stand as he moves toward the door. He pulls a set of keys from his pocket, attached to a keyring with a metal tag. I've never seen that set of keys before.

"Where did you get those?"

"Not a good start." He says, inserting the key into the security door lock. He turns it, and the lock clicks as it retracts.

He completes one full turn and then half of another. The lock clicks with a metallic sound, and he pushes the door open without further noise.

Inside, it's dark. I move closer to him, touching his coat and hiding behind him. He takes a step inside, his figure blocking the light coming from the landing. With his right hand, he searches for a light switch. I can hear my breathing getting heavier. The lights come on. There's a large entryway. The walls are bare, but the finishes are modern, recently done. A white lacquered shelf is against the wall in front of us, with an unused key tray on top. It's made of aluminum, shaped like a fluid conch shell. The officer steps inside and looks around. The light comes from several LED spotlights embedded in the ceiling, four of them. I follow him. To the right, there's another shelf, and above it, attached to the wall, is a white video intercom. On the left wall are four coat hooks fixed to the plaster.

I gently close the door, guiding it until I hear the lock click shut. Then I turn to follow him. He's already in the next room, lit by more LED lights. I follow. I step into a large open space, more than ten meters long and about six meters wide. Two rectangular pillars stand in the center of the room. On the left are three windows covered by shutters. At the back is an aluminum desk, clear of any clutter. Behind it, there's a large black–and–white photograph of two gears.

The man walks straight ahead, toward the desk. To the right, there's a closed door. I turn and notice a living area with a sofa and a chaise longue facing a flat–screen TV with a light gray frame. A glass coffee table sits between the couch and the TV. The room's lights aren't all on, some areas are in shadow. The TV is mounted above a cabinet housing several devices, which seem to be amplifiers. Two vertical speakers stand on either side of the TV, each about a meter and a half tall. They're black, with fabric covering the front. The side panels seem to be wood, ebony, judging by how dark they are. Or maybe they're just painted. Speakers. There are more black–and–white photos on the walls, all sharp and clear. One shows an empty cinema in the dark, its screen bright white. More than a cinema, it looks like a theater, judging by the decorations around the screen. It looks like a theater dressed up as a cinema.

The man in front of me reaches the desk and stops. He examines the surface, running his fingers over the smooth top. He stands there, still, silent.

I head toward the living area. Behind the pillars are shelves full of CDs and DVDs. Classical music, '70s rock. The prog rock I could never listen to for more than five minutes straight. And then post–rock, Mogwai, EF, Explosions in the Sky, GYBE. Those I liked. I liked them a lot.

"There was a computer here."

I lean out from behind the pillar.

"What?"

"There was a computer on this desk." He taps his finger on the surface. "And now it's gone."

"How do you know?"

"There's an imprint left by the monitor stand here, and on the floor, there are power outlets and an Ethernet socket."

I pull out my phone and turn on the Wi–Fi. I search for networks. It finds a couple, but the signals are weak. They don't belong to this house.

"There's no Wi–Fi here. That's strange. Marzio would never have been in a house without Wi–Fi."

"There was a computer here, and now it's gone."

I lean against the back of the couch, looking at the music Marzio listened to. I exhale slowly. I scan all the titles, one by one. I recognize them. We listened to them in the car, each with its own particular flavor. I smile. On the bottom shelf, I see Tori Amos. All her albums. I kneel and reach out. I grab Under the Pink, then From the Choirgirl Hotel, and Little Earthquakes. You gave me this one after our first month together. I still remember. We sang it together. You, with that ridiculous falsetto that always made me laugh.

I laugh silently. I miss you.

I put Under the Pink back. But something feels off. I can't quite figure out what. It's as if the side of the pillar is scratched or maybe dented. I pull out a few more CDs, then a few more. I empty half the shelf and crouch down for a better look.

There's a numeric keypad. It's gray. At the bottom, I see a straight slot, slightly less wide than the shelf, rising at the sides and hiding behind the upper shelf. I remove all the CDs from the upper shelf as well and see the last side of the rectangle carved into the pillar.

"What are you doing?" The officer peers around the pillar.

"I found something."

He crouches down next to me.

"Is this a damn safe?" he clasps his hands over his knees.

Above the numeric keypad is a five–digit LCD display. He points at it.

"Do you know any codes? Any important dates? We need to open it."

He brings his finger close to the metal of the door. It's painted white like the pillar, with only the keypad standing out in its metallic color.

I exhale very slowly. My hand is in the pocket of my jeans. I feel the paper under my fingertips. I pull it out and unfold it under the officer's wide eyes. He looks at me but says nothing.

I extend my finger, watching it tremble as it approaches the keypad. I type the first number, and a red asterisk lights up on the display. Then a second, and another, until it fills up. I keep typing. All the digits.

Here's the last one.

I press the button.

The asterisks disappear.

The word OPEN appears, and the automatic lock opens with a faint buzz.

The door tilts toward me. I reach out and open it. A dim light illuminates the contents.

An aluminum–bodied MacBook.

"Perfect." I hear his enthusiasm behind me.

I pull the laptop out of the safe. We both stand up. He points at it.

"Shall we turn it on?"

I nod.

"Let's sit down." He gestures toward the desk.

I walk quickly, my strides long, with him half a step behind. I pull out the chair and sit down. The laptop in front of me. I sit there, motionless, drained. I stare at the apple logo on the casing.

He's standing in front of me, waiting for me, I guess. He puts his hands on his hips. I can't see his face. He decides, reaches out, and opens the screen. He walks around the desk, tilting his head to look at the screen.

"You knew him well, didn't you? Well enough to know his passwords. He presses the power button."

I shrug. He resumes walking and heads toward the door on the right.

"Take your time."

The chair is comfortable. Soft. The seat is low, just the way he liked it. The computer has started up, waiting for the password to unlock it.

I try the one. His password. Our password. I tell myself I'm just trying, but I know it will work. I press enter after typing the last letter. The login window disappears, and a second later, the desktop appears.

"Done." I say aloud.

I open the mail app and the Finder. I search through the documents while waiting for the emails to load. The folders are well–organized, files arranged in a tree structure: correspondences, accounting, various documents, divided by year and then by category. It's easy to navigate. I know this world. It's vast, deep, and sprawling. I can almost see his hands, his eyes in this screen. I click through the folders, imagining his hands on the keyboard. His profile illuminated by the screen, the faint nighttime glow lighting up the room. It's as if I'm standing three steps away, watching him as I explore his computer, and he is me.

His arms, his face, they are me. And this sense of merging is a fleeting moment. It overtakes me, and I realize I'm overtaken. I return to my own body, suddenly. I stare at the screen, unsure of what I'm looking for.

"Have you found anything?"

His voice echoes faintly from the other room, reverberating softly off the walls. I breathe.

"I don't know what to look for." The words drain the strength from my shoulders.

It's the truth, the simple truth. And it leaves me powerless. A fragile framework where I rest my skin, and the darkness is lit only by the tiny flicker of a candle so small it can't even illuminate itself.

"You don't know what to look for, huh?"

He steps out of Marzio's room, holding some letters, unopened envelopes. He flips through them, reading the senders on the back. He opens one, the paper making a crisp sound as it slices through the air. He walks over to me and glances at the contents, distracted. Then he places it on the table in front of me.

"That's normal. Happens to me every time. What comforts me when I don't know what to do is that, most of the time, the things we're looking for aren't hidden." He says, his gaze wandering around the room. "You just have to see them." He looks at me. "And to see them, it sounds silly, but you shouldn't search for them. In fact, the less you search, the more they'll appear right before your eyes... Is that the mail program?"

The inbox window has appeared on the monitor. There are many unread emails. Ads, recently arrived, and other emails I've already seen on the Gmail account. All already checked.

"There's nothing here." I say. I don't want to scroll down too far, don't want the emails from Lili or Cardia to appear.

He stands beside me, reading the subject lines with me. I feel uneasy. I don't want him to know about those conversations. I look for a distraction, something to say or do, when I see it. Another email account. With a dedicated folder. The folder is called 'Me.' Without thinking, I hover the cursor over it and click.

"What did you do?" He asks behind me. "I was reading."

"Sorry." I say, my heart pounding.

I'm afraid of discovering something with him and then having to explain what I know. But it's too late now. The folder is already open.

Both of our eyes are fixed on the first email in the list. Dated a week ago. Sent by the law firm Grassia. Lawyers. The subject line is Challenge.

In the preview window, there are just a few lines.

Dear Marzio, I've reviewed the documents, and we're ready to respond to the challenge of Dr. Cardia's will. As you mentioned, the key issue is the transfer of the Golden Share to you. We have plenty of room to address this. Come by the office tomorrow so we can discuss the matter further and decide on the best course of action.

"What's the Golden Share?" I ask, my voice almost childlike. I immediately feel a bit ashamed.

"It's a right. A right that Marzio's father gave to Cardia. And that Cardia seems to have given to Marzio when he died."

"What kind of right?"

"A right that concerns Prosud. A right that would have given Marzio significant power."

"I don't understand."

"There's not much to understand. Are there any attachments?"

I check the header, no attachment icon, but the quoted text in Marzio's email refers to an attachment. I click on the sent folder and search for the email. I find it, open it, and there it is: Challenge.pdf. I open it.

We stand still, reading.

The challenger is Umberto Solimena.

I lose my breath.

"I don't understand, were they fighting?"

"They were fighting. And the fight was resolved. With a winner, I'd say."

The words hit like a punch in the stomach. He places a hand on my shoulder and leans over me.

"Sorry, I was being an asshole. Sometimes, stuff like that just slips out. I'm sorry."

My eyes are full of tears, but I shake my head.

"It's fine."

"Open this email, please."

He points at the screen, indicating a few lines below where we're looking now.

The email is from Prosud. The subject is Convocation.

It's from the CEO's secretary. It's a notice for an extraordinary shareholders' meeting. The date of the meeting is the day after Marzio's death.

"What's happening?" I ask, scared. I knew nothing about this, Marzio never told me anything about this.

"Family business, it seems. Strange stuff."

I turn to him. He's jotting something in his notebook.

"Do you know what's going on?"

"I have an idea that's becoming clearer, piece by piece." He doesn't lift his eyes from his notes.

I'm afraid. I feel like things are slipping out of my hands. I feel like I know something important, and I feel like talking about it is wrong. I remember exactly what the girl on the phone told me. I mustn't talk about it with anyone. No one. But I can't keep it to myself, I don't know how to use this information on my own. I look at him. He's absorbed in his notebook, writing, crossing things out, and drawing lines. And I feel there's a reason he stepped out of that elevator at that moment. I need to get rid of this weight. I need to share it with someone before it crushes me. Even if it puts me in danger? Even if it puts her in danger? Even if it undermines Marzio's efforts to save me? To save himself?

"What is it?"

I'm staring at him. He looks back at me, and I lower my eyes.

"What is it?" He asks more insistently.

I look at Marzio, he's close by, his face dark, staring into the void. He's so close that if I stretched out my hand, I might be able to touch him. You're so close, Marzio, that if I focused, maybe I could smell you, your scent.

"What aren't you telling me?" He presses. "I recognize that look from a mile away."

I curl into myself.

"It's nothing. I was just thinking about him."

"Bullshit."

"It's not bullshit." My voice is whiny. Why do I do everything to sound like a two–year–old?

"Yes, it is. You know something you want to say, but you're not sure whether to say it or not."

"What?" I look at him, surprised.

"Look, it's simple. I figured it out right away. That's why you're here in this room. I chose to trust you. I did that by exposing myself. If you're here with me and doing this." He gestures broadly, indicating the house "If we're in here together and not just me alone, it's because I chose to trust you. Because I believe you're a good person, trying to understand what happened to the guy you loved, and you're doing it in good faith. I believed in you. Now you need to believe in me. You have to believe that what you tell me will help nail the person who killed your Marzio."

He watches me in silence.

It's a thin veil of ice covering my face, and it only takes a breath to shatter it. It presses onto it with force, pushing into my cheeks, sending blood to my temples. It wraps around me like a red snake, covering my eyes, and a cloudy film drops over them, making everything gray and uniform. The contrast fades until the overwhelming sea of my thoughts leaves only a faded image of a placid lake, ready to explode. It's like a sharp point drawing closer, building tension until it releases a burst that shatters this imperfect stillness, melting me into a liquid memory on the floor.

His touch on my shoulder breaks the spell.

Reality is more solid than my thoughts, and I crash into it helplessly. Nothing happens. No glorious explosion, no disintegration of my body as I had wished. I remain motionless and weak under the weight of my own flesh. None of it leaves me, even though I desire it so intensely. It all continues until my lips begin to move on their own.

"There's someone. His name is Ligresti. He's a finance expert. Somehow, he's connected to all of this. I don't know how or why, but I know he's involved." I stare into the void.

"How do you know about this person?"

"I can't tell you."

"This isn't going well."

"I can't." I say, lowering my head.

"Tell me something else."

"He works for Solar Finanziaria or something like that, in Luxembourg."

"Solar Finanziaria?"

"Solar Financial."

"He knows Marzio's brother. They have connections."

"How do you know?"

"I called, and they mistook me for the brother's secretary." He writes something in his black notebook. "I tried calling him, but his phone is off. From what I understood, he's in Italy."

"And he's not answering, then?"

"The phone's off."

He closes the notebook and nods.

"I see. Thanks for telling me." I nod without looking at him. "I just got an idea to speed things up."

He pulls out his phone and selects a number from his contacts. He holds the phone to his ear. After a moment, someone answers.

"Olivieri. Here we go. Still at work?" He pauses. "Listen, I've got something for you. But you can't do anything with it for two days." He steps away toward the windows. "Yes, yes, I get it, but I don't care about ethics or any of that. I do you a favor, you do me a favor. But…" The person on the other end interrupts, but he presses on, "But, but I don't care. It's either this way or no way. Got it?" He listens, then continues. "Okay. So, we're agreed. Get a pen and paper. Write down Ligresti."

He turns to me.

"Livio Ligresti." I say.

"Livio Ligresti. Works at Solar Financial in Luxembourg. Find out every-thing you can about this guy." A pause. "Okay, okay." He straightens up. "And say it... say that again" He walks quickly toward me and puts the phone on speaker.

"So, the lady finally answered me after a hundred calls." The metallic voice from the phone says. "And then I asked her, 'So, ma'am, what do you think, about the loss, the boy.' And she responds in a resigned tone, 'Marzio had problems, many, and he kept them to himself. He was a lonely, sad, introvert-ed boy, and the losses we've faced only made his situation worse.' So, I ask her, 'Ma'am, so Marzio was down, he was sad?' And she says, right off the bat, 'Yes, unfortunately, almost to the point of depression.' And then I ask her, 'So, did you expect something like this?' And she says, 'It was a possibil-ity to be considered.'"

"Pretty explicit, huh?" Says Cardona

"I'd say so." Responds the voice on the phone

"Except, let's say, it doesn't match the scenario I have in mind?"

"Cardona, you've got one hell of a scenario."

"Do your job well, and I'll tell you about my scenario."

"At your service, Commissioner. We'll talk tomorrow afternoon."

He ends the call.

I swallow loudly.

I look at him and shake my head.

"You're full of fear." He says softly. I remain silent, staring into his eyes. "There's something to be afraid of in this story, for real." He straightens up and extends his hand. "I'd offer to take you home, but I know you wouldn't stay there." I take his hand. "So, let's do this. Come to my place. There's a comfortable couch. I live alone, and maybe we can have another chat if you feel like it. Tomorrow morning, after we've had a good rest. What do you say? We've got plenty to talk about and do."

I think about it for a few seconds.

"Okay." I say in a whisper.

I don't want to be alone tonight.

24.

"Hello?"

"So… he left."

"Are you following him?"

"No."

"What do you mean, no?"

"I went to get the car." The voice on the other end of the phone is breathless.

"But wasn't he on foot?"

"He left with a girl, from the building. They were on a scooter. They both got on and left."

"What the hell… And you just watched them leave?"

"I got the license plate number."

"I couldn't care less about the license plate! You're supposed to follow them. Otherwise, I'll spend the money I pay you on a funeral wreath!" He yells.

"I'm following them now. I'm heading to the car. I'm running."

"Damn it!" He shouts, slamming the phone down.

He slams the phone onto the desk, placing his hands on the wooden surface and gripping tightly.

He counts to twelve, then picks up the phone and redials the last number.

"Hello?"

"Send me the license plate by message."

"Yes, sir."

"What does the girl look like?"

"Blonde, thin, not very tall. In her twenties."

He hangs up without listening further.

He rests his elbows on the desk and clasps his hands in front of his face, staying in that position for a few moments.

The phone lights up with the message containing the license plate. He grabs it and forwards it to another number, adding, 'Let me know.'

He bites his cheeks.

He exhales.

He picks up the phone again and checks the time.

It's late.

But not too late.

He makes another call.

"Hello? Yes, it's me. We might have a problem. I wanted to tell you right away."

25.

The door opens. A narrow, dark hallway stretches out in front of us. He walks in and switches on the light. The white walls are dotted with stains and peeling paint. The floor is covered in gray terrazzo tiles, giving me a feeling of melancholy. The door on the right leads to the corridor. It has two brown wooden panels with frosted glass in the middle that doesn't allow you to see what's on the other side. I run my hand over it, the waves in the glass feel soft and cold. He walks to the end, where there's another open door. He enters, turns on the light, then disappears beyond the wall. From here, I can see a sink and a closed window. As I move forward, I glance around. There are no decorations, no photos, no paintings on the walls. It feels like the house of someone who has just moved in and still has everything in boxes. He reappears, stepping out from the doorway.

"If you're hungry or want something to drink, this is the kitchen." He gestures behind him, showing it to me. "There's not much in the fridge, but we'll manage." He exits and enters the last room on the right. "Sorry it's not the most comfortable place." He shouts as he moves around the other room.

I reach the entrance of the room he entered, it's a bedroom. He's facing away from me, bent over a messy desk.

"Where's the bathroom?"

"Next to the kitchen." He points without looking at me. "It has a white folding door."

I turn and see it, three steps, and I'm touching it. I try to open it, but it jams after a few centimeters. I have to push it with both hands to fully open it, the sound of the plastic bending is unpleasant, like it's about to fall apart. The bathroom is rectangular, narrow, and uncomfortable. The floor and walls are covered with small white tiles, blackened in the corners. To the left is a shower platform with a small showerhead sticking out of the wall. There's no curtain or plastic shield around it. On the floor, in a corner, there's a towel, still wet, folded against the wall.

I look at myself in the small mirror above the sink, my eyes are red, hollow, tired.

I want to splash my face with water, but I realize I'm still holding Marzio's computer. I could put it down somewhere. I step out of the bathroom as he passes by me, entering the kitchen. I see a table covered with a yellow oilcloth. I follow him and place the MacBook on the table. I suddenly notice that my legs hurt. I sit down for a moment.

He opens the fridge and pulls out two beers.

"Want one?" He asks, shaking them with the necks held between his fingers.

I don't have the energy to say no, and maybe I do feel like having a sip of beer.

He opens a drawer, pulls out a fork, and with a quick motion, pops open the first bottle, handing it to me. The kitchen is so small that he only needs to take half a step for the bottle to reach me. I take it and sip. He takes a sip from his own.

"This place is really a dump. I'm sorry."

"No, no, it's fine." I say, but what am I even saying? "No, I mean, it's not true. It's okay."

He laughs and takes another sip from his bottle.

"No, it's not. This place is a mess, and I keep it even worse. It's not the kind of place you'd bring a girl, but it's all I've got."

I shrug.

"So, have you ever gotten any threats, pressure, strange phone calls, or had anyone approach you during this time?"

I look at him. He waits in silence.

I sigh.

"No, no one."

"But you started looking into things. And you found something. How did you come across this Ligresti?"

I bite my lips. I didn't come here to be interrogated, but I'm afraid to say it out loud.

The room goes quiet, letting the hum of the city outside vibrate through the closed window.

"Why don't you tell me what you know, and then I'll tell you what I know?"

He looks at me, then makes a face that ends in a challenging smile. He raises his hands and takes another sip of beer.

"Okay. I'll tell you what I know. Then it's your turn."

"You'll tell me what you know and what you've figured out" I respond firmly.

"You're worse than the journalists." He smiles. "Alright, then. So, I know Marzio was a smart guy, who lost his father young and was taken in by Augusto Cardia like an adopted son. I know he was a researcher, developing new products for his company. I know Cardia died some time ago, and Marzio decided to change departments. I don't know why he wanted to do that. I've talked to a lot of people, and everyone has a different idea, but I know one thing."

He leans against the windowsill, sipping his beer.

"I know they all got it wrong, and no one really understood him. Everyone says Marzio was intelligent, and I believe that. I believe he knew exactly what he was doing and who he was dealing with."

He pauses for a long time.

"I believe he had many enemies. Enemies who were very close."

He looks at me intensely.

"Do you know anything about Cardia's will?"

Will?

I shake my head.

"You mean that thing about the Golden Share? No, nothing."

"Well, I think that's important. Good old Cardia gave Marzio a right when he died, the same right Marzio's father had given to Cardia while he was still alive. A heavy right. The right to veto any decision made by the top brass at Prosud."

I swallow. This doesn't make much sense to me.

"But wasn't he the owner?"

The commissioner frowns.

"Yes, he owned forty percent. Then there's the brother and the mother. I think that's why we found that email about contesting the will. I believe the family had something to say about Cardia's decision. We need to dig deeper, but that's the direction." He pauses for a second, then looks at me, curious. "What do you think of the mother?"

"Never met her." I think for a moment. "Marzio never talked about his family. Not to me, at least."

"What do you mean, 'at least'?"

"Nothing." I shrug.

"Oh no, we're not doing that. I'm telling you what I know, and you can't hide what you know!" His tone is accusatory, and he leans toward me as he says it.

I stay silent, lower my gaze, and the conversation dies.

He picks it back up.

"I'm saying he was a smart guy, and I'm saying that I think he cared about you. Because he kept you in the dark about all the bad things happening to him and kept the people who wished him harm from looking at you. To protect you."

He pauses for a long time.

"Did you know that in his office, on his desk, or anywhere else, there are no pictures or signs of you."

I stay silent. Were you protecting me Marzio?

"Or he was just doing his stuff, I have actually seen him in photos with other girls, photos that he kept secret."

I tremble as he says this. A current of electricity runs down my spine from the back of my neck and radiates into my legs, which turn to lead. I place my heavy hands on the table, my mouth hanging open. I can't believe his words.

He watches me. My reaction surprises him. I break eye contact and retreat into myself. Maybe it's her? Maybe she's the one he keeps with him when I'm not around? My heart feels like it's being torn apart. She told me to never tell anybody, keep the secret. But I can't bear it. And what if she is another girl? What if he is bluffing? Can I take the risk. My hands reach on their own for the back pocket of my jeans, it's like my body wants to just escape this nightmare, share the weight. My hands pull out the photo. I look at it, my eyes burning as they fill with tears. I turn to him, trying to hold back the sobs. I need to be strong.

"Is this her? Is she the one in the photos?"

He looks at me, astonished. He takes half a step forward, as if he can't believe it, then another full step toward the table. He looks at the photo in my hand, then stares at me.

"And where did you get this photo?"

He's genuinely surprised. He's sincere.

"Is it her?" I ask as a tear rolls down my face.

He stands still, like a statue. Then he shakes his head.

"Yes."

It's her.

I exhale, inhale, and exhale again. My chest deflates, and the tears stop. All that's left is my heavy breathing.

"Where did you get that photo?"

I shift my gaze from the void to his eyes.

"I took it from Cardia's house. It was taken at his vacation home."

"Vacation home? Where?"

"His wife took me there." I swallow the mucus running down my nose.

"Where?"

"In Sorrento. We both say at the same time."

We fall silent. I put the photo of Marzio and her back in my pocket. Then, from the front pocket, I pull out a packet of tissues and wipe my face.

"Did you know Marzio went to Sorrento a few days before he died?"

It shouldn't surprise me. It doesn't. Maybe my skin is getting tougher, or maybe I'm just tired. I shake my head.

"Tell me the truth, it's that girl who told you about this Ligresti, right?"

"Yes, it's true, it's her." I nod.

"She plays an important role in this story. She's central. Do you know who she is?"

"No, I don't."

"Do you have a way to contact her?"

"No, she…" I take a breath, I can't breathe "She's very scared, she says we're in great danger and that Marzio was also facing big dangers, and if he didn't make it, now we risk that they'll get us. I have no way of contacting her, she… she finds me, I don't have her contacts."

He drinks his beer. He finishes it and places it on the windowsill. He moves towards the fridge to grab another one.

"You see? Step by step, we're getting closer to the truth. You need to stay calm. And you don't need to be afraid because I'll make sure they don't hurt you."

He closes the white fridge door and, with the help of a fork, opens this other bottle as well.

"If we manage to talk to this girl, we've hit the jackpot. Believe me."

He looks out the window. The red streetlights illuminate his face.

I'm tired.

"Go to sleep, there's a couch in the living room."

"Yes, you told me."

"See you tomorrow."

"Goodnight."

I get up and head towards the hallway. I drag myself with exhaustion with every step. The room is tidy, at least more so than the others. The couch is made of green faux leather, I sit down, it's fairly soft. That's enough for me, I stretch out my legs and rest my head on the armrest. The last glance before closing my eyes is for him. As always.

26.

The dawn wakes me up.

The window faces exactly east, and the horizontal light of the sun hits the wall, enveloping me. I look beyond the glass; the ball of fire is pale yellow, veiled by a thin layer, difficult to tell if it's clouds or just the morning mist, peeking between the silhouettes of two gray buildings. Its blade of light enters directly here, filling my eyes.

It's another day.

Marzio is sitting in the corner, next to the window. He's sitting cross—legged, his figure is dark, and I can't see his face. Lying on his lap, coiled like a snake, is him. His back is to me, sleeping on Marzio's lap. His jacket takes on a silvery hue in this light.

He's sleeping. I can feel it, the air is not heavy with his cruel spirit, but I still don't want to be here, with him. I get up, grab the laptop lying by my feet, and leave. As I turn to go into the hallway, I catch a glimpse of him moving out of the corner of my eye, adjusting himself on his legs.

I quicken my pace and head to the kitchen.

He's there, where I left him, holding a cup of coffee.

"Good morning."

"Hi." my mouth is dry.

"I made some coffee. The machine is still hot. Take some."

I want it, so I approach. I put the laptop on the table. He extends his hand and points to the cupboard.

"The cups are in there. Rinse them before using them."

I open the door and reach in to grab a brown coffee cup. I do as he says, turning on the faucet to rinse it. I feel the roughness of the dust washing away under the water.

I turn off the faucet and pick up the coffee maker.

"It's already sweetened." he says.

I nod and pour myself a cup. Then I sit down where I was last night.

"Here we are again." I say. He smiles.

The coffee isn't bad. Maybe a bit bitter, but it's good.

"How much stuff is on that computer?"

I listen to him in silence and don't respond. I shrug as I keep sipping my coffee. Sleep still clouds my thoughts.

I think I slept deeply. Maybe for the first time since… since that day. That cursed day. I feel heavy. But I think that's what it feels like when your body is rested.

"What time is it?"

"Seven fifteen."

"Do you have to go to work?"

"It's Saturday."

I nod. His answer comforts me. I won't be alone today.

"How did you sleep?" He tries to be caring, you can see he's making an effort.

"Better than usual." I appreciate the effort.

Another tense silence. I drink my coffee. I finish it now. I place the cup down. The question is in the air. I feel it growing, nurtured by his tension. He was waiting for it. My awakening. What he wants from me. And in the end, it's fine by me, maybe with him by my side, the fear softens. Sharing the same goal lightens this burden weighing on my shoulders and soul. I shouldn't share anything. Nothing, I promised silently to her, but this is fine, it's fine for me, fine for him, and in the end, fine for Marzio. I'm okay with it.

"So. Shall we carefully see what we find on this computer?"

That was the question I'd been expecting, I smile. I stay still for a few seconds, he watches me, and I can feel it.

"Ok."

I place my hands on the aluminum frame and open the Mac. I type in the password, and the laptop comes to life. Exactly where we left off before. I pause, waiting for instructions.

He places his empty cup down, almost tossing it into the sink, and quickly moves toward the table, grabs a chair, and settles next to me with a decisive gesture.

"Let's start with the sender, see who it is."

I click on the mail app and select the sender from the header.

Do a search, see if there are other emails from this address.

I click the search bar and paste the address; two emails appear, then a third after a moment. He leans toward the monitor.

"Let me read them a bit." He says, extending his finger almost to touch the screen.

I click on the first one, and it opens. He leans in and reads it carefully. I try too, but after the first two lines, I get distracted. My gaze drifts to the window, to the city that seems so far away but is right here, just steps away. The traffic is still flowing smoothly. After all, schools haven't opened yet, and the only people on the streets are the parents who are work slaves. If only we were blessed with a bit of sun today, a warm ray. I would be grateful, truly grateful. I breathe in the aroma of coffee, it feels good to feel at home for small things like this, the small habits that make you feel that here, at least here, you are safe.

"Move to the next one."

Reluctantly, I turn my gaze back to the screen and follow the cursor until it hovers over the second line in the search results. Double–click, and the window with the email text appears. I move the cursor away from the words to make it easier to read, stopping on the dock. The icons enlarge, giving the illusion of a smooth, wave–like motion. I've always liked that effect. But now, the feeling isn't complete, something disturbs me. The largest icon of all is blue, round, with a white 'S' on it, and the cursor is resting on it.

I had no idea Marzio had a Skype account. Clicking on it feels like the most natural thing in the world.

A few seconds, the cursor turns into a spinning wheel that spins a couple of times, and then the Skype chat window opens, covering the email the inspector is reading.

"What are you doing? Put the email back, let me finish reading." He complains, waving his open hand and pointing his fingers at the monitor.

But his words mean nothing now.

There is only one name in the contact list.

C.

And Marzio's username is M. just 'M.' with a period next to it. Exactly like in Cardia's photo.

"What are you doing?" The inspector complains again, this time more firmly.

There are three missed calls, two on September 7th and another on September 8th, just after midnight. The inspector looks at me, then at the monitor. I point at the name on the screen.

"It's her."

And at the same moment my finger stops a few millimeters from the screen, the dot next to the name turns green.

I should think about it, but I don't.

Double–click, and the video call starts. With my hands, I push the officer aside so that he doesn't appear in what the webcam captures.

It rings. The cold, hoarse Skype ringtone. It rings again.

A sound alerts me that the call is active. The recipient's window opens, but the screen is black. No image appears.

It's my turn.

"It's me." I swallow. "I managed to recover his PC. I opened Skype and saw the account. I called. I hope you're okay."

There's a long moment of silence after my words. So long that I feel like asking whether my words reached the other side clearly, whether they arrived at all, or if there's truly someone on the other side of the camera.

"You're a beautiful girl. He always told me that. He was right."

That's his voice. It has a light, pleasant French accent. Feminine, delicate.

"How are you? Everything okay?"

"Yes, I'm fine, I'm safe. And you?"

"Yes, everything's fine. Yesterday, I managed to get into his house and took the computer home."

"How did you get into his house?"

"I found the keys."

"Where?"

"In one of his coats."

Silence.

"You told me to check the beige trench coat, and then I tried all the ones in the closet."

The inspector slides a note across the keyboard. I read it.

"Listen, there are a couple of things I'd like to ask you. Otherwise, I can't make sense of anything. May I?"

More silence.

"Go ahead." She replies coldly. Tense.

"I saw you tried to call Marzio on September 7th."

"Yes."

"Did you need to tell him something?"

"Yes."

"What?"

"He had to do something at the office, the last in a complex sequence, and once it was done, we would have been free of a burden, both of us." The sense of affliction is strong in her tone.

"And then?"

"Then what happened, happened."

"But you didn't know what he had to do?"

"No, not in detail."

"I see." I pause. Then the inspector taps a couple of times on the second question. I don't read it, running my hand over my chin. I need to ask her this first.

"Listen, can I ask you a personal question?"

"Yes."

"I..." My voice trembles "I saw a piece of paper. A sheet where Marzio wrote some things, a formula, a kind of oath, and then two drops of blood on the paper."

I get the impression she's holding her breath. The line goes silent; there's only an electric hum in the background, letting me know there's still a connection between us.

"Where did you find it?" Her voice is tense.

"At Cardia's house. In Sorrento. In his desk."

"Who took you there?"

"Isabella."

160

Again, silence.

I lean back in my chair. I stare into the Mac's camera. I know she's watching me.

"Who are you?"

My voice fades into the background of urban traffic, slowly rising and filling my ears. There's breathing next to me, it's the inspector, kneeling and watching me in profile, listening to what I'm saying. I only hear his breathing; he's otherwise motionless.

She tries to say something, then gives up. She's struggling with herself.

"You can tell me."

"Yes, that's true, but also not." She says "Because this thing belonged to the three of us and only us. That's the meaning of the oath. It was Augusto's idea."

"But what's your connection with them?"

She sighs.

"But in the end, none of us are left. I'm the only one carrying this weight."

"I'm here too." I say with a touch of bitterness.

"Yes, you're right. You're here too. You're the extension of Marzio now. His hand, the last thing that ties me to him and Augusto."

"Who are you?" A long pause separates us.

"I helped Marzio. To do what he needed to do. Augusto introduced me to him. He called me one day and said he needed me, so I took a plane and came. Augusto never called for nothing." Her words flow freely, her French accent mixing with her desire to free herself from this burden "And when I heard him that time, I knew he truly needed me, so I came."

"How did you know him?"

"Augusto?" She pauses. "You've been to Sorrento, haven't you? You said you were in his study. Well, there you must have seen a painting, assuming Isabella left it there."

"Yes, I saw it."

"That's a portrait of my mother."

"Your mother?"

"From when she was a child and lived there. That was my mother's face when my father fell in love with her."

My breath catches in my chest.

"You're Cardia's daughter?" The question escapes my lips without control. She pauses.

"Yes, it's me." She says in a somber tone.

We stay silent for a few seconds, then she continues.

"Augusto didn't raise me. But he always loved me. I lived in Paris all my life. He always supported my mother and me, even during her failed marriage. And when she fell ill for the last time and everything ended, the only one left here for me was him. He never failed me. He loved me; I felt it and still feel it. He loved me like he loved my mother. He could never take her with him; it wasn't their destiny to be together. They both knew it and accepted it, but the truth is they never let go of each other, always bound by a double thread that kept them close and far at the same time. It's hard to explain, but that's how it is." She speaks like a flood, a dam that has burst. "Then came the call. I went down to Sorrento, and one day he arrived with Marzio. Both had tense faces. Marzio needed to know something, to access some information that was hidden, concealed, and the only way to do it was through a third person, someone far from him or Augusto. A person unsuspecting and trustworthy."

My gaze is fixed on the camera, but I can feel the inspector moving, jotting down what she's saying in his notebook.

"You."

"Me." She replies.

"But what did you need to find out?" A sense of anguish rises from the pit of my stomach toward my throat. But I'm curious. I need to understand.

"It was about Prosud." Then she corrects herself "It is about Prosud."

"In what way?"

"There are strange things, things Marzio didn't understand. Things related to the capital increase."

The inspector writes a big question mark in his notebook and shows it to me. I get it.

"What capital increase?"

"It was decided." She pauses "It was imposed, a capital increase for Prosud."

"When?"

"At the beginning of the year."

"What was wrong with it?"

"Marzio had suspicions, that it was a political maneuver, meant to damage him, to weaken him."

"Why?"

"Because the capital increase was large. Very large. It affected the personal finances of the partners. He would have needed to go into debt, and he suspected that it wasn't truly necessary. He suspected that was a move to dilute him, and pushing him away from corporate control"

"And then?"

And then they called me. Augusto knew the situation, and Marzio's suspicions struck him and convinced him that something was wrong. I arrived and listened to their story. Then they proposed their idea to me."

She pauses, and I wait for her to continue. In my mind, I picture Marzio, Cardia, and her talking in the study in Sorrento, seated at the desk.

"I accepted, and I gave myself for them, doing what they asked me. I went through with it to the end. I didn't fully understand what I was doing. I didn't grasp the scope of my actions, but I did it. Then Augusto died. He died, do you understand?" She addresses me with urgency, suddenly changing tone. "He died. And I never understood. They say a heart attack. They say he died suddenly. I only know that I always saw him strong, vigorous, never worn down by fatigue or pain. And at that time, he was too focused. He could never have died. He had to clear the fog he and Marzio were caught in. He could never allow himself to die. He never would have allowed it, never."

I'm afraid. I want to ask her what she did, but I don't have the courage.

"Do you think they killed him?"

"I feel something, something inside. The same thing you feel now." She says disdainfully.

I lower my gaze. I stay silent. Long seconds pass.

"From that moment, our spiral began. From Augusto's death, we found ourselves in a stormy sea. I stopped working. I was afraid. Marzio was strong. He continued, even though he was scared. In those days, he talked to me a lot about you, about how much he loved you, how important you were to him, how much peace his life with you brought him. He felt an intense, visceral love for you. I saw Augusto and my mother together in their dream of a possible, realized love in you two. When he talked to me, I fell in love with the two of you, and I never wanted to stop listening."

"Did you talk often?"

"Yes, first on the phone. Then eventually in person too. He would come to visit me."

"Where?"

"I stayed in Sorrento. In the last days."

"Until when?" I ask, following the commissioner's suggestion as he shows me the question written in his notebook.

"Until he told me to leave."

"When?" Anxiety grips my throat.

"A few days before the end. He came to me one morning in Sorrento and told me to run away. And to never let anyone hear from me again, for my own good. His face, his words, and his gestures frightened me. I saw him again on the sixth, last Wednesday. He explained what to do in case." She stops, trying to hold herself together, and I do the same, once again feeling the urge to cry. "In case something went wrong. I had given him some documents, papers I had recovered from his company. He carried them with him, in his car. He told me those were the ones that worried him. I was supposed to leave early the next morning. He explained everything to me, gave me the name Ligresti, and then…" She stops. "And here we are now."

Once again, our thoughts are wrapped around Marzio, his face, his fear, his attempt to save himself and us, the parachutes he set up along the way, one by one opening to keep us from plunging into the abyss, into ignorance. His will to give us a chance to atone for him, for what had consumed him in the fire.

I see the flames, the red heat surrounding him, his hidden face turning into a black shadow of ash and burning coal. His figure growing darker and darker until it loses substance and transforms into smoke.

The commissioner nudges me.

He's waving the next question under my nose. I hadn't noticed. I read it and mechanically repeat it.

"What were the documents you gave him?"

I slowly bring my gaze back to the camera to reestablish eye contact.

A few moments pass.

"They were invoices. Purchase and sales. Prosud related stuff."

The commissioner takes notes, and I feel drained. I wonder when I will stop feeling like this.

"I'm tired, you know." She says. "All of this terrifies me and fills me with sadness at the same time."

"Yes, I feel the same. It's terrible." I pause and then say it. "I see Marzio all day. He's always in front of my eyes, and I don't know how much longer I can handle it."

"Yes, I understand. He's inside me too. I can't forget him. I don't want to." She sighs. "He didn't deserve all this."

"None of us deserves this." I reply.

"Yes, that's true. And I hope the truth can be uncovered. To give him justice. To give him what he wanted, what he was seeking."

I remain silent. My spirit is curled up inside me. Weak and tired. It has retreated into the deepest, warmest part of me. My heart beats weakly, though quickly. Sadness envelops me.

The commissioner shakes a piece of paper over the keyboard. I look at it. Then I turn toward his eyes. He looks at me and nods, as if to encourage me.

"You know, Marzio's car keys weren't found with him at the crime scene."

"How do you know that?"

"I know a policeman investigating the case. You know, he doesn't believe Marzio killed himself either."

"So there is someone else."

"Yes." I smile. It's true, we're not alone now.

"I need to tell you something. It's important. Do you know about Augusto's Golden Share?"

"I read the emails."

"Yes. That was the last straw. What broke the balance."

"Between Marzio and the family?"

"Yes. Do you know how the shares are divided after Marzio's father passed away?

"No, I don't."

"Forty percent to each child and the remaining twenty to the mother, Margherita. Augusto knew that Margherita's views were, how can I say… She always sought a strong figure to cling to, and she developed this form of worship for an undisputed leader. Indisputable, I would say. And as long as Marzio's father was alive, she was satisfied. When he died, she desperately searched for a replacement. In the end, she found one. She gave herself entirely to this cause, the cause of making this person her absolute reference point. But in her selfish version, her own needs became everything, and in the end, and I'm sure of this, she chose to make one final move to free herself from her anguish."

"What anguish?" I don't think I'm understanding much.

"The anguish of seeing two currents clash, two rivers flowing parallel but separate, neither gaining full control over the other. Do you understand? The absence of one 'I' above all."

The commissioner rubs his thumb and forefinger together a couple of times. I watch as his lips seem to mouth the name 'Marzio.'

"That's why she chose to give up her twenty percent." I stay silent, thinking I understand. "So that it could be definitively decreed who was on top and who was beneath. To restore order. Maybe she would have done it with a mother's heart, dividing it nine and eleven, but she would have done it anyway. For her, the principle mattered above all else. Even her own soul was at stake for this.

Augusto knew. He felt deep down that it would happen and took precautions. He had the authority, and he did what he thought was right. The Golden Share to Marzio nullified all of Margherita's claims, leveling what she was trying to do. And from there, everything spiraled. The reading of Augusto's will was…" She pauses. "Let's leave it at that."

What can I say? I knew nothing of all this. Nothing. Marzio, if you loved me so much, when were you going to tell me all of this?

"But I have to tell you something."

I listen.

"I have to tell you that Augusto would have been proud of you, of what you're doing, and the courage with which you're doing it. Marzio would have been proud too." I smile. I don't know whether to believe it. I don't know if it's just to comfort me. "I'm glad we talked. That I told you these things. I felt the need to tell someone, and you were the only person I could confide in. There's one last thing you need to know before I go. When I met with Marzio for the last time, he told me that if something happened, he had left one last thing for you. He had kept it safe at the company. He was going to give it to you the next day, before the meeting. He never told me what it was. But when he said it, he seemed at peace. As if… he felt reassured. Did he ever give you this thing?"

I shake my head.

"He never gave me anything."

"Then he didn't manage to." Her voice fills with sadness. "That thing is for you. He made it for you and hid it for you. It's yours, waiting for you. I don't know how to help you, and that destroys me, because I saw in his eyes how important it was to him to give it to you."

My heart pounds. My Marzio.

"You have to recover it. I don't know how, but he would want it that way."

My Marzio. I turn toward the door. He's there. The demon holds his left hand and clings to his right leg. I can't see his face, I don't know if he's sleeping.

My Marzio is here for this. To finish what he chose to do. That's why he's here. His death wasn't enough to break his will. He's here for me.

"Everything okay?" She asks with her slight Parisian accent.

"Everything okay." I say as I turn my gaze back to the monitor.

"I have to go." She says quietly.

"Okay. Thank you for everything."

"There's something terrifying behind all this. It's already taken Augusto and Marzio, one after the other. It's Umberto. He's ruthless, all he cares about is power. Money."

"Did he kill them?"

"I don't know. All I know is that if Augusto and Marzio discovered any shady dealings, then Umberto wouldn't have hesitated. I'm scared they'll track me down. When you called me, I froze. I don't want anything to do with this family. Please, don't call me again."

"Okay."

"I hope this ends the way Marzio would have wanted."

I look at her. In the camera, I think I can see her light eyes. The monitor is pitch black.

"Marzio wouldn't have wanted it to end this way. But his will is so strong that it will take us where he wants in the end, even if he's not here, in our flesh."

"He's in our hearts, isn't he?" She responds immediately.

"Yes, in our hearts."

"Exactly."

The conversation ends.

All these words leave a bitter taste in my mouth. Yet they recharge me with energy, with how many things I didn't know but now do, how everything seems clearer. How much fog has lifted now.

How much of Marzio was hidden from me, and how cruel it is to discover it like this. How much I would have wanted to be a part of this life of Marzio's. How far my image of him is from this suffering. Why? Why did you exclude me from this pain? Why didn't you want to share it with me?

The commissioner's phone rings, startling me. He gets up and walks over to it. It's on the windowsill. He looks at the display, and his face lights up.

"This is a morning of revelations, let's see what this is about."

He exclaims, satisfied. He presses the green button to accept the call and then another. He comes over to me, sets the phone on the table, then leans forward, resting his elbows on the tablecloth–covered surface.

"Olivieri, good morning! Did you fall out of bed this morning?"

"Cardona, don't joke around, as usual, it's me saving your ass every time, including this one." The journalist's voice is beaming. "I've been up all night digging for you, and I found something interesting."

"You're a sly one. That's the one and only truth." Says the commissioner, amused.

"So, listen up. I did some digging. Ligresti is a big shot in finance, he was doing well. Then he kind of lost it, or who knows what, and dropped out. You following me?"

"Yes." Cardona says, nodding.

"He was big on international transactions, but I think he made a couple of risky moves and disappeared before the waters could stir. So, he vanished. He wasn't talked about for a few years, people looked for him, but not too hard, and then he just faded away. But..."

"But?" Repeats the commissioner, knowing he has to play his part in this ritual.

"But he reappears, and now he's heading Lunar Finance, not Solar like you said." The commissioner gives me a slightly reproachful look. Then he turns to the phone. "Sun... moon... it's the same thing. Get to the point.

"Yes, yes. Okay. So, Lunar Finance is a financial company, but it doesn't have that big of a business, at least not compared to what Ligresti is used to. So you wonder, why would this guy come back from nowhere to manage a finance company that's peanuts for him? Maybe he had a nervous breakdown and just wants to work in a smaller, more comfortable environment? You know what I think?"

"What?"

"That's all bullshit. These people are sharks swimming through bank transfers, invoices, and checks like cannibals. Trust me, he smelled money and dove right in. And here's where it gets interesting." He pauses, and we hear the sound of papers being shuffled. "So, from the little I managed to see, and I won't tell you how. Because you know, I've got someone up there who looks out for me, but I know you don't care, but I like repeating it because you need to get it in your head that you always have to say yes to me."

"Get on with it, talk."

"So, Lunar owns a ton of shares in various companies, but here's the kicker: through a series of cross–holdings, it owns the majority of shares in only two companies. They're controlled indirectly, but the decisions that move them are Ligresti's. Want to know which ones? "He says smugly, with that metallic voice coming from the commissioner's old phone."

"So, I'll tell you: Chem It S.p.A. and Concrete Works GmbH, a German company." He pronounces it all with a fake German accent. "Do those names ring a bell?

"No. Says the commissioner.

"Not to him, but they do to me, and I freeze. It's the same name I saw in the balance sheet found at Cardia's house in Sorrento."

"Well, bad news. Because the first is the main supplier of raw materials to Prosud, the Solimena company, and the second. He pauses as if holding his breath. "And the second is its best customer, from what I've heard. They say it alone moves over thirty percent of Prosud's revenue."

We all stay silent. All three of us. Motionless.

"So?"

"So what?" The commissioner replies.

"So what do we do?"

"So I'll take care of my business. And you can't publish any of this before Monday. Understood?"

"Come on, Cardona, Monday is a lifetime away!" Olivieri exclaims, dissatisfied.

"I don't care. Today and tomorrow are mine. Meanwhile, keep looking into what else you can find."

"Where else will you find someone like me who, in one night, in one night, finds you this mountain of information? Say it, come on, say it."

"Go shoot yourself." Says the commissioner, and hangs up.

He looks up and stares at me. I look back at him. I see his excitement growing. I'm scared, but I feel a shiver down my spine. I see the truth, and I'm afraid to discover it.

"I need to tell you something." I feel the commissioner's gaze on me.

"Go on."

"The first time I spoke to her, she told me to look through Marzio's things for a clue. I did, and I found this."

I pull a small piece of paper from my pocket and show it to him.

Lili is the key?

168

"Yes, see, that's the code that opened the safe."

"Who is Lili?" Asks the commissioner.

"I thought it was just a code, but now I think it's the initials of Livio Ligresti. When I found the note, I received a cryptic call, and in the call, there was a recorded message. It was a description of this Ligresti's Wikipedia page.

I open the browser and navigate to the page.

"See? It seems this guy is an expert in moving capital to tax havens or something like that. And you said the secretary knew Umberto's secretary?"

"Yes. And after discovering this, I went to Sorrento. There, in Cardia's desk, I found this." I pull out the photo of Marzio, Cardia, and his daughter. "And the financial statements for the companies your friend mentioned on the phone."

The commissioner tilts his head to get a better look at the photo.

"So Marzio and Cardia were reconstructing the financial structure, probably orchestrated by Ligresti and Umberto, and through C., they were gathering the documents needed to prove some illegal act."

Yes.

He pulls the photo from my fingers. He brings it close to his face, studying their expressions. He seems to be thinking of something. I see a grimace of anger. Long moments pass, then he looks at me seriously, but I can feel his excitement.

"We need to go back to the company site"

"I've never been there."

"We need to recover what Marzio left for you. I'm sure that's the last thing I need to close the case."

I sigh. What Marzio left for me. My heart feels heavy. I want to know what's there for me. But I'm afraid.

27.

The phone rings. He's in bed, his eyes have been open for a while. The wrinkled sheet is on his knees, his gaze fixed on the ceiling.

"Hello?"

"I'm still here. In the end, no movement. They went up last night and haven't left."

"Did you see them go up?"

"No, but their scooter is still parked here."

"But you haven't seen them since?"

"No." Silence. "I did what you told me. Everything's fine."

"Can you see anything?"

"Nothing. Nothing will be seen."

"Stay there. Let me know of any movement."

He places the phone on the nightstand.

The room is dark. The shutters are closed. The light from the screen briefly illuminates the walls with a grayish hue before going dark again.

He brings his hand to his chin, his beard unkempt, rough. He tugs at it, trying to release his frustration. The relief is brief, not enough.

He jumps out of bed and heads to the window, opening it with a sharp gesture. He throws the shutters open, letting in air and light.

He looks down at the street and sees the cars already parked in double rows.

He grabs the phone from the nightstand and heads to the kitchen for his first coffee of the day. Walking barefoot, he enters the room, grabs the moka pot, opens it, and cleans it before filling the tank with water and the filter with coffee. The powder spills along the edges of the split machine. He grabs a cloth from the counter and tightens it forcefully. He places the pot on the stove and lights the flame.

He looks at the black ring left by the coffee powder. With a quick hand, he wipes it away. He moves toward the window and opens it with another sharp motion. The shutters thud dully against the building's walls.

He touches the phone in his pocket.

He takes it out, unlocks it, and dials a number.

The phone rings.

It rings for a long time. It rings until the call disconnects.

He stares at the display as it returns to standby.

He sits at the table. Counts to ten.

He tries calling again.

The phone rings.

It rings for a long time.

Someone answers.

"It's me. The situation is complicated. I don't trust it. I feel like we need to do something."

He pauses and listens to the other person.

"Yes, you're right, but I don't think that'll be enough. And this business with the girl, no one knows this girl, I don't trust her."

Another pause. Then he continues.

"Yes, I understand, we should've met her, but we didn't. What do you want to do? Complain to someone?"

The other person responds, raising their voice

"Man, your money's worth as much as a joker card. I'm telling you what's best to do now to manage the situation, otherwise, if you want to handle it on your own, I'll wash my hands of it, and it'll be your problem. It's not hard for me to disappear."

He stops, but there's no response from the other side.

"So." He says more calmly. "If you want to listen to my advice, which you paid good money for, you'd better act. After all, didn't your friend already jump ship and vanish?"

A brief pause

"So we're clear. We switch gears and close this case. We sweep away the dirt with a couple of strong strokes. My way."

He ends the call. He puts the phone on the table and stands up. The coffee is starting to brew. He returns to the kitchen with a hammer and a pair of scissors. He grabs the phone with his left hand and sends a message:

Proceed with the alternative plan.

He opens the phone cover, removes the SIM card, and cuts it in two with the scissors, setting the pieces aside. Then he wraps the phone in the cloth and strikes it four times, violently, with the hammer.

The coffee is ready.

172

28.

He's ready, wearing a light blue shirt and the same dark raincoat he wore last night. I've washed my face, neck, and armpits. I feel refreshed, but I don't like the smell of the soap. The clothes I'm wearing are old, but it doesn't matter. It's fine.

"Are we all set then?" He says enthusiastically.

"Yes, we're set."

A thunderclap explodes outside. The glass vibrates powerfully.

"Do you have an umbrella?" I don't have one, so I spread my hands to show him.

He walks ahead into the hallway.

"Listen, I've thought about it. I don't think it's a good idea for you to come in with me."

"What do you mean? I have to go in."

"Yes, that's clear. It's just that…" He walks into the living room and disappears from my sight.

"I absolutely have to go in." I don't understand what he means, and it irritates me.

He reappears, handing me a dark blue umbrella.

"I think this should work." He says, walking past me again. "But do you have any idea what he might have set aside for you? Even a vague one?"

"No, I have no idea at all." I don't need to think about it.

"So we're practically going in blind." He says loudly as he disappears into his room again.

I lean against the wall and sigh.

He emerges triumphantly from the hallway, holding his umbrella. He walks up to me and stands in front of me, also leaning against the wall.

"You've never been to the company, right?"

"No, never."

"Good." He pauses. "So, you don't even know where the offices are or anything."

"No."

"Okay. Listen closely. Marzio and the others went to great lengths to hide you. There has to be a reason for that. Clearly, it's about your safety. I can't think of anything else. But you have to get inside. So we need to come up with a way to sneak you in. Once inside, we'll search together for what he left you."

He gestures dramatically as he speaks, unlike yesterday.

He seems… excited.

"The plan is this. You'll come with me in the car, and we'll enter Prosud. It's raining, and there'll be a downpour."

A flash of lightning lights up the bedroom and living room doors. He raises a finger and exclaims "Right on cue! The way to get you inside is to hide you. You'll travel in the trunk of my car. It won't be comfortable, but it'll work. Once there, I'll come up with something with the guards, the rain, and the rest. They'll let me in. Once inside, I'll open the trunk, you'll get out, and head off on your own. We'll meet in Marzio's office, and together we'll search for what he left for you."

He watches me intently. I nod.

"I know, it's not the most refined plan in the world."

"The important thing is that it works."

"Exactly. The important thing is that it works. Listen carefully, the plant is built around a main road. Marzio's offices are on the left side of the road, in a two–story building. I'll park so you can get out of the trunk and head straight to the left, walk about fifty meters, and then get into the building."

He puts his hands in his pockets.

"You can't miss it." He says, showing me three sets of keys. "Listen carefully, these are the keys to Marzio's house. We'll leave them here, near your computer, we won't need them. "He clenches them in his left palm, then points to the other two sets. "This one has the keys to his office. I'm convinced there are other keys in here that open doors in Prosud. Keep it."

He takes the keyring between his index finger and thumb and hands it to me

"This other one…" He pauses. "I don't know what it opens, but it was his. It was in his car. So far, everything I've found there has been useful, so you should take this too."

He puts it in my hand and then gently closes my fingers over the keys, taking my hand between his. They're a bit rough

"If I'm late, start without me. Don't be afraid. We're almost there."

"I won't be afraid." It's become my mantra.

"Very well then, let's go."

"He heads to the door, and I follow."

"Where's your car?" I ask as he opens the door and gestures for me to go out.

"In the garage." He closes the door and locks it.

"You have a garage?" I'm surprised that a place like this has a garage.

"Yes, these are condos built in the seventies for police officers. After all sorts of changes and mix–ups, the garages stayed. I don't know how, but this house ended up with a garage. It's convenient for me because I use the service car, which is why I rented this place. It's not too expensive either."

174

We descend the stairs, him in the lead .

"There are also benefits for police officers, they deduct it directly from my paycheck. It's worth it."

We reach the small entrance hall leading to the closed park. The glass of the aluminum door is blurred by rain.

"Open the umbrella." He says before opening the door.

The wind and rain hit us, and we move toward it. He turns left, and we walk single file for about thirty meters before stopping.

"One drawback is that the garage opens manually!"

He shouts as the wind whistles through our hair, inserting the key into the lock at the center of the wide garage door. Above it, there's a handle. He twists it, then gives it a shove. The door moves a little, then returns to its resting position, pushed back by the wind. He tries again, harder, and the overhead door opens, rising to the ceiling. I step inside, all the way to the back of the garage, where the water doesn't reach.

The room is empty. On either side, shelves hold cardboard boxes spilling over with documents and odds and ends.

His umbrella is half–broken, and his hair is wet.

"Sorry, I left the car outside the park. I'll go get it and come back. Wait here."

I nod and watch him disappear into the rain. The wind swirls at the garage entrance, the door shakes and rattles, it seems fragile. I take a few steps back, afraid it might fall, pulled down by the gusts.

I'm alone. I lean against the back wall, shake the water off my small umbrella, and secure it with the strap. I wait, arms crossed, for him to return. I check the time. The morning is wearing on. I sigh. I don't like being here. I move closer to the door, leaning as far out as possible without getting wet. Outside, the rain makes everything hazy. But in the distance, I see a flashing yellow light. Squinting, I see something moving, maybe a gate opening. Behind it, there are two yellow headlights. The gate opens, and I see the car approaching. I step back as he pulls up and turns to reverse into the garage. I press against the shelves as the car slowly backs in.

It's a black Alfa 155 sedan. It passes in front of me. I see Marzio's head through the window. He's sitting on the back seat, gazing placidly ahead. The car moves further, and then there's him. Sitting in the front passenger seat, leaning toward me, grinning malevolently, baring his rotten teeth, and reaching a hand toward the window. I don't know if he's waving or trying to grab me, maybe both. I shake my head and look away. The commissioner has gotten out of the car. He's already soaked. He walks to the trunk and opens it. He starts emptying it, and I approach. I look inside. It's empty now, though it seems a bit dirty.

He gestures at it and shrugs.

I'll be in the dark inside.

I cross my arms. I have no other choice but to go in there, under this rain, toward Marzio. In the dark. Fine. I'll stay in the dark. And when I get out, I'll face the truth.

I sit inside, pull up my legs, and crouch down.

I see the policeman's face. His eyes are gentle.

"Don't worry. It won't take long to get there."

I nod, then stare into space. He gently lowers the trunk lid, gives it a firm push at the end, and it closes.

The sound of the rain is muffled. Distant. I'm here, curled up in the belly of this car. Once again, being transported.

I hear the car door close. The engine starts, faint but with vibrations that reach me here. I slip my left arm under my head and close my eyes. The car moves, then stops. The door opens, and the sound of rain becomes louder, drumming on the trunk above me. A few seconds pass, and then I hear the metallic sound of the garage door closing. The commissioner gets back in the car, and I feel the weight shift on the left suspension. He shuts the door and drives off.

"Everything okay back there?" He shouts from beyond the seats.

I take a deep breath and shout back.

"Yes!"

"Okay, let's go."

He shifts gears.

"Here we go." He says, but after a few meters, we stop again. I hear him shuffling papers and objects on the dashboard. "Damn remote." He mutters to himself.

Then he stops, perhaps finding it. I wait a little longer, and we're on the move again.

I keep my eyes closed. I try to breathe steadily, to relax, focusing on the sound of air passing through my nose. The bumps of the road distract me. I can't believe how many potholes there are on this road. It feels like we're driving on a dirt track. As time passes, I feel the grooves of the trunk pressing against my bones.

"I'm making a call." He says. I have nothing to say. I stay silent, focusing on my breath.

"Ventriglia? How are you? It's Cardona."

Another of the commissioner's friends.

"Hi, hi. Listen. I'm on my way to the company. I need a favor... yes, perfect. I need you to come to the company and let me in. Yes. I'll say I'm coming to see you. That you need to show me something. Yes. Yes, perfect. Listen, how long will it take you to get there?"

He pauses to listen.

"No, listen, I'm already in the car. I can go slow, but it won't take more than half an hour. Can you make it?" He asks, worried. "You have to make it. I need to do this now. I'll explain later. No, no, nothing special. I just need to figure something out. Quick stuff, not more than half an hour. Yes, okay, fine, got it. Yes. Okay. See you later. Make sure you get there first. Yes, bye."

The conversation ends. The car is moving less now, taking a long left curve. I'm pushed toward the side of the car. I hold onto the felt lining the dark space that envelops me to keep from slipping. The curve ends, and the commissioner shifts gears. He accelerates.

"We're getting on the highway. I called a friend. He worked with Marzio, knows him well. He'll help us get in. It'll take about half an hour to get to the plant. It's pouring, so we can't drive too fast."

"Okay." I reply curtly.

He's right, the sound of rain hitting above me has taken on a darker tone. It feels like drops of lead, pounding down. Now the dull whistle of the wind joins in. I keep breathing. Each breath feels endless, my belly expands, and my chest swells. I inhale until it hurts, then a bit more, and I exhale with my belly, pushing the diaphragm up, emptying my lungs. I do it once, then again, and again. Each time, I feel my eyes grow lighter, my sense of self stepping back, away from my body, each time a little lighter. The noises fade, and I drift away from here. I enter a dark but comforting room, warm. The sound of rain is like a hypnotic lullaby. I no longer feel my body, and my consciousness becomes weaker, calmer, relaxed, undisturbed. A placid lake. And it stays that way with each breath. Until everything becomes soft. I settle into this pleasant drowsiness. Each breath is an eternity. I see figures and faces forming behind my closed eyelids, I see smiles, fluid shapes of shifting colors, dancing in a black cauldron like a graceful ballet. Sometimes I see a pair of familiar eyes, familiar features, I see home, the room. The bed, the dishes, and the food, his smile, my peace. The windows and the sun. She's there too, Cardia's daughter, outside on the balcony, which is a huge terrace full of flowers overlooking the blue sea. We have breakfast together. He spreads jam on my croissant. He's wearing a shirt with the collar up, concentrating on the knife. His knife. No one speaks. There's soft music in the background. Then we all raise our arms and open our mouths in joy as the roller coaster car takes a sharp left and sends us into a loop. My hair flies away, obscuring my face. I can't see anything. Everything is black. I hear him shouting with joy. And again, we go up and then down. He holds my hand, with the other I try to push my hair away from my face, but I can't, they're stuck and tangled, thick, too many. I really want to see his happy face, screaming with joy with me, and I try again to see, but the more I touch the hair, the more it tangles, around my face, around my neck, around my chest. I squeeze, and they hold me still. I grab scissors, afraid of blinding myself, but I want to see him. I

177

slide the blade in, I'm scared, and I cut. Something falls, and I see a little light. Again the blade goes in, I cut, and I bleed, my cheek is torn, but it's only superficial, so again and again, each cut strips away my skin, the hair is bloody, my cheeks red, I cut and free myself, I push the hair from my face, and the room is dark. The jester's face is next to mine. He's looking at me, laughing with his mouth wide open. It's huge, dark, and empty. I feel like I'm being swallowed by it. He puts his hand on my shoulder, pulls me up to him, squeezes, and laughs, laughing like a demon.

I jolt back and hit the back seat. My eyes are open, gasping. Everything around me is dark. Just like in the dream. But now I hear the rain beating on the metal above me. My hands touch the felt lining this cell. The car has stopped. We've arrived, I tell myself. Stay calm. You'll be out soon.

The car door opens, and someone gets in.

"We're in. They're letting us through." It's the commissioner's voice. – I'll park, and then I'll leave the trunk open. Wait a few seconds and then get out. Okay?

"Okay." I say loudly.

We keep moving. Then the car slows and turns left.

"Walk along the walls. Don't get noticed."

We stop.

He turns off the engine and gets out. The rain still falls heavily on us. I hear the automatic lock of the trunk release. I see a sliver of light.

"Commissioner." Calls a distant voice, the sliver of light closes again.

"Yes?" The voices are distant, the rain makes it hard to hear what they're saying.

"I told you, Ventriglia isn't here yet."

"So what?"

"Commissioner, I can't let you wander around the plant alone. It's dangerous, I can't allow it."

"And what do you suggest?"

"You have to leave, commissioner."

"Leave? I just got here."

"I'm sorry, but I can't let you stay."

"Fine, I'll come with you to the gatehouse and wait for Ventriglia there. Okay?"

"And the car can't stay here." Says the guard.

"You're soaking me to the bone, we'll move the car later. Open the door."

The commissioner's voice fades. I hear them talking, but I can't understand what they're saying. Then the sound of an engine accelerating and moving away.

I exhale the tension. I raise my hand and lightly push the trunk lid. It moves. I see light.

My heart races. Maybe I should wait here a bit longer. Give them time to reach the gatehouse. The air coming through the crack is fresh. It fills my lungs. I feel the need to get out of here. I push the lid open further and lean out to see. There's a figure moving in the distance. A car. I can't see much. The rain is heavy.

I pull up my hood. I go.

I open the trunk and climb out. My legs are trembling. I close the trunk, shove my hands into my pockets, and lower my head. I head left, just as he told me, watching my feet alternate in front of me. My shoes are getting wet. The muscles in my legs are sore but gradually loosen with each step. I haven't opened the umbrella. I'm afraid of being noticed. To the left, I see a two–story building approaching. It must be the one the commissioner mentioned. I quicken my pace and reach the door, there's a covered corner where the rain doesn't reach, or at least not as much. The door is made of gray aluminum, with the word 'Prosud' written on the glass. Inside, it's dark. My fingers touch the keys. I pull the sets from my pocket and look at them for a moment. Then I look at the door.

The left door doesn't have a lock, and neither does the right.

I look around and see that there's a magnetic card reader with a keypad to the right, but again, no lock where I can try my keys. Panic sets in. I look up and see a camera pointing at me. There's a red light under the lens. It's recording.

I press myself against the wall, trying to avoid being caught on camera. I turn my back to it. I don't know what to do.

I see the cursed demon a few steps away from me. He's watching, hunched over, rubbing his hands together. He grins. I can't stand it. He disturbs me. I can't stay here much longer. I look across the street. There's a figure standing there, watching me. I squint, trying to focus, but it's hard to see clearly from here.

The rain eases for a moment. The watery veil between us thins, and I can finally make out his shape. It's Marzio. He's on the other side of the street, watching me. And suddenly, he turns left and starts walking.

He grabs my hand and squeezes it.

His skin is rough, scaly. It feels like it could crumble at any moment.

"He's happy, you know?"

His voice is shrill and unpleasant. I had almost forgotten it. Hearing it again sends deep shivers down my spine. All the awful sensations of these past days return. Nausea knots my stomach. I try to pull my hand away, but he grips it tightly. And he squeezes even harder when I try to shake him off. He points.

"He's going, he's going!" He says excitedly, shaking his finger at Marzio, who's walking quickly.

I have to follow him.

I move into the rain. One hand in my pocket, the other in the demon's grip. He's heavy, I feel him dragging me down. I feel my shoulder being pulled toward the ground, but I walk quickly. And he comes with me. I can't quite understand how I manage to keep moving; I feel bent in half, leaning to one side, but my balance holds. I follow Marzio. He's on the other side of the street. I follow without crossing, not yet. The rain grows heavier again, and even with my hood pulled tight, it seeps into my collar, soaking my hair. The drops are heavy, falling fast, each one a sharp sting. At the end of the road there are metal structures, tanks nestled within them, surrounded by shiny pipes coiling like snakes, winding between tall pillars and blooming atop the round cylindrical heads. They look like needles plunged into fingertips, sucking the lifeblood from a patient no longer visible, enveloped by the machines keeping him suspended in midair. There are crosswalks, and I cross them.

The steel monster looms closer. Marzio is in front of me, about twenty meters away. I fall in behind him. He heads straight for a large metal tower. It rises before me, and I almost hear a murmur in my ears, reminding me to show respect. It feels like I'm approaching a temple dedicated to some pagan deity of iron and water. Each idol is guarded here within. Iron gargoyles standing watch on the sides are shadows cast on the balconies, extending meters beyond the frames, to protect the treasures within. I approach the structure's legs. They are thick, wide, set deep into the concrete and bolted with bolts as wide as three fingers. Rust drips washed away by the rain like blood. Inside. Here the shadow is even darker, the rain is only a sound behind my back. I shake the water from my shoulders, pulling my hood back.

Marzio is in front of me, closer now. He has his back to me, continues to walk among the silent machinery. The lights are dim. Large round electric motors lie lifeless, pipes coiling from their ends to form strange geometries. It looks like everything here has been built, disassembled, and rebuilt again. Some pipes are old and rusty, while others shine with new life, untouched. He moves quickly between these sculptures, leading me into its heart. Where it's darkest. There's a metal staircase. It descends into a dark pit. I see him disappear into it.

I follow, placing my foot on the first step, and feel the demon's hand pulling me back. Away from there. I can't stop. I step down the first stair and take him with me. The dim light from the surface fades after a few meters. I pull out my phone and light the way. At the bottom of the stairs, there's a button emitting a faint red glow. I reach it and press it. Some neon lights flicker on, illuminating the narrow pit. My feet are on a steel grate. I look down through it but see nothing, just darkness. I raise my eyes, searching for Marzio. He's not there. Around me, concrete walls, light gray. I can still see the marks of the wooden boards that held them in place during the pour. Just above my head, a bundle of pipes spreads across the ceiling, snaking into every crevice.

Out of the corner of my eye, I see movement to my left. There's Marzio, slipping through an opening. I follow, my footsteps on the grate make a dull noise that's quickly absorbed by the concrete walls. There's no echo. Who knows how deep this pit goes. I reach the opening where I saw Marzio disappear and step into it.

Darkness again. The demon's hand slides up my forearm, wrapping itself under my elbow. It grips tightly. His fingers are cold and long. In the distance, I see a faint red light. It looks like the button I pressed earlier. I keep walking. There's a handrail, I brush it with my hand to guide myself in the right direction. The last bits of light from the opening behind me fade away. Now I only look toward the button. Above me, the pipes run in the same direction. They're made of iron, some are wet, dripping. The heavy sound of my footsteps echoes. I keep brushing the handrail, remembering to breathe. Deeply, deeply. I reach out, touch the button, and the red light disappears. A new set of neon lights flicker. To my left, there's another set of stairs. I can see it because at the bottom, a neon lamp lights up the last few steps. Marzio must have gone this way. I descend the stairs, one step at a time, counting them. I reach the bottom. The staircase is narrow, only wide enough for one person at a time. Nine steps. Once again, I'm standing on a grate. This is a narrow corridor, no more than sixty centimeters wide, with iron railings on both sides. I can't see the bottom beyond my feet or the walls beside me. I inhale. My legs are like marble. My face, stone. The air stops inside me, unable to escape.

His hand grips tightly. The thumb digs into my armpit, and the four fingers wrap around the head of my humerus. He pulls back, and I bend my shoulder to the right and then down. Pain. I groan between my teeth. It hurts, he wants to tear my arm off. Beyond, I can see nothing.

Nothing.

But Marzio passed through here.

I take a step. Then another, and another. Around me, everything is dark. The only sound is me, trembling with fear in the air. One centimeter at a time. On a path that seems endless. I walk, and the light behind me fades, I can't see anything, I guide myself by the hand on the metal, not to stumble, I could fall, a shiver runs through me, it could overtake me then, one step after another, I am here. How much farther I must walk, I don't know. I am alone here. I want to turn back and see how far I've come, but I'm afraid I won't see the light that brought me here anymore. Lord, what have I done? Where am I? Where am I going? Marzio, where have you taken me? Where are you?

The darkness is total.

I stop. I slip my hand into my pocket, take out my phone. I activate it and raise it in front of me, trying to shed light on this deep darkness.

I see nothing. Only the long steel walkway I'm standing on, I don't see walls, I don't see the bottom of this pit. I look up. There are shadows of pipes, I can't see them clearly, but they seem enormous, at least two or three meters in diameter, above me, the fingers of a giant crossing perpendicularly over the path I'm following.

Where am I?

The grip tightens, stronger, more violent. I'm shaken, and I lose my balance, I grab onto the handrail to keep from falling, and there I see my phone fall, its blue light fading into a distant dot in this darkness.

I scream in despair with all the breath I have in me and reach out toward it, but it's useless. It's falling. I am here. Crying and screaming in terror, the terror that comes from my gut, a dagger twisted and turned to tear me apart. The light vanishes. Only emptiness remains, and my choked scream becomes a soft sob. A distant echo, bouncing off walls I don't know where. I hear no other sounds besides my own. I am only fear and brokenness. Broken deep within my soul.

A whistle of wind brushes my skin. And a rustle in my ears. I open my eyes, filled with fear. My heart races wildly. I want to stay here, but I'm afraid, I want to move forward, but I'm afraid. I feel the walkway shift, a dull sound, a low wave spreading through the metal and air. Like a call, a warning to tell me I cannot stop.

I exhale all the air trapped in my throat. I can't stay here. I have to move forward, or I'll fall, into the abyss, with this metal pulling me down.

I take a step forward. I move. Then another, as if I'm limping, then another. The first step is the hardest. Then I find my rhythm. And I keep going like this. I close my eyes. I cry silently. In my darkness. At least that belongs to me. My hand guides me. It brushes the metal handrail lightly, without really touching it, leading me in a straight line toward an unknown destination.

Oh, Marzio.

I think of you and see your face. How I wish I could hold you now, my love. How I wish you were here. So we could do this together.

I press my lips together until they disappear, they burn. I open my eyes, they're red.

I take my left hand off the handrail for a moment and wipe my eyes with my wrist. I sob.

I look down. I can't even see my feet. Then I look up.

I open my mouth. I can't believe it.

There's a light up ahead, faint. But it's there, I see it. It's in front of me. I feel a tiny sprout of joy bloom.

"Marzio?" I whisper softly.

"Marzio?" The echo responds in the same tone. Then again, and again, dissolving into the void.

The walkway sways as if something hit it hundreds of meters away.

I move toward the light, my steps steady.

The light keeps getting closer. I can see it more clearly now. It's a naval–type lamp, oval in shape, with a metal grille protecting the domed glass. The light it emits is warm, yellow. It's mounted above a narrow green wooden door. Surrounding it is a large concrete wall; I can't make out anything else. I'm getting closer, there's a rectangular landing at the end of the walkway. The door is right in front of me, but the landing continues for another meter to the left. I'm close. Just a few more steps.

I reach it, there's one last step between the walkway and the landing.

I step down.

I'm on the landing. I hear the sound of rushing water, like a river approaching a waterfall and then plunging down. It gurgles and then explodes. A distant roar. It comes from the left.

I look at the door. The knob is round. It's brass, yellow, I touch it. It's warm. Almost like gold. I turn it, and the door opens. I step inside.

The light is on. I close the door behind me. A large pipe blocks my view of the room, supported by an L–shaped iron bracket. I have to crouch to get around it.

The room is small. To the left is a desk, with its short side against the wall. There's a blank sheet of paper with a pen on top of it. There's also a candle, its flame tall and thin. It burns quietly, and its warm light fills the room with soft tones.

To the right are some filing cabinets, made of wood, painted green, lighter than the door. They protrude from the wall. Each has three drawers.

In front of me is Marzio. The color of his skin is warmer than what I've become accustomed to seeing in these recent days. He still doesn't show any emotion, but at least now… at least now he doesn't seem dead. I don't know if it's because I'm happy to be here, seeing him, or if it's the candlelight enchanting me. He stands motionless. His gaze is still lost in the void, as always. Behind him, I see a painting. The wooden frame is simple, smooth, and entirely black. At the top, in the center, there's a tiny glowing dot. A star in the cosmic void.

Behind the desk, there's a wooden chair with a curved, worn backrest. Further back, there's a small hallway leading to another door. I see another pipe, one that would require you to crouch to get through.

My gaze returns to Marzio.

He's looking at me.

I feel the other arm wrap around my waist. I feel its legs pressing against mine, and its weight bearing down on me. It squeezes and climbs. The right hand is on my shoulder. It tightens and climbs higher. I feel pain. The weight is too much, but I look at Marzio. His gaze is so gentle. Anything could happen to me now. Anything at all. I'd be happy. My Marzio. My Marzio is here.

I see him move, his arm... his arm lifts. His index finger points to his side, to my right.

Is there something I need to see, Marzio? Is this why I'm here? Is this what you wanted?

He stares at me and points to his left side. He's pointing at something I can't see.

I take a step forward. He's pointing beyond the filing cabinets. I still can't see, so I take another step. I get close to the desk. He's moved to the left and keeps pointing there.

I lean past the last cabinet.

Down below is a green metal cube. The surface looks painted, matte. I get closer. There's a dial with numbers around it and another concentric dial with a slot to insert a finger and turn it. Beside it, there's a keyhole. It's a safe, a heavy–duty one. Very heavy. I slip my hands into my pockets and grab the keyrings.

Of the two, only one has a long key that might fit in the keyhole. The keychain has the symbol of a zodiac sign.

I bend down, I have to kneel to insert the key.

The demon is at my neck, squeezing in a deadly embrace. I feel his cold skin pressing against my right ear.

"We're here." He says.

His lips brush against my ear, they're dry. Harsh. Rough.

"How many things will we find? How many toys did the child leave us? They'll be our toys. Our toys. We'll play with them forever."

The key slides fully into the lock. I try to turn it, and it turns. The mechanism makes a noise. It seems like it hasn't been opened in a long time, but the key turns easily in the lock. I make a full turn until the key returns to its starting position.

The door opens. I pull it toward me by the keyring.

Inside, there are papers. Ochre–colored sheets. I gather them up.

It's a file inside a folder. On the cover, there's 'UF–11' written in block letters. It's Marzio's handwriting. I open it. There are diagrams, formulas, and calculations. There's data on chemical composition and the production process. Is this your work, Marzio? Is this what you wanted to leave behind? I close the folder. There's another sheet beneath it. I take it and place it on top.

It's handwritten, in his cursive. I recognize it.

I, Marzio Solimena, in full possession of my mental faculties, hereby declare my sole and exclusive heir to all...

I stop.

I can't read anymore. Tears fill my eyes. I bring my hand to my mouth and sob once again.

"I don't want all of this. I just want you. I just want to stay with you."

I get up and try to turn around, the weight I carry on my shoulders is too heavy. It's such a struggle. I bend under the burden. I can't see Marzio's face.

"Let's stay here, let's stay here for a while. Let's talk. Let's be together. Tell me how you feel, like we always did. Let's stay together. Please. Time flies when it's just you and me, doesn't it, my love? An eternity could be nothing if spent with you. I'm not afraid now. I just want you. I don't want to go back up. Not without you. My love."

"Beautiful words. But now step away from there and give me what you found."

I startle. I turn abruptly. At the door stands a tall man. Blonde. His long hair is wet, hanging to his neck. His soaked gray sweater clings heavily to his shoulders, and his dark jeans are drenched. He holds a pair of pliers in his hand. His arm extended toward me, he gestures for me to give him the documents.

"Who are you?" My voice chokes in my throat. The weight of the demon presses heavily on my shoulders. I gasp.

"A friend of Marzio. Give me the papers."

I step back.

"Bullshit."

"Listen, bitch. I've already taken care of your pig cop. Now it's just you left. Give me the papers, and I promise it'll be quick and painless."

He steps forward.

I keep moving back. I feel the safe press against my knees, I can't retreat any further.

He comes closer. His face twisted with rage.

"It's here, close now. He wants you." The demon's voice hisses in my ears. Surprised, with a hint of disappointment.

The man keeps advancing. The deep lines around his mouth carve black furrows. The light casts sharp shadows over his brow. His eyes dark pits beneath them.

He circles the desk. He's close. I glance around. I could jump over the desk. I could run for the door.

He's right on me, Marzio beside him, his gaze lost in the void.

It's over. I raise my left hand to shield my face, clutching Marzio's will and the project's formulas to my chest with my right. My legs buckle.

"Oh my God."

It'll end like this. Like a sob in the dark.

It's not fair. It's not fair. Not after coming this far. So close to justice for you, my love. You don't deserve this. You don't deserve to be forgotten like this.

The blonde man raises his arm. The pliers glint in the air. He's coming.

I look up. My final goodbye to my love. I'm coming back to you. Finally.

He grunts, flexing his arm to gather strength. He aims for my head. I close my eyes in fear.

Every muscle tenses. Mortal tension.

A sharp blow to the back of my head. I feel the bone shift against the others. My skull vibrates. Everything spins around me, and the drum beats a violent march against my eardrums. I'm spinning, I'm about to fall. I feel wetness. I bring my hand to my head, then to my eyes. There's blood, red blood, fresh blood. My knees bend involuntarily, I go down.

The blonde man in front of me, his hand raised to the sky again, the expression of animal fury on his face.

"Oh." The jester whispers in my ears, surprised. "If that's what you want. Go on."

The man's arm pulls back, one last strike ready for me. My head spins. I can't understand. My thoughts whirl chaotically. Control over reality slips away. I feel my senses abandoning me. His hand, his outstretched hand. The blurred figure of Marzio beside him. I think I'm afraid now. My eyes close, as if a gentle hand has been placed on my forehead.

An electric explosion, glass shattering. I feel it on my face, my head. It falls on me.

I open my eyes, jolted awake as if from a nightmare.

Marzio's hand is raised. He's gripping the man's wrist. The man struggles, terrified. The lamp flickers. White flashes in the night.

"What the hell is this?" He screams.

Marzio's eyes are open. They glow with white light. The lamp goes out. His eyes are the only thing illuminating the room. The profile of the blonde man. His hooked nose. He brings his other hand to his wrist, trying to free himself. Marzio stands still, like a pillar of steel. The man doesn't see him, writhing like a venomous snake.

"Is this our game? Our toy."

The jester's voice is a sharp hiss in my ears.

"You didn't want me to touch him, did you? Yet he gave himself to me, piece by piece. To save you? How important are you? Do you even know?"

Marzio, no, what have you done? What have you sacrificed? I'm afraid. I can't afford to lose you. But I have no strength. I remain still, a helpless spectator. I hate myself. Images spin around, madly.

"It's inevitable, child. We are all slaves. Evil doesn't take us. It pervades us. We are made of it. So delicious." The monstrous voice booms in my ears, only I can hear it. "The unnecessary must be eliminated. The relics you call humanity, love, just illusions. Accept me, for I am the truth."

No. I can't accept that. How much evil has taken you, how much has consumed you, my love. More than I can bear, more than I can understand. I know now. The same fear gripping my heart now. Wrapping me like a cloak of thorns. I wanted to be with you. In every moment you were alone, scared. To heal your pain with mine, to find refuge in each other. It hurts, like walking barefoot on broken glass. But I know it would have taken us where we wanted. Where we deserved. Our home.

"As you wish, foolish girl. I'll show you the substance, then. And you'll decide, in the end, what's to be believed."

My shoulders are free. On the desk, the jester advances. Slowly. His long arms dangle at his sides, attached to his stocky body. He approaches the man, who continues to thrash violently, trying to free himself.

The jester places a hand on his shoulder.

The man freezes and turns.

His scream of terror fills the room. I cover my ears.

The jester leaps onto him, wrapping himself around his neck.

The room shakes violently, as if struck by an earthquake. My side hits the edge of the desk, and a sharp pain stabs into my flesh. Another tremor causes the filing cabinets to open. Dust puffs out from the papers now exposed to the light. I see Marzio on the other side of the desk. The star in the painting behind him shines intensely. I look at it. It stings my eyes. I hear footsteps outside the door. Heavy footsteps. Advancing. With each step, the room shakes. I'm afraid.

The man collapses to the ground. The demon is on him. His scream is cut short. His back arches in a spasm of pain and terror. The jester raises his hands to the sky, as if in a blasphemous prayer.

Then everything goes silent. We fall back into the darkest black.

And yet.

And yet, his breath is near.

Hands tighten around my neck, squeezing, squeezing until I can't breathe. With one hand I try to loosen the grip with the other I reach out toward where I think Marzio is. But he's too far away. I can't reach him. The weight pushes me back. I'm scared. I hear the wind blow hard, like a door suddenly opened and a cold gust of death rushed in. I'm afraid. I hear papers fly from the cabinets, scattering away. Terror grips me. I can't stay here, the walls will collapse. Marzio will die, I will die, it will all be over.

I crawl backward and turn

The weight on my shoulders

A single effort.

I stand with all my strength.

I try, and I feel him climbing with me. Pressing on my chest.

"I'm hungry, my love."

I scream. I can't bear the demon's voice inside me.

Everything spins, and the drum beats of my heart a violent march against my eardrums.

I am spinning, I'm about to fall. I bring my hand to my head, then in front of my eyes. There's only black. I look toward the door I came through. I only know it's open, but it's far away. I can't see anything.

I can't see anything.

29.

Ventriglia enters the guardhouse, accompanied by a gust of wind that flips the umbrella in his hand. He closes the door and greets the others.

The commissioner is bent over the reception counter. He stops chatting with the guard and turns to the technician, who is trying to fix his umbrella.

"Ventrì, took you long enough." He says mockingly.

The technician glances at him sideways, trying to shoot him a dirty look, but gives up once he manages to close the umbrella.

"I made it, didn't I?" He points to the door "Shall we go?"

The commissioner moves away from the counter as the guard calls out to Ventriglia.

"Doctor, your badge." He reminds him.

Ventriglia steps back and walks past the commissioner.

"You're right." He says, pulling the badge out of his coat pocket and passing it over the magnetic reader, which beeps. "Now we can go." He says to the commissioner.

They make a run for the car. The rain is pouring, and the commissioner can't help but get soaked. He left his broken umbrella with the guard, but by now, a few more drops don't make much difference.

"You're drenched, Commissioner." Ventriglia says as he starts the car.

Cardona runs a hand through his wet hair and shakes it.

"It's not a big deal" He mutters.

"Where are we headed?"

"Let's go to your place." He points forward to indicate the direction.

"Research and Development offices?"

The policeman nods.

The gate lifts, and the car enters the plant.

"We'll park right by the door, right? So we don't get even more soaked."

"How long do we need to stay?"

"An hour, two at most."

Ventriglia grimaces, then checks his watch. He keeps driving.

"Is someone here?" He gestures toward the commissioner's Alfa.

No, no. That's my car. They let me in earlier, then made me leave. They're a bit strange around here.

"Just a little." The man at the wheel replies. "Let's do this, Commissioner. I'll park next to yours so no one complains about yours."

"As you wish."

Ventriglia parks the car.

"I'll get the umbrella for you."

"Don't worry, I'll run for it."

Cardona opens the door, stands up, and dashes toward the office entrance. He's careful not to slip, watching where he steps. The rainwater flowing down the sides of the road has become a torrent. He reaches the entrance and stops. He takes off his coat and pulls out his notepad and pen. He's completely drenched and feels the need to dry off.

Ventriglia arrives with his umbrella, which is still struggling against the wind. He approaches the magnetic reader and offers it his badge. The doors open, and they enter.

The commissioner eyes his Alfa; the trunk is closed. She must have gotten out. Everything should have gone well. He exhales, a smile spreading across his lips. He glances upward. Across the street, he sees a man in jeans and a sweater, holding a large blue umbrella. But the man is completely drenched, as if he had rolled in the mud. Blonde, with long, soaked hair hanging down his neck. In his hand, he's holding a pair of pliers. The man realizes he's being watched and quickly walks away.

"Who's that?" The commissioner asks Ventriglia.

The technician turns and squints, watching the figure disappear into the rain.

"I don't know, maybe someone from maintenance?" He replies.

"In jeans and a sweater?"

"Maybe they called him in for an emergency?"

"Does that happen often?"

"Commissioner, let's go inside and talk about it. Out here, we're getting soaked."

Ventriglia sets the umbrella down on the floor, and the commissioner does the same with his coat.

"Commissioner, wait. Bring your coat, and I'll take it to the office. We'll put it over a convector to dry."

Cardona nods, picks it up, and follows the technician to his office. They walk down the corridor, looking around. It's empty. No wet footprints on the floor. Cardona whistles as if to call someone. No response.

"You whistle, Commissioner?" Ventriglia asks curiously.

"Sometimes. Is no one here on Saturdays?"

"Rarely. And it's a quiet period. There's no reason for these offices to stay open on Saturdays."

"How many people are usually in the plant on Saturdays?"

"It depends on the production lines. Right now, we're only producing five days a week. The market is slow. So there's just some maintenance staff and the emergency crew, but the personnel is kept to a minimum. It's different when we're running three shifts, seven days a week. Then the plant is alive day and night. It never stops. But it's always pretty calm here."

They reach his office door. He opens it, and they enter. Ventriglia approaches a white plastic convector to the left of the door and turns it on. Then he brings the coat rack closer to the warm air.

"Put your coat here." He says, fiddling with the controls "Some warm air will come out now."

The commissioner does as instructed, then walks over to the desk and sits down. Ventriglia follows suit, sitting on the opposite side of the desk.

"So, are you going to tell me what we're doing here?"

The commissioner coughs, pulls a cigarette pack from his pants pocket, and puts a cigarette to his mouth.

"Can I smoke?"

"You're the boss."

He lights it.

"I came to check something out. I'm close."

"Close? Close to solving it?"

Cardona nods. He takes a long drag, and the cigarette's tip glows brightly. "Where's the bathroom?"

"Go out of here, right down the hall, just before the stairs."

The policeman gets up and leaves the office. He walks down the corridor, reaches the stairs, but instead of going to the bathroom, he climbs the steps. He arrives on the first floor. There are still no wet footprints on the floor. He whistles again, but once more, there's no response. He sighs.

"It's me, where are you?" He says softly, but no one answers. "Are you here? It's Cardona!" He says, raising his voice.

The only sound in the hallway is the rain hitting the roof and walls. All the doors are closed. No one is here.

He walks briskly toward Marzio's office. When he reaches the door, he knocks three times.

"It's Cardona. The commissioner. I'm alone. Open up."

But no one opens. A look of disappointment crosses his face.

"Where the hell are you?" He asks the door.

His phone vibrates in his pocket. He pulls it out and looks at the display.

"What do you want, Cesarano?" He snaps.

"Commissioner, where are you?"

"Minding my own business, why?"

"Commissioner, I'm at the station. Prisco's here looking for you. He's going nuts."

"What do you mean he's going nuts?"

"Commissioner… he's going nuts, shouting about you, saying all sorts of things. You'd better come here. You'd better hurry, trust me."

"As far as I'm concerned, he can go to hell. That guy's an idiot."

"Commissioner, come. Before we have more drama on top of what's already brewing. He's really serious about this."

Cardona sighs. He scratches his chin and rests his hand on his hip.

"Commissioner?" Cesarano sounds genuinely worried.

"I'm coming. I'll get in the car and head over. I'll be there in half an hour."

He hangs up and heads back downstairs to Ventriglia's office. The technician is sitting at his computer, his face illuminated by the pale glow of the monitor. The policeman grabs his coat from the rack.

"Don't say anything, I need to step out for a bit. Can you wait for me here?"

"Where are you going, Commissioner?" Ventriglia asks, surprised.

"I'll be back soon, meeting someone quickly and then I'll return."

"What can I say? Go ahead, I'll be here. I had some things to finish on the computer anyway."

"I need to tell you something before I leave."

"Go ahead, Commissioner."

"I didn't come here alone today."

"What?"

"A colleague came with me. Young, blonde, in her twenties. She was in the car, but I sent her ahead while I waited for you in the guardhouse. No one knows she's here."

"But why, Commissioner?"

"We're looking for some important documents that could shed light on Marzio's death. It's important that she works undercover. I've been trying to find her around here, but I don't see her. Maybe she couldn't get in without a badge. While I'm gone, I'd like you to look for her, or at least leave the doors open so she can enter if she comes back."

"Alright, I'll leave the doors open and take a walk through the accessible areas."

The commissioner nods in thanks, grabs his coat, and leaves quickly. The commissioner gives a quick salute, takes his coat, and leaves in a hurry.

He reaches the door, opens it, and steps back into the rain.

He runs to avoid getting soaked, but it's useless. He's drenched within a few meters. He turns the corner and heads toward his Alfa. He unlocks it with the remote and jumps inside.

On the seat, he struggles out of his coat and throws it onto the seat beside him. He starts the car, turns on the wipers, and reverses onto the main road of the industrial complex.

His phone vibrates again.

It's a message from Olivieri.

Something's wrong: Concrete Works closed its last two balance sheets with a loss of €15 million. Guess who CW's client is? CHEMIT!

Cardona glances at the road, finding himself in the middle of the lane. He steers back to the right, passing by the burned engineering building.

Ventriglia's words come back to him:

'Ground floor, Engineering. First floor, Administration.'

He stops at the guardhouse, gets out of the car, and walks inside.

"Here's your badge." He hands it to the guard over the counter.

You need to check out.

The commissioner leans over the magnetic sensor, which emits its sound, then returns to the counter.

"Thanks, goodbye." The guard collects the badge without looking at the commissioner, who turns to leave.

First–floor administration. Marzio moved there. Invoices and various documents.

He stops. He turns back to the counter and pulls a photo from the inside pocket of his coat. He folds it in half and shows it to the guard.

"Excuse me, just curious, do you know this girl?"

The guard is surprised. He looks at the commissioner blankly. Then the commissioner waves the photo in front of his face.

"Do you know her?" He asks brusquely.

The guard looks at the commissioner's hands. He squints, opens his mouth, then closes it again.

"Yes, I know her, she's Camille, the intern from the finance and administration department. But I haven't seen her for a while. Maybe she's sick. Why?"

"Thanks."

"Is she connected to the investigation?" The guard asks.

The commissioner is already outside the guardhouse and back in his car. The gate is open, and he pulls out onto the highway.

He accelerates, phone in hand, selects the number, and calls.

"Hello, Commissioner."

"Explain this to me clearly."

Olivieri laughs heartily.

"Well, it's not entirely clear to me either, but I managed to get my hands on the financial statements of the two companies Ligresti controls. And there's something really off. Listen, Concrete Works buys additives from Prosud, they buy a ton. Like, a lot. They should be using them to mix into their cement, right?"

"Yes."

"Except that Concrete Works doesn't make cement. They're supposed to do civil engineering works. I say 'supposed to' because they haven't done any civil works in the past two years. They barely have any contracts."

"So what are they buying additives for?"

"The commissioner reaches the highway ramp, accelerating toward the city. The rain pounds down, and he sets the wipers to maximum speed. The noise is so loud that he tries to raise the volume on his phone call, but it's already maxed out."

"And here's where it gets interesting. One of the company's biggest clients in the past two years, guess who it is?"

"ChemIt?"

"ChemIt! From what I'm reading, they're selling them excess additives as waste material."

"What the hell are you saying?"

"And then ChemIt sells raw materials to Prosud."

"It's a feedback loop!" Cardona growls, a mix of surprise, excitement, and anger.

"I haven't quite figured it all out yet, but I think it's a system to hide profits."

"To inflate the company's apparent value."

"That too, but I need to think about it for a bit." The journalist pauses for a moment, then continues "Commissioner, listen to this. You really need to hear this."

"Go on."

Olivieri laughs again.

"So, Concrete Works, based in Germany, with German clients, German workers, etc., etc., was working up until two years ago, doing good work too. Then something changed, they switched direction. Listen: they laid off eighty percent of the staff. And do you know what happened two years ago?"

"No."

"Don't you want to guess?" Olivieri's voice has a mischievous tone.

"I want you to tell me."

"Two years ago, Lunar Finance acquired majority control of Concrete Works!"

"There it is."

"There we have it!"

They both fall silent. The car races along the wet road. The asphalt is empty. He's the only one on the road. Everyone else is at home, getting ready for lunch.

I understand it all now. Thanks. I'll get back to you later for updates.

"Come on, Commissioner, this stuff needs to be published immediately. Tomorrow we'll release a small article."

"No way. I said Monday, and it'll be Monday."

"Come on, Commissioner, do the right thing!"

"We'll talk later."

He ends the call and throws the phone onto the passenger seat.

The way is clear now. The flood has broken the banks.

"It's done." He slams his fist against the steering wheel.

He searches for his pen and notebook, they're in his coat, but it's too hard to grab them and write while driving, so he changes his mind, grabs his phone again, finds the voice memo function, and starts speaking into the microphone.

"It's clear. There was a struggle, a power struggle. Something that's been brewing for years. The brothers didn't get along? Doesn't matter. One of them started it, probably…"

He reflects for a moment.

"The older brother, took control, managed things. The younger one grew up with Cardia backing him. The father must have known or suspected something, that's why he gave him veto power. And so, the younger brother grows under Cardia's wing. He distances himself from the family. The mother adores the older brother. How long has the younger one been out of the house? He meets a girl, settles down. But something doesn't add up. He talks to Cardia. There are strange financial movements. Papers he doesn't have access to, and the explanations he gets don't satisfy him. There's the 2008 financial crisis, everything stops. The company doesn't go into emergency mode? Is it a safe haven?"

The commissioner speaks quickly, never pausing

"The revenue streams keep flowing because they're playing the game of selling to Concrete Works, which resells to ChemIt, which resells to ProSud. He senses something is wrong. I don't know, but the idea holds, and he's in too deep. Things get darker. His doubts grow, and he doesn't know what to do. His brother. The brother isn't trustworthy. Marzio doesn't believe him. He feels like he's being cut out. The power is shifting against him. The mother sides with the older brother. Marzio needs to understand. He needs to study, to dig deeper. So, in agreement with Cardia, they infiltrate someone into the administrative office. It's his illegitimate daughter. The one in the photo. She lives in Paris but comes here out of love for her father. He gets her hired as an intern in the finance and administration department, so she can get inside and find what he needs. He moves to engineering, which puts him closer to her, giving them more freedom to move. She does it, she gets the documents and hands them to him. Meanwhile, Cardia dies."

He coughs, the car fixed in the passing lane.

"Big problem. Things are moving below the surface. He continues his investigations: ChemIt and Concrete Works. That's how he gets to the name

Ligresti. Somewhere around this time, something happens... how does Ligresti fit in? Here it is: there's proof that Ligresti personally knows Solimena, the elder. Because their secretaries knew each other well. And then... Ah!"

He jolts in his seat

"I almost forgot the capital increase. He's faced with a choice. Invest in the company and drain his own assets, or refuse and dilute his share. This is the spark of doubt. His doubt. He has to figure out how the money is moving. He knows there's a trap. He knows, and he finds it. He studies the system, understands it. Profits are siphoned out of the company? To prevent him from receiving the profits due to him for his shares? He's cornered. On one side, his brother is artificially inflating the company's value with false revenue, and on the other, he's siphoning money off to tax havens. A pincer move to push him out. I'm just missing the details, and I'll figure them out as soon as I get out of this damn car. And in this twisted game, he has to defend himself."

The dashboard lights up, but he doesn't notice. He's caught up in his story.

"And then the mother! The mother! Another line of attack. Rumors say she would give her share to just one son, obviously the eldest, or distribute the shares to ensure an absolute majority in the company. That's where the waters get muddy. She wants to give him the majority, but then, out of nowhere, Cardia's will reveals the Golden Share. He can veto anything. Can he stop the capital increase? Doesn't matter, the will is contested. Endless arguments. They can't let him have that power. He feels hunted, that's where the fear sets in. He goes to Rome, Ligresti is in Italy on the same day. Then he disappears."

He pauses to think

"Marzio must have tried to reach out. Maybe he tried to bring him over to his side, maybe he blackmailed him with what he knew. Ligresti disappears, the meeting is a failure? It's unclear. But Ligresti's disappearance is notable. It doesn't go unnoticed. Maybe Marzio got a signal from outside, something that scared him? Maybe someone was following him? I don't know. They would have found the girl if that were the case. Either way, he gets scared. He sends Cardia's daughter away. Maybe he slipped up at the company. Either way, the board meeting is on the seventh. Maybe he's planning a final showdown, fireworks, yes, it must be. Then suddenly, he returns to the office on the night of the sixth. Why? Someone calls him? Maybe a last attempt at mediation with his brother? I need those damned badges. He goes to his office, and bang. It's over. He's on the floor. The office goes up in flames. Someone takes the car keys. Maybe they even opened it. Maybe the documents explaining the dirty dealings between ChemIt, Concrete Works, and ProSud were in the car. Maybe they took them and felt safe. So safe they forgot the keys outside the office. But by then, it's too late. The office is on fire, and the keys aren't there. They're not inside. The rest of the story is written in my notebook. Simple, easy, smooth as oil, right?"

He clicks the stop button, and the recording stops. Satisfied, he tosses the phone onto the passenger seat.

The speedometer reads 160 kilometers per hour. He sinks into his seat and smiles.

Ah, Prisco, Prisco. And you? Do you have a role in all this, or are you just the regular bastard your mother made you? Ah! Believe me, now we're going to have some fun. Real fun. I can already picture you, all fired up like a bull, on a thousand. But I'll sort you out, you piece of shit. I swear on whatever you like, I'll let you talk. I'll give you the benefit of the doubt. I will. But if I see even a sliver of bad faith in your pressure, I swear on everything I hold dear, I'll skin you alive.

He laughs, laughs heartily, drumming his fingers on the steering wheel. The sign for his exit flashes by, he didn't see it, but his exit is near. He lets off the accelerator and veers right to merge into his lane. The rain seems to be easing up now. Maybe this storm is coming to an end. Maybe we'll see some sun this afternoon. He looks up, leaning toward the windshield, but there are only clouds.

He straightens up and presses the brake.

His heart leaps into his throat.

His hands grip the steering wheel in a tight vise.

His foot presses down, all the way, all the way to the floor. The car doesn't stop, doesn't even slow, it keeps speeding straight ahead. He tries again, lifting his leg and stomping down once more. He feels nothing, nothing. The brakes, the brake system, someone tampered with my brakes. He grits his teeth, biting down so hard it cuts into the roots of his flesh. The exit looms closer, so close. The blond man. The blond man with the pliers. The guardrail is wet, so close. He grips the wheel, braces against the seat. The seatbelt. He doesn't have his seatbelt on. He never wears it. He didn't put it on. The guardrail is so close. The exit is narrow. Seconds stretch into hours. He could swerve. He could swerve. Turn. The car veers right, skidding. The wet asphalt. The rain. The screech of the tires, the guardrail is so close. The car spins. He sees the concrete barrier in the middle of the road. The car lifts. Spins. Flies, then the sound, the crash, the noise. Everything is gray, a single moment, everything condenses, the senses merge into one, him, the car, the rain, the metal, the world. Everything is one.

30.

What I see is black. It's the blackness that envelops me.

I float weightless. In this vast sea, I move in a direction unknown to me.

It's always been here. It needs no real explanation.

I'm descending, that much I can say. I'm descending, and it's a gentle embrace for me. I feel the soft caress of your thought wrapping around me, and I'm at peace, I'm down here, I'm with you.

It feels like an infinite space. Yet I can sense its boundaries. It's so vast that I can stretch my arms inside it and still have time to breathe. Your sound rises on my skin, leaving white imprints on my rosy surface. Timeless is this dance. Pure pleasure. Varied notes, harmony, and a distant rhythm. A faint drum beating in the shadows, marking the time, the steady pulse. The snap of skin, the vibration of wood. My face is turned downward, and I descend. Eyes open, and I smile. It's dark, but I can see. Flickers in the distance. Soft sails bringing a cargo of shivers, pure emotion. Unfiltered. I am consumed by it. Throughout my soul, I don't know where it begins, I don't know where it ends. There's no break in it. Do I have limits? It's hard to perceive them. It feels like I completely belong to this, like I am this place.

There's a reflection below. The color is dark, blue, dark blue, and black. A fluid movement, liquid, where my descent is headed. I see it getting closer, a circle expanding in size, perfectly round, a placid lake, water lying at the bottom of this cavern with no walls. The surface is still. I approach it, and I see myself falling, my hands reaching toward it. It's peaceful. Silent. Pure. I approach, and I see a figure in the water. It's my reflection, reflecting me as I fall, arms outstretched. My head. My shoulders. I'm a light feather. The closer I get, the larger the figure grows. Its edges sharpen, and I see.

I see that it's not me.

It's not my reflection in the water. It's Marzio.

I'm close now, and so is he. Just centimeters apart, and I stop. I look at him, and he looks at me. I smile, and he smiles.

He smiles at me.

My heart breaks seeing you like this, just as I've always adored you. My heart is yours. You know that, don't you? I think it, and he nods. He nods. His hair moves gently in the water.

I long to kiss you. To hold you. To keep you with me. The water is so close.

The closer I get, the closer you are.

I close my eyes. I feel the water touch my nose. It's warm. My lips, my cheeks, and my forehead. I submerge my face in this dark lake. I breathe deeply. I feel calm here. I open my eyes. You are there, watching me. I see you clearly. Right in front of me.

I stretch out my arms, immersed in this water that feels like amniotic fluid, home. Toward you, my fingers, toward yours that reach out too. We laugh, we laugh together. In unison. Just a few millimeters, and I'll be able to touch your fingers, finally.

And from behind you, he emerges. From the darkness, with his hat, his nose, and his grin that's a fierce grimace. He grabs me by the shoulders, furious. I try to break free, I don't want this. You are below, far away, at his feet, and he's huge here next to me, yanking my hair, screaming horrible things at me. I scream, I don't want to go, I don't want this. I can no longer see your face, and he's too strong, too much of everything. He pulls my arms, my shoulders, my hair, my head downward. I can't resist. He drags me down, and the water swallows me. I sink like a heavy stone. The air turns cold, thick. I fall freely. Into the void. There's nothing here but pressure, pressing down on me, crushing me, making me small. I fall, and I don't know how long I've been falling.

I've been falling for an eternity. I don't even know if I'm breathing anymore.

A flash envelops me.

It's you. Crying. A child. In elementary school, wearing a white apron. Crying. You're filled with fear and sadness. Crying desperately in a corner. They left you alone. Your sobs surround me, filling my lungs. They're my sobs. The sound echoes in this giant classroom, distorted, the low rasp of a baritone clearing his throat.

I see your house. Your parents' house. I know it's theirs. You know it too. You're outside the kitchen. You're ten years old. Shouts come from the door. It's a fight. Your mother and father arguing. The words are harsh. You stand there, listening. You hear it all. You turn, and there's your brother's huge face. It's your fault. He says. It's your fault. You were never supposed to be born. His eyes are fiery, his tongue green, his lips purple. He's a snake with a forked tongue slithering between my legs.

You should be ashamed. It's your mother speaking, looking at you, fourteen years old. Her face disdainful. The mortification shakes your spine and reverberates into your eyes. Everything vibrates, everything is doubled. No. And then No, another No. Not today. Voices all around repeating only this, No. A wall of No, in every possible intonation. I said no. I said no. I'm sorry, but it's no. The doubt, the certainty. My hands crumble. I look at them, and they're sand, in a yellow desert. Where I'm all alone. Why do people want to hurt me, I wonder. It's Marzio's voice that echoes. On the walls of my mind, this theater with endless walls, balconies filled with mannequins, immobile spectators. And him, and me, in the center of the stage. A child on his knees, crying, fists pressed to his eyes.

A violet flame emerges from the darkness, writhing, twisting, a woman's voice, a seductive laugh, sultry. She's beautiful, with wide hips like the alpine valleys, a narrow waist like a fjord, breasts full and firm like grapes on the hills, nipples hard and red, pointing upward, toward pleasure. Her hands move, gliding down, from her ribs to her navel, stopping there and then lower, into the darkest depths. A flash of pleasure illuminates the room. Her lips are wet, pink. She turns. The face is there, her hair pulled back. I look into my own eyes. I'm looking at myself. It's me. It's me moaning. The pleasure envelops me deeply, and I feel the pressure, the control fading away, the sharpness of a scream, a trill. The color red, the color violet. The depths advancing. Grabbing me, rising. All the way to the tip of my tongue, spreading like a beacon over the sea of shadows. It shines sharper and sharper. And it goes out.

Silence.

A door closes. A desk. Not bad. A voice nearby says. I look up. It's Cardia. He sets the papers on the desk and looks at me. There's a hidden smile on his lips.

The room is far away. A cube in the void. It's the only light. The only light I see. The only light that fades. Gone. And I'm alone again.

A café table. 'Caffè degli Artisti', says the sign outside, green and gold. A taxi pulls up nearby, its plate reading Rome. You look up. A man gets out. Behind his sunglasses, I see him with you. He approaches. His expression is grim. Your heart races. He steps into the shadow of this tall umbrella protecting us from the sun. His gaze falls on you. He comes closer, and I move away. With every step he takes, I'm further away. 'Are you Marzio?' you nod. 'The flight was a little delayed. I read about the situation, I know how to help you, I can give you the key to understanding.' Lili. You are Lili. You are the key.

Standing. There's the sound of a car behind me. It approaches. It passes behind me. Its headlights illuminate the asphalt, it slows, and turns, stopping further ahead. It parks. The lights go out, the engine stops. The door opens, and you get out, Marzio.

It's you, with your shirt, your pants. You get out and close the car behind you. A computer in your hands. Your face is tense, steely. You walk briskly. There's a gray aluminum door. You reach out and open it. The corridor is dark, there's a door at the end, it's your door. Your office. You touch the handle. It's open. You flinch. Why is it open? Why should it be open? You always lock it. Fear rises inside you. Your breaths grow heavy, but you're here, you have to go in. You have to get it and put it somewhere safe. For me. Before you leave.

The door opens. It's a massive stone slab, kilometers thick, with roots deep into the center of the earth. The darkness beyond is so black. Your hand reaches out, the light that appears is dim, veiled. A curtain falls, and the stage opens. The same shiver runs through me when you turn and see a man behind your desk. Few hairs on his head, his gaze fixed on you, his eyes cold. Determined. A single thought. You stand there, frozen, with your hand on the handle, trying to figure out what. When. Oh, Marzio, you wanted to leave. To escape. Your shoulders pull back. And a hand grabs you. Pulls you in before anything else. You feel like you're giving in. That you have no strength left. Another step, and you lean forward to keep from falling. The door closes, and a man behind you watches. Blond hair, long on his neck. He reaches into your pockets and takes what you have. His blue eyes stare down at you. What do they want from you? What they want, we know. Please, have a seat, and a hand gestures to the chair. Beyond the desk. What game are we playing? You sit, they make you sit. He smiles. He's playing. Where are the papers? What papers? He laughs. A fist lands on your neck. It's so strong you sway, you feel like you're losing balance, you bend over, trying to understand what's happening. Where are the papers? He repeats. You raise one arm, then the other, and set the computer on the desk. He smiles. It's an evil smile. It's all been written already. You realize it now. You knew before, but now it hits you. Another punch, in the same spot. It knocks you off the chair. Hands on the floor. They lift you and put you back in place. Don't try anything funny. We'll break you. Is there a way out of here without being broken? The fear is inside you, inside me. There's a thought. Money. Offer them money, offer them what you have, do it. Save yourself, save yourself. Survive a little longer. But you don't. It will end here. You know it. How much more to do, how much more to say, count your breaths. One by one. One less with each second. It's all started. There's no stopping it. You know it, they see it. They try again, but what more is there to say? Everything you need is here. You're still missing something, can we end it like this? They make you stand up. In the center of the room. Kneel, then. No, not this. Please, no. Your knees won't bend. They repeat it. Until two blows from behind do their work, and you fall to the floor like this. Hands clasped to your chest, lips pressed tight. Tight together. Hands clasped to your chest. It will be quick, you say. It will be quick. They wet your head. It runs down your hair and then your neck. The smell of gasoline seeps into your skin. Oh God. It's done. My name, my name, my name fills the air, fills the room. You cry. Tears mix with the liquid soaking you. A stronger blow hits the back of your head. It's strong, you stagger, the world spins, my name, my name. It can't end like this, it can't. It can't. Consciousness fades. And you float above it all. The ceiling holds you back. Looking down. The two men are on opposite sides, and you're on the floor, the piece of paper in hand. Go out. He says. A flame. The paper ignites. You're there, you see yourself, you see the fire fall.

And then it begins. It burns. The flames rise high, the heat unbearable. Everything around burns. The desk, everything on it, the cabinets, the papers, the chairs. The walls blacken, hell on earth. You raise your hands to the sky. One last desperate prayer. My name, my name. On all the papers, there's my name, in every image, there's my name, my name.

Your shirt, your pants. They turn black. Your skin shrinks away.

Up there on the ceiling, you remain, you need to fly away. Complete your journey. Return to the source. But you can't. You don't want to. The name, my name. There's still more to do. The black seed grows from your stomach. The pain, the love. The two weights that still bind you to the chain of suffering. A life that isn't life. You can't integrate them anymore, they separate. Superfluous layers fly away. Only the core remains. He clings to you like a malignant tumor. The last two elements left. Love and pain. A blasphemous embrace, yet so natural.

I see the both of you. The both are you. I'm here outside. The flames shatter the glass, exploding into a thousand pieces, and the fire rises, rises higher. I feel the heat on me. It's so strong that I want to step back, but I stay still. Long shadows stretch across the ground. My eyes hurt, but you are there. Your body is there, and it's ending. It's ending like this. Oh, my love, my Marzio, what have they done to you? How could they do this to you? With what courage, with what strength?

I cry. I cry in silence. My tears have no weight. How much I love you. How much pain.

What I feel now.

What you feel now.

My love.

Where is the chill of death?

I hear in the air a distant chord, a major chord. It rises, rises in intensity. It vibrates with the flames. And it comes to me. The chill of death, where is it?

Something happens, and my hand moves. It's full, oh Lord. It can't be this way. It can only be this way. Tonight. Tonight, I am with you.

My hand is full. Full of you. Your hand is inside. I see it, it's there, and it holds me. Oh, Marzio, you are here. You are here with me. I look at you. At my side, and you smile. You smile, happy. You know how much I love you, don't you? How happy I was to be your girl. You, mine. Being one, we could have, for a lifetime, my love. You knew it, I knew it. They took us away, but we will always belong to each other, us. One single thought of love.

You smile, you smile for me. Your smile.

Oh, Marzio. How I've missed you.

Everything will be alright.

All right.

His hands leave my neck, and they slowly fall from my shoulders, slipping away like a wet cloak, heavy with water, sliding off my skin. The cold is no more. His hands have no reason to exist anymore, and they fall away. Fall away. It is finished.

Marzio looks at me, glowing, shining from his heart, his eternal smile radiating. His eyes are alive, alive forever. The wind catches us, moves our hair, the warm breeze stirs his clothes, everything turns white, he smiles, he smiles for me, he smiles with me.

White drops of love rise, a sea of candid white surrounds him, I see his eyes still fixed on me as they rise, rise up, his hand holding mine, my arm lifting, he's there, he's this infinite light moving away, cradling something close to his chest. The last black drops fall away. It's a child, sleeping peacefully, looking newborn. It's you, it's you both. The pain washed away. Purified. Freed by one last sacrifice. There is no more anger, terror, or fear. They have all vanished. Your sweet eyes on me, and you say goodbye with your gaze, in my hand, you dissolve, and yes, you can go now. You can go in peace now.

You can be at peace now. I loved you like I'll never love anyone else.

I remain here. Watching this black ruin rise before me. Everything turns dark again, and I'm still here.

Yet at the end of the road, I see it. It's there.

The glow of dawn beyond this black gate. The profile of the horizon. The backlight blinds me, fills me with energy. The weight of my body on my feet, I feel it. The firmness of flesh. The cool breath filling my lungs. Alive. New for a new day. A new life.

The sun rises.

It hits my face. I raise my hand to shield my eyes. The folder casts a shadow over me. Inside are Marzio's words, his thoughts, and his work. His handwriting gleams golden against the sun.

"It is all over."

And All begins.

Table of Contents

–

www.ingramcontent.com/pod-product-compliance
Lightning Source LLC
Chambersburg PA
CBHW022145240626
47153CB00007B/2525